Just Right

SWEET HAVEN FARM
BOOK THREE

JESSIE GUSSMAN

Contents

Acknowledgments

Cover art by Julia Gussman
Editing by Heather Hayden
Narration by Jay Dyess
Author Services by CE Author Assistant

~

Listen to the unabridged audio for FREE performed by Jay Dyess on the Say with Jay channel on YouTube. Get early access to all of Jay's recordings and listen to Jessie's books before they're available to the general public, plus get daily Bible readings by Jay and bonus scenes by becoming a Say with Jay channel member.

Chapter One

Maybe if she hadn't been bitten by the neighbor's pug when she was eight.

Maybe if it hadn't taken twelve stitches.

Maybe if she hadn't spent three nights in the hospital after it got infected... Maybe, maybe, maybe.

Avery Conrad had to quit blaming everything on her childhood. Especially since she was almost thirty and currently hanging from the light pole in front of Greg's Hardware Store on Main Street in Love, Pennsylvania. The giant red-and-white candy cane strapped to the pole had blocked her from shimmying to the top. There was not enough money in her bank account to pay for any damages to the town's Christmas décor. Even if they had enough of said décor to tastefully decorate a town four times the size of Love.

Currently, considering the events that had necessitated her precipitous climb, she was very thankful that her best friend for the past five months just happened to be a former circus performer who had tried, with minimal success, to teach Avery a few "tricks."

The next time she saw Jillian, she'd have to report that she'd mastered the pole-climbing part of the contortionist-hanging-by-her-hair routine. Necessity was the mother of survival, or however that old saying went.

Pursing her lips, she looked at the dogs sniffing the bottom of her temporary residence. Black, long-eared, long-haired, and quite loud. Their teeth were rather large, too, thank you very much.

Her eyes drifted a little farther to the scuffed hiking boots of the man who had spoken to her less than a minute ago. In what had to be only the second or possibly third time in her life, she'd not been able to gather her wits to answer back. Yet. She'd have to get down from the light pole before she could comfortably read him his pedigree. There was just something gauche about her current position that negated the authority she hoped to convey.

"I said they're harmless. I promise."

His deep voice reached her, reminding her of the tympani part in Nielsen's 4th symphony.

"I was bitten when I was younger." She tightened her grip, thankful she hadn't put her gloves on. She probably wouldn't have gotten up the pole while wearing them.

He gave a low command, a word she couldn't hear, and the dogs trotted the few steps to his side. Once they had stopped barking and his voice could be heard, they seemed to listen fairly well.

Avery put her forehead against the cold pole. Flakes of snow drifted past her nose. She could pretend to be comfortable and want to stay in her current position, which would be ridiculous and an obvious lie, of course, although hardly shocking to anyone in town. She could get down and give the guy the tongue-lashing he deserved, but that would mean getting close to the despicable dogs. Or she could slide down and stride away, ignoring the very large man and his ugly dogs.

Avery slid awkwardly down the pole. It was high time she faced her fear of dogs.

Her feet landed with a plop and a scrape as her right foot slipped on a soft patch of ice. Her legs shot out from under her and she flailed with both arms and feet, trying to regain her balance before she landed with a thump on her bottom, one leg stretched out on either side of the pole.

Her butt stung, but her pride stung more.

She could make this look like she did it on purpose. It would be a stretch, but she could bluff her way through. She had to get up first.

A single car ambled down Main Street. The horn honked. Avery threw up a hand without looking at the driver. Better to assume they were laughing with her and not at her. Although, the close-knit folks in Love had already pegged her as crazy. Sometimes, it was just better to play along.

With one hand on the pole, she scrambled to her feet. Unfortunately, because she was being careful to avoid the ice patch, she leaned too far to the left, lost her balance, stumbled, and smacked her head with a hollow *bong* against the green metal of the pole.

Pain pulsed in her head and radiated down her arms to the tips of her fingers, which throbbed. A small shower of red and silver confetti rained around her from the candy cane at the top of the pole. Any second now, it would cut loose, dropping down and smacking her on the head. That seemed to be the direction her life always went.

She might have been able to pretend she landed on her butt on purpose, but there was no way she could pretend she meant to smack herself in the head with the pole.

At least she was on her feet.

She glanced up, only to meet the beady red eyes and glistening white teeth of a ferocious hunting dog. Saliva dripped to the ground as the dog licked its chops, no doubt thinking her Armani wool, cashmere-lined jacket looked an awful lot like a hot dog bun, and thinking she, of course, would taste an awful lot like a hot dog.

"Please call off your dog." She meant to say it with authority to the man now in front of her, but it came out on a scratchy whisper. What kind of man allowed his dogs to stand over a helpless woman, salivating and dreaming of banquets and hotdogs? A total jerk, obviously.

His hand fell back to his side. Probably, he had extended it to help her up, but she hadn't noticed and it was too late now.

"Gladys, sit," the man said with a suspicious hitch in his voice.

Her jaw clenched. He was laughing at her. Usually she didn't have a problem laughing at herself. After all, this kind of thing happened to her all the time. *All* the time. But to have this arrogant stranger and his snarling, starved dogs...

Wait. "Gladys?" What kind of person named their dog Gladys?

"Yeah. I guess I should have called her Bruiser or Fang or Eats Ladies for Leisure..." There was that deep, tympanic vibration again. The vibration struck her right under her diaphragm and caused an unfamiliar heat to expand under her heart. She sucked in her stomach to stop the odd sensation.

"You can stop laughing at me anytime. Don't you have somewhere to go?"

"Wanted to make sure you were okay. That was quite a hit you took." He jerked his head up, pointing with his chin. "Thought the candy cane might get loose and make it a two-for-one."

"Wouldn't have surprised me," Avery mumbled, for some reason finding it hard to let go of her irritation. Maybe because both dogs were now looking at her like she was lunch. At least the throbbing had slowed to a dull thump focused solely in her head.

The man bent and picked up the bags she'd dropped. He held them out to her, his fingers long and calloused. Brown. The thumb nail was black, like it'd been smashed by a hammer.

The man nodded at the pole. "I'm sorry about that. They know they're going hunting tonight and they're excited."

The vibrations hit her diaphragm again. Taking a deep breath to shove the unfamiliar sensation aside, she snatched the bags filled with Christmas decorations and lights out of the man's hand.

Avery looked up. Way up. Man, sometimes it sucked to be short. She was going to drown in snowflakes if she looked this guy in the eye while she talked to him.

"Whether or not they're going hunting, there are still leash laws in this town." It was never easy to sound condescending to someone who was almost a foot taller than she. "In the future, you could avoid this whole, unpleasant scenario if you simply remember to keep your animals leashed while within the town limits."

"Yeah, lady, I could." One side of the man's mouth hitched up, revealing a fascinating dimple at the edge of his lip. "But I don't know why I'd want to. It was pretty impressive watching you shimmy up that pole. I sure hope you're registered for the lumberjack contest at Love's Christmas celebration later this month."

Avery planned to march in the parade, playing her tuba. Nothing more. Hopefully, shortly after that she'd know if she had been accepted to the Washington D.C. Eveningtide Orchestra. "I've never been mistaken for a lumberjack," she said, unable to soften her words with even the hint of a smile.

His lip hitched up a little more and the dimple deepened. "It wasn't a mistake."

"Of course, it was a mistake. I'm barely five feet tall. Your wrists are bigger than my biceps, which you'll have to take my word on, since I'm not taking my coat and sweater off in this cold. Not to mention, if I took off my outerwear, your dogs might decide that's a dinner invitation."

"Yeah, I suppose that little old lady they had for breakfast didn't stick to their ribs very well."

Avery couldn't keep her mouth from dropping and her eyes from widening in the second before she realized that he was kidding. Probably.

She eyed the dogs and inched backward. Just in case. Her back hit the pole and she stopped.

"Have a Holly, Jolly Christmas" grew loud, then soft again as a young teen opened the hardware store door and walked out. He nodded at them before he turned and shuffled down the otherwise deserted sidewalks. Unfortunately, the dogs didn't take their eyes off Avery.

Something that looked like regret or possibly pity flitted across the man's face. "I'm sorry my dogs scared you."

"You're not acting sorry, and they're still here."

"They'll leave when I do." A muscle ticked in his strong jaw. "When I was training them, I never thought to include a command for them to go sit in a corner while I helped an otherwise elegant woman down from a light pole. I'm shortsighted that way."

Avery's lips twitched. She buttoned them down. After all, she would have walked away from this conversation five minutes ago if she weren't terrified to turn her back on those ferocious animals. "Where I come from, dogs do not go off their leashes. For any reason."

"I was born in this town. And these dogs were born and bred to be off-leash."

"Not in town."

5

"They haven't touched you."

"They don't need to touch me to make it clear as day they want to eat me."

Something close to a growl came from the man. The vibration in her diaphragm did double time. But she was a classically trained musician who had never been the slightest bit interested in the tough, outdoorsy type of male. Plus, in her experience men didn't stick around any longer than it took them to catch the eye of something prettier and younger, so they weren't worth her bother. Double that if said man came with boots and dogs.

Whatever those vibrations were, Avery knew what they weren't—not interest and not attraction. Not for the tough, boot-wearing, dog-owning mountain of a man in front of her.

A muscle in the man's cheek worked back and forth. He knelt slowly, placing a hand on each dog's collar. "I'll hold them until you leave."

Avery tilted her head and smiled the smile she used after a wretched performance that the audience clapped for anyway. "Fine. Now I can walk away, unworried about whether or not I'll get eaten before I make it to my car."

She turned. Before she'd taken three steps, she heard whining behind her. From a dog, she thought. Tempted to ignore it and continue on—after all, she had holiday cheer to spread—she shifted the heavy bags and glanced over her shoulder.

The man had stood up and started to turn, no longer having his hands on the dogs' collars. He, too, was glancing back over his shoulder at the animals.

One of the savage beasts had Avery's leather glove in its large jaw. It whined again.

Avery froze. Fear, like a cold hand, gripped her neck. It was like the dog was doing to her glove what it wanted to do to her.

"Hey, Gladys," the man said softly. "The Fancy Lady dropped her glove and you want to give it back?"

He turned completely around. Avery felt his gaze on her, but she couldn't lift her terrified eyes from the beast that held her captured glove.

"How about I do it for you?" he said as he bent and plucked the glove from the Jaws of Death. "Stay," he commanded before he strode to her. In unison, the dogs sat, watching Avery with evil eyes and polished fangs.

"This is yours?" the man asked when he stopped in front of her, holding up the glove.

She tore her eyes from the beasts of prey and licked her lips. "Yes." Her voice was barely a squeak. "It is," she said more forcefully.

He cleared his throat.

She imagined he was trying hard not to laugh at her.

"Do you want to take it?" he asked slowly, waving it as he spoke.

The bags of decorations meant to cheer Mrs. Franks made her arms ache. Transferring them to one hand, she snatched her glove. "Thank you," she said through her teeth.

"I'll pass that on to Gladys," the man said, failing to hide his smirk.

Avery's eyes lingered for a fraction of a second on the dark stubble of his angled jaw.

No interest. Not on his part, since he could barely contain his derision for her. And most certainly not on hers.

"Tell her she'll have to find her supper somewhere else." Avery craned her neck to meet his dark eyes before she turned and strode away.

GATOR FRANKS OPENED the back door of his mother's house slowly. It creaked. He didn't want to wake her if she were sleeping, as she often was before supper.

He'd finally shaken the unsettled feeling from the unfortunate confrontation in town with the fancy woman and the light pole. The whole thing really wasn't his fault, since little Braydon Carper, all of nine years old, had opened Gator's pickup door to pet his dogs, accidentally letting them out. But he hadn't been able to explain that to the woman, because it would have been too much like admitting she was right, and his experiences with his ex had taught him it was a huge mistake to admit weakness to a woman. Give them your throat and

7

they'll go for the jugular, rip it out, tear it to shreds, then go after your heart. Every time.

It really didn't matter that the woman had been as opposite from Kristen as could be. Except for the money angle. They were the exact same there.

His toe stubbed something in the dark and he grabbed the hall table to keep from falling. His fingers bumped into something cold, which wobbled. He grabbed for it in the dark, but only succeeded in knocking it over. It hit the edge of the table before tumbling to the floor and shattering. Something glass, obviously. He hesitated, not remembering anything either on the floor or on the table early this morning when he'd left the house.

"Gator?" his mother called from the living room where he'd probably awakened her from her nap. The treatments made her tired.

"Yeah. It's me. I don't remember seeing anything here earlier when I left."

"Avery was here. She helped me decorate for Christmas."

Gator filed through his memory, but came up with a blank on anyone named Avery. He'd been living out west for ten years, but the town hadn't changed that much. "Avery?"

The couch squeaked as his mother moved.

"Don't get up, Mom. I was trying to be quiet and not wake you."

More squeaking indicated that his mother ignored him. "Avery Conrad. She's related to Fink or Ellie Finkenbinder somehow, and she came out from Philly or near there this summer to help with the farm. I thought she had a teaching job there, but she never went back this fall, so I guess she didn't." A light flipped on. So much for his mother's nap. "She offered to decorate, and since I know that you hate the knick-knacks and what-nots and wouldn't want to mess with them for me, I took her up on it."

His mother was right when she said he hated knick-knacks. And this was a big part of why. He was big and they always made him feel like an elephant in an antiques shop.

Gator flipped the hall light on and grabbed the broom and dust pan. He knelt to sweep up the pieces of— "It looks like I killed one of the wise men."

"We'll pretend Herod found that one and ordered his head chopped off." She gave the pieces a sad look. He guessed they were expensive, but her tired eyes crinkled as she smiled at him.

He shrugged. "Looks more like he planted dynamite under the camel's saddle."

"If you toss the pieces in the can, it'll get rid of the evidence and the cause of death will be whatever we make it."

"I'm sorry. I was trying to sneak in and not wake you. I didn't know you'd decorated." As he stood holding the pieces in the dustpan, he realized that he'd tripped on the most grotesque snowman he'd ever seen. "Is that thing made out of burlap?" Lights wrapped around the dumpy brown body, sort of like a droopy hangman's nose, and a shiny orange plastic carrot stuck out from its face. It brought to mind an ugly Christmas sweater, only in 3D and sitting in his house.

"I bought that at the elementary school's annual holiday sale. The lady I bought it from said her third-grader made it herself."

"I believe it," Gator said. If it'd been him, he'd never had admitted his child made something that hideous. "Are you sure it was meant to be a Christmas decoration?" The lights might have been sort of an indication, but if he'd had to guess, he would have said it was some new-fangled way to scare mice and rats. Or possibly some type of anti-theft device. His lips twitched as he thought of the fancy lady going up the light pole. If his elderly hunting dogs had scared her that badly, that hideous looking burlap creature would have her high-stepping it to the nearest jail cell and locking herself inside.

His mother tugged her bathrobe tie tighter around her waist and gave the burlap snowman a warm glance. "There was something about the snowman that made me feel like I'd met a kindred spirit."

Guilt tightened Gator's throat. He didn't love his mother less because she'd lost a breast and all of her hair, and she'd not complained. Not to him, anyway. But he could see, now that she'd mentioned it, how she might feel like she had something in common with the ugly snowman.

He couldn't give her back her breast, or her hair, and his heart hurt for the pain she couldn't talk to him about.

He set the dustpan on the table and bent over, wrapping his arms around his mother, feeling the unfamiliar frailness, swallowing against the fear that the disease would continue to eat at her until there was nothing left.

"I think you're beautiful, Mom." He managed to get it out without choking. Hopefully, she couldn't tell that her thirty-two-year-old son was trying not to burrow into her arms and sob. "And I think your snowman is beautiful too. On the inside."

His mother laughed, as he'd hoped she would.

She patted his back. "Come on. Avery left us some tofu salad."

He didn't groan. Honest.

With a sigh his mother said, "I hate the stuff, but it's supposed to be good for me."

Because of that, he could shove it down his throat too. And try to be thankful for Avery, who decorated with the knick-knacks his mother loved and made her tofu salad because it was good for her. "I'll pretend it's steak."

How hard could it be?

Chapter Two

This is fun, Avery said to herself. *This is really fun. I actually really enjoy this.*

She was a liar. And not a very good one.

After using her shoulder to push the Finkenbinder's barn door closed, she hefted her tuba up. Normal people did not get up before dawn and go outside in sub-freezing temperatures to practice their tuba away from sane people, just so they didn't wake said sane people up.

No one had ever accused Avery of being normal.

If she was going to beat out all the men who played the tuba and get that position in the Washington D.C. Eveningtide Orchestra, she had to be way better than normal. After all, what good was a tubist who didn't have a chair in an orchestra? It's what she'd practiced all her life for. And it's how she proved that her dad walking out on her and her mother didn't really matter. He said she talked too much, had too much "hot air." Well, she had taken what he considered a fault, her "hot air," and made a successful career out of it. Of course, it was only successful if she were employed. Which she would be, once she aced her audition, which she would do since she was going to practice harder than anyone. No matter the cold or dark or the fact that she had to do it outside so she didn't wake the Finkenbinders or their children.

Thankfully, she could practice her tuba with gloves on.

She looked over at the pink sky, then back at the house. Not quite far enough away. The tuba was rather loud, and the Finkenbinders had been kind enough to allow her to stay at their home while she pieced her life back together. The least she could do was keep her tuba in the barn and make sure she was far, far away from the house when she started practicing at this ungodly hour of the morning.

It was pretty out, with the sunrise reflecting on the pond. And she wouldn't notice the cold once she started playing. Like all her other problems, the cold seemed to fade away once she got into her music. She might have started taking lessons because her dad had said that she might as well put her lungs to good use, but she'd kept playing because she loved it. Kept playing until she was good enough to be the first woman tubist of the Philadelphia Waterfront Orchestra. No small feat, thank you, and a position she'd held until she lost it last spring. To a man. Drat their bigger lung capacity and the automatic stigma that came from being a female tubist that, oh, say a violinist or harpist did not have to deal with.

But there was an opportunity in Washington D.C., and she was going to get her chair back, just in a different orchestra.

She glanced back at the house again and decided she was far enough away. She had her stand and music tossed in a small bag over her shoulder, but she could get started on a few pieces from memory. Shifting her tuba, she brought it to her lips and puffed into the mouthpiece a few times to warm it up.

Taking a deep breath, she launched into the O Madonna warm-up that she almost always started her practice sessions with. No need for music, and since it was broad and expansive, she could really get into it. The piece never failed to get her in the mood to practice and work hard.

Before she'd made it through two measures, a flock of birds, ducks maybe, startled by her playing, flapped and flew from the direction of the pond. The unexpected motion made her miss a note, but she'd played the song enough that she picked right back up with barely a hitch and sailed smoothly into the meat of the piece.

As always, the music pulled her in, surrounding her, filling her, chasing away the worries and concerns clouding her mind, and pouring peace and joy into her soul. Practice was work, no mistake, but there was something uplifting about playing an instrument with competent skill.

She was almost at the end of O Madonna when two shadows came streaking around the far side of the pond toward her. Wolves. Her heart tried to escape out the back of her throat. She'd never heard of any around these parts, but she hadn't been in "these parts" very long.

In eighth grade, she'd read half of a Louis L'Amour book. The only western she'd ever picked up in her life. As she struggled to lift her tuba off, she tried frantically to remember if the book had mentioned wolves and whether or not they could swim.

She couldn't outrun them.

She might or might not be able to beat them to death with her tuba.

If they didn't swim, the pond was definitely the best option since there were no trees or light poles handy.

Tossing her tuba down, and praying the wolves didn't eat it either, since it represented more money than most people paid for a small car, she careened down the hill and crashed into the pond.

She realized right away what she had failed to take into consideration a few seconds ago: it was December and she was quite likely going to die from hypothermia. She just as quickly decided that hypothermia was preferable to being mauled to death. Probably.

The wolves had almost come around the edge of the pond, but Avery couldn't quite make herself duck under the water. Too cold. She did, however, manage to make her almost numb legs carry her in until the water was up to her chest.

Stopping at the spot where she had splashed in, the wolves stood and barked at her, which triggered a memory. Maybe from the Louis L'Amour book, maybe not, but she thought she remembered that wolves didn't bark.

The first rays of cold December sun were coming over the horizon when she turned and squinted at the two animals. Did she recognize them? Same evil eyes. Same polished fangs. Same hungry look.

Gladys and her wicked twin, for sure. And, wouldn't you know it, the same booted mountain man striding along behind. Only now he had a gun slung over his shoulder and the look on his face wasn't benign humor. He looked mad.

Her chest burned. She was the one standing in freezing cold water to escape being eaten alive by his ill-bred, unmannered canines. She was obviously the one who should be angry. She narrowed her eyes.

At his command, the dogs stopped barking, but paced along the water's edge, both looking ready to jump in any time.

She didn't give him a chance to speak. "This is the second time your dogs have—"

As she started speaking the man stopped so fast his boots skidded. "You?" he asked incredulously, interrupting her tirade.

"Yes." Her teeth had started chattering in earnest, and her feet and legs had gone from cold to painful. "It's me. This is the second time your wild animals have required me to run for my life."

"You," he said again as though he couldn't believe it. "You're the one that was making all the unholy noise. I had everything set up for duck hunting, which took me hours, and you scared them all away."

"I'm glad I could save a life," Avery mumbled. For some reason her tongue wasn't working very well. At least her legs and feet had gone numb.

"Oh, crap." The man walked to the edge of the pond. "Get out of there. Now. Before you can't."

Take your dogs and leave first was on the tip of her tongue, but she couldn't get her mouth to work. The second time in two days, which was some sort of record for her. If she were still on speaking terms with her dad, she would have made a note to mention it to him.

"Come on, Fancy Lady. I have no idea what you are doing here, at this hour, making that horrible racket, but you can't stay in the water. The dogs didn't bite you yesterday, and I already fed them two small kids and a teenager this morning, so they're not hungry."

By this time, Avery had stopped shivering, which was nice because she could grit her teeth. Later, when she wasn't so tired, she would decide for sure whether she would associate with someone who might, or might not, be feeding his dogs humans. Her eyes wanted to drift shut. She could sleep standing in the water.

"Frig." The man shrugged off his gun. "Open your eyes, Fancy Lady."

She managed to keep her eyes cracked slightly as he bent down and unlaced his boots. Everything seemed to be in slow motion. She could lie on the water and float away. How nice that would be. That irritable man could go blow. His dogs could turn into cuddly, long-haired Persian kittens. Maybe she'd give them a bowl of warm milk. Very warm milk.

He splashed into the pond, toward her, his dogs beside him. She wanted to turn and run away. To get away from the dogs and away from the big mountain man, but her body wasn't cooperating. If only she could take a nap. If she could rest for a few minutes, she'd be able to run from the dogs again.

~

THE CONFOUNDED Fancy Woman didn't have the sense God gave a goose. Or a duck, for that matter.

Swooping her up right as she closed her eyes completely and started to sink into the water, Gator turned and strode with confidence out of the frigid pond and toward Fink and Ellie Finkenbinder's old farmhouse. They probably wouldn't be up this early on a Saturday, but having grown up beside Ellie, he knew they wouldn't mind a bit opening up their house to someone in need. It might not even be locked.

Gator tried to shrug off his annoyance that the fancy woman had scared his ducks away. It wasn't exactly easy to go duck hunting. He'd gotten up before dawn and been down by the pond for over two hours in this freezing weather. If it hadn't been extreme stupidity on her part, he'd not be so upset. But seriously? What kind of woman walks around in the dark, making a ridiculous racket on some kind of overgrown trumpet, then, for no reason whatsoever, walks straight into a pond that could only have been a few degrees above freezing?

Not one with a brain.

She was smaller than she seemed. He hurried his already fast walk. He might be irritated, but he didn't want her to die. "And if you do die, I'm not really going to feed you to my dogs."

"I don't believe you," she slurred. Her lips were blue, her face pale.

The eyes that had spit fire and sass last night were closed. Dark lashes rested on porcelain skin.

He grunted. Even suffering from hypothermia, she wouldn't be silenced. But her eyes hadn't opened.

"I should call 911," he said to himself as much as to her. In order to do that, he'd have to go back to his duck blind to get his phone.

"No insurance," she whispered.

That gave him pause. Yesterday, he'd judged her as privileged by her clothing. Today, she wore the same fancy coat and what looked like expensive jeans and boots. He had to admit, everything he knew about fashion he'd learned from his ex-wife. He tucked that mystery away for another time.

He could commiserate with the no insurance. He'd actually been formulating a plan to try to pay his mother's astronomically high deductibles and co-insurance, and Fink was the man he needed to talk to. His idea hadn't exactly been to barge into Fink's house just after dawn on Saturday morning, but...

He took the porch steps two at a time and pounded on the door with his elbow. It opened as he shifted to try to reach the knob.

"Gator?" Ellie Finkenbinder, in bright purple pants and a tee shirt, her hair in wild tangles around her head, blinked up at him like she expected him to disappear with the morning fog. Then her eyes widened. "Avery?"

The woman in his arms nodded weakly. Gator's jaw dropped. Was this his mother's Avery?

"She was in the pond." He couldn't quite bring himself to say that she walked into it of her own accord. Ellie seemed to know her. If Avery was certified crazy then Ellie wouldn't be surprised, but if Avery was truly that petrified of his elderly hunting dogs, then he didn't have enough time to explain it.

Ellie bustled him through the kitchen and into the living room where she directed him to lay Avery on the couch. "Go to the laundry room off the kitchen and start the dryer. There's a load of towels in there that I haven't gotten out and folded yet. We'll get them warm. Put some hot water on the stove."

Gator headed out of the room.

"I'm taking her wet clothes off, so don't come back in until I say, and be sure to stop Fink and the boys if they come down the stairs."

"Got it," Gator said.

The laundry room off the kitchen was easy to find. He started the dryer, then kept an ear out for footsteps while he put water on the stove to boil. The heat of the kitchen felt good on his wet clothes and stocking feet.

Ellie appeared in the doorway.

"Bring me two towels, then start the dryer again."

He obeyed.

As he handed the towels over she said, "She's awake, but still slurring her words. I know she doesn't think she can afford to go to the hospital..." Ellie bit her lip and gazed off into the distance.

Because of his job as a forest ranger out in Montana, this wasn't the first case of hypothermia he'd seen. He'd actually suffered from a few mild cases himself. Ellie was doing all the right things. "I've dealt with hypothermia before. I think she'll be okay. As long as she's breathing and her heartrate is steady."

"I'd feel more comfortable if you'd check her. She's covered."

Gator glanced into the room where Fancy Lady Avery lay on the couch. Something tugged at his heart and his feet started moving before he'd even decided to go. "Make her a cup of tea and you can make sure she gets a few swallows." Warming from the inside out. He'd feel better if she were in the hospital, but he could respect her desire to not go. He'd rather die than rack up a bill he couldn't pay. He also would have bet a boatload of cash that Fancy Lady Avery could have paid for an ER visit. Appears he'd have been wrong.

"I'll do it." Ellie grabbed the towels and hustled back into the living room. "I'll also get more warm towels."

"Great," Gator said, as his feet took him to Avery's side. Her teeth chattered together, her small body shaking under the blankets, and immediately his anxiety dissipated. For a hypothermia victim, shivering was good.

He stopped beside the couch, somehow wary of touching her. Maybe because of her sharp tongue, but more because he found himself *wanting* to touch her. To run his finger down her cheek, curve his hand

17

around the angle of her chin, and bury it in her hair. Which was crazy. But he couldn't tell that to his heavily thumping heart.

Shaking the feeling off, he reached deep for a mask of clinical dispassion as he touched two fingers to her neck, searching for a heartbeat, praying it was strong and even.

Her eyes snapped open. He almost yanked his hand back, like he'd been taking advantage of her. Their eyes met and the thumping in his heart became painful. He pushed his fingers forward, murmuring, "Just want to make sure your heartbeat is strong and steady."

"Really?" she asked weakly. "Are you sure you weren't planning on strangling me and feeding me to your dogs?"

Her pulse was steady, and even a little fast under his fingers. "They prefer to kill their own victims."

Her hand slipped up and out of the blankets, grabbing his wrist. Her fingers didn't quite make it the whole way around. He broke eye contact to stare at the contrast of the pink shine of her nails against his dark skin.

"So, you're saving me so you have dogfood tomorrow?" she asked, with a little more of the familiar sass back in her voice.

Oh, yeah. She was going to be fine. He was actually more worried about himself.

"I have a whole basement full of people chained to the wall. You're safe for at least a month."

"I'm Christmas dinner, then?"

"You're too small for Christmas dinner. Maybe an appetizer."

"You're one of those people who discriminate against people because of their size. Like you did one thing to be as tall as you are. There's nothing wrong with being short. Short people have feelings too."

Avery took a breath to continue, but before she could, Ellie spoke from over his shoulder. "You're feeling better. I have to admit, I was a little concerned when you came in and didn't have much to say."

Gator stretched to his feet, hoping Ellie hadn't noticed he'd had his hand on Avery's neck way longer than it took to grab a pulse. His wrist tingled with a funny feeling of awareness, and he fought the urge to hide his hand behind his back. He hadn't been doing anything wrong.

Avery's cheeks reddened. "Sorry. Some people seem to have this ability to raise the heat level in others. But I guess that's what I needed." She narrowed her eyes at Gator.

"Fink's in the kitchen," Ellie said to Gator with a smile. "Maybe you can help him finish the tea."

He could recognize a dismissal when he heard one. Without looking at the frustrating Fancy Woman again, he grabbed the pile of cooled towels, and headed out of the room. Fink sat at the kitchen table.

"Gator. I thought I heard a deep voice in there." Fink looked askance at the cool towels in Gator's hand.

He explained about Avery while walking the towels back to the wash room. "She's on the couch warming up. I'm on tea duty."

"I see. Wow." Fink rubbed the back of his neck. "Avery has been so considerate about practicing her tuba where she won't wake or bother us. It never occurred to me that it's getting cold outside. I thought she stayed in the barn with it."

"Maybe she usually does."

"Is the tuba still outside?"

"Yeah. I'll run out and get it once the tea is done."

"I'm sure her case is in the barn," Fink said.

"Okay."

Fink rubbed his head. "That old barn is liable to fall down any day. I've been looking for someone to either re-side it or tear it down."

"I wanted to talk to you about that."

Fink, with his straight carriage and serious expression, looked every bit the high school principal, even in the matching striped pajamas. He rubbed his chin. "You used to do construction work."

"Yeah. In high school, during summer break, I worked with my grandpa. Old barn boards are bringing top dollar right now. In fact, I have a buyer in mind, but I wanted to talk to you first. If you're serious about tearing it down, I'll give you a competitive estimate. You can even price match it." After trying two cupboard doors, Gator found the mugs and grabbed one.

Fink walked to a canister and pulled out a teabag. "I actually have three estimates on my desk. Ellie wanted me to get a price on re-siding it too. She's attached to the old thing and thinks it would be romantic to keep it."

Gator sniffed. "Probably would be. I'm guessing the re-siding estimate might have debased her on the romanticism of keeping it."

"Large sums of money have a way of shooting holes in the best-laid dreams. She did say that Avery and she had a few ideas of how the barn could make money and could be an asset to our business. But the cash out up front is considerable."

"If you decide to tear it down, I'd love to be able to submit an estimate." Gator took the tea bag and dropped it in the mug. Steam rolled from the water on the stove.

"I'll show you what the other guys offered; you let me know if you can match it. You're my neighbor. Even if you can't match them, if you're in the ballpark, I'm hiring you. I know Ellie will feel the same." He paused with his hand on the refrigerator door. "If we decide to re-side, would you be interested in that?"

Gator hated to turn down the work, but on his limited leave of absence from his job, he only had time to do one barn. He needed the extra money he'd make from selling the old boards. There were two or three other barns in the area he could make an offer on. "I can only do one job before the New Year's when I have to be back in Montana. Mom has some bills, and I wanted to make enough to take care of them before I leave. To do that, I need the extra from selling the boards."

Fink set a carton of orange juice on the table. "I get it. Let me talk to Ellie and make sure we're on the same page. She, Avery, and Jillian spent a whole afternoon here at the kitchen table last weekend dreaming up ways for the barn to make money."

"Jillian?"

"A relative. Same as Avery. They came to help out this summer when I was laid up, and they've both stayed through the busy season."

"Hmm." Another woman just like Avery? He wasn't sure the world could handle two of her. But he didn't say anything. Fink seemed fond of her. He rubbed his wrist where her fingers had clasped it. "What are they going to do with the barn? Get a herd of Holsteins and start milking them?"

Fink laughed as he pulled a glass from the cupboard. "No. They did talk about putting a dog kennel in, which Avery was not overly fond of." Fink's voice lowered like he was telling a secret. "She's not a big dog person.

"Or turning it into a storage facility for boats or RVs. We've used it as a haunted barn in autumns past, but the insurance company is balking at insuring it unless we do some major upgrades. We need to justify the expense with anticipated income."

"Yeah, I get it." Gator poured the boiling water onto the teabag in the mug.

"I think we decided it wasn't worth it, but it's not worth my wife giving me the silent treatment for the next month if I came to the wrong conclusion from our conversation."

Gator's face twitched. Knowing Ellie, Fink was probably joking, but Gator knew all about getting the silent treatment. Kristen had given him that for the majority of their marriage. "That's fine. I'm going to run down and gather up the oversized trumpet. While I'm down there, I'll look around, but to do a proper estimate, I'll need to come back some other time with a tape measure and some other stuff."

Fink drained his glass. "That's fine. By the time you get back, I should have those estimates dug up."

"Great." Gator walked over to the doorway and peeked in. "How's she doing?"

Ellie turned from her position on the chair beside the couch. "She wants to get up."

Gator glimpsed Avery's sparkling eyes. Something pulled him toward her, but he resisted. "I'm getting the trumpet thing."

Avery's gaze lifted to meet his. His heart tripped, and that annoying protective instinct caught at his neck again. He couldn't read her expression. It didn't matter anyway.

He turned and strode out of the kitchen.

Chapter Three

G ator fingered the long envelope in his hands, waiting for the pole-climbing, frozen-lake-swimming woman to look up from where she stood beside the cash register. A small table directly in front of him held small homey-looking Christmas decorations. Large, beautifully decorated wreathes and other pine-type decorations hung on the walls.

Because of his size, he often felt boxed in when indoors. The small trailer that served as the tree farm office amplified that feeling.

She still hadn't noticed him. He squelched the disdain threatening to pucker his lips. Apparently, Avery was a cat person. Hard to label her as anything else with the long-haired fur ball she had strapped to her chest in one of those carrier things a normal woman would put her baby in. No wonder she panicked so fiercely over his dogs.

He shifted his feet awkwardly in the small tree farm office. Apparently, she didn't hear the jingle of bells on the door when he walked in. Or the door opening and closing. It's not like he had snuck in. He wasn't duck hunting, after all. Not today.

She rearranged the photos on the counter next to the cash register and bit her lip. That same oddly protective, tingling feeling bloomed in his chest again. The one he'd felt as he stood at the bottom of the light pole and again when he charged into the pond.

This woman was way too much his opposite for him to want to have anything more than a passing acquaintance with her. He looked at the cat again. It was ugly enough to be some kind of purebred.

He cleared his throat. "Excuse me."

The woman jumped three feet into the air with a screech that only barely drowned out the cat's startled meow. Her hand flew out, knocking over the soda can beside her.

More frenzied flying and screeching occurred as Avery grabbed the can, set it upright and struggled to save the pictures from ruin. It was odd that she even had pictures. Digital had taken over actual hand-held pictures for the rest of the world.

"I'm so sorry. I didn't hear you come in." She finished gathering her pictures up. One hand stroked the ugly cat strapped to her chest. Its face looked like it smashed into a wall at some point in its life, but then Gator thought of his mother and the snowman. He still didn't like cats, but he allowed that a dreadful face didn't necessarily equate to a nasty disposition. Although, the thing *was* a cat.

"You should have said something," Avery exclaimed. "I was working on this and I get so focused on things that I lose all track of everything else that's going on around me. And, oh, I forgot to thank you for rescuing me from the pond." Her lips turned down. "Although, it was your nasty, mean dogs that chased me into it."

Gator opened his mouth to inform her that his dogs were not nasty or mean. They were actually elderly and quite nice, having never bitten a single person in all their long years. But she had continued on. And on. Confirming his suspicion that in that area, at least, she wasn't like most women who excelled at the silent treatment. He tilted his head as words continued to flow out of her mouth. A woman like her might drive a man to appreciate the silent treatment.

Avery put her fingers to her mouth. "Oh, I'm sorry. I'm doing it again."

She stopped talking and looked at him. Quiet. So, it must be his turn to speak. He stared at her as the seconds ticked by, suddenly and inexplicably at a loss for words. Her cheeks grew pink and she reached a hand up and stroked the cat again.

The sight broke his stare and he turned his head, tapping the envelope he carried against his palm. Right. He'd forgotten why he was even there. Probably stunned by the ugliness of that stupid cat.

"I'm looking for Fink."

She tilted her head and looked up at him. Something about her eyes, which were clear blue like a bottomless glacial lake, gave her an glow of sincerity that he couldn't shake. It didn't matter what her eyes looked like. This woman wasn't any less mercenary than the rest of her species.

But today his mouth wasn't taking orders from the thinking side of his brain apparently. Because it opened and said, "I'm sorry my dogs scared you. Twice now. They're really not mean or ferocious."

"They just want to eat me." The lady shrugged fatalistically.

"Actually, scientists say that if a human dies in their apartment, their cats will eat them. But a dog would starve to death first."

"And they've proved that how?" she asked, with a wave of her hand and a flash of her shiny pink nails.

How had she climbed the light pole with nails like that? "By killing a cat and studying the microscopic clump of cells that passes for a brain in that animal." He lifted a shoulder to indicate it didn't matter. "I don't know. The article I read didn't say." And he hadn't needed any further proof since the article simply put into words what he had known as fact forever: a cat couldn't be trusted any farther than a woman. Except if he died in his apartment, a woman would pick his body clean of anything that might have any monetary value before skipping town with his credit cards, money, and bank account information. He didn't think a woman would actually eat him, although with women, one could never be completely sure.

"You can't believe everything you read on the internet. In fact, most of it is fiction. Why I read the other day that string musicians have bigger frontal lobes than brass musicians, but everyone and their step sister knows that brass musicians are the most intelligent people in the orchestra." Avery's perfectly bobbed hair swung around her head as she spoke, giving even more life to her personality than the ruffled blouse and saucy skirt. The only thing that was a downer on her whole body was the sour-looking cat that glared at him through half-closed eyes.

"If you value that sort of thing."

Her hands stilled over the pictures she seemed to be sorting. "And that means?"

"Uh, playing an instrument has nothing to do with how smart you are?"

"Oh." She brightened. "Exactly right. Do you play?"

"No."

The hopeful expression melted off of Avery's face. "I'm marching in the Christmas parade next week with Love's professional musicians, and we could use some new talent."

"Can't help you out." And wouldn't want to. Funny that the idea of marching in a parade gave him the stomach heaves, but he'd always done the lumberjack competition without a second thought. "Does the farm still donate the trees for the tree trimming contest?"

"Yep." She gave a decisive nod that set her hair to swinging again. "They'll be cutting those next week."

"Well, if Fink needs help getting them cut and into town, I'll give him a hand."

Her eyes widened like she was surprised he'd offered to help. "Okay," she said. "He and Ellie had a late doctor's appointment with one of the boys. I'll tell him when he gets back."

"Great. And could you give him this? I'm headed out of town for a few days." He held up the envelope in his hand. "It's the bid on tearing the barn down."

Avery's mouth flattened. "You know, just because something's old, doesn't mean that it's worthless."

"I never said it was worthless." He laid the envelope on the counter beside the pictures that she had spread out. "But, now that you mention it, it's funny the way a woman's mind always goes to the money. How much is it worth?" He shook his head. Avery had that captivating energy about her, but he wasn't fooled. All women, with a few notable exceptions, his mother being one, needed money, and plenty of it, in order to be happy.

"You want to tear it down! With a small investment that barn could be making Fink and Ellie a nice, tidy sum."

"It's an eyesore and it needs to go." And he needed the money for his mother. Even more so since just this morning as he'd been walking out, he'd noticed the pink foreclosure notice on his mother's desk. His throat tightened and his forehead throbbed. Surely, they couldn't foreclose just because the home equity line was six months behind? But he knew they could, and would. If only his mother had told him. It would have been tight, but he could have paid those payments with his regular salary. Or close to it. But now, with a lump sum needed to stop the proceedings, he really had no choice but to convince Fink to tear down that barn.

"It's not an eyesore. It's an historic building that deserves the dignity of being restored to its former grandeur."

Her cat glared at him with evil yellow eyes.

He ignored it.

"It's just an old bank barn that has seen better days. They cost more to maintain than they're worth."

"Sometimes you think things are old and worn out, but they just need the right person to come along and show them some love."

"We're talking about an inanimate object." He shook his head. She acted like he suggested shooting her grandmother. It was a barn, for goodness' sake. It shouldn't matter to her if it got torn down or not. He opened his mouth to tell her just that, when the door opened, little Christmas bells jingling, and a couple strode in. After a Christmas tree probably.

He had thought, for a few moments, that maybe Avery was different. Exactly what his lonely heart wanted to think. He stuffed down something that felt a lot like disappointment and strode back toward the door, nodding to the couple who looked vaguely familiar.

He wouldn't feel guilty for wanting to tear the barn down. To get Avery on his side, he should have pointed out how much money Fink and Ellie would make from the sale of the old boards and beams. Too late. And he didn't care what she thought. Not much, anyway.

"Mrs. Franks' son must be some kind of super-craftsman if he made these in high school." Avery replaced another burnt out light in the wooden cutout of a skier doing a flip. It was the last in a seventeen-cut-out line, which started with the skier on his feet heading downhill.

"A super electrician too, since Mrs. Franks swears that these things work in perfect time." Jillian Powell sat with one ankle behind her head as she untangled a string of blue lights for over the walkway arch. Mrs. Franks' entire large front lot was stuffed with motion coordinated Christmas decorations her son had made for her before he graduated and left home. They had yet to turn everything on and confirm that it all worked together, but Mrs. Franks swore it would.

"I like Christmas just as much as the next person, but this seems a little excessive, even to me." Jillian dropped her leg from behind her head and stood, bending down and throwing one leg up in the air in a perfect split as she gathered the lights from the ground.

"You can never have too many decorations." Avery started up the ladder under the arch.

"At least not at Christmas. You can't look at all this and not smile."

"And that's what Mrs. Franks needs. Cheered up. A reason to be happy."

"It should make her happy that her son is back from out west." After hooking the lights on the end of her shoe, Jillian did a slow handstand, lifting the lights up to Avery.

With anyone else, Avery might assume she was practicing a routine or maybe showing off. With Jillian... Avery had decided you could take the girl out of the circus, but you apparently could not take the circus out of the girl.

"Have you seen him?" Jillian asked, her voice sounding perfectly normal, despite the fact that she was upside down and holding herself up with her hands.

"Mrs. Franks said he'd left for a few days. Something about a project he promised to do." As she spoke, she remembered Gator saying he was going out of town for a few days and Avery's gaze fell on the G. Franks printed on the underside of the arch where she pinned the lights. The same G. Franks that was on all the decorations in the yard. Her hands stilled. "Has Mrs. Franks ever said what her son's name is?"

"Nope." Jillian dropped her feet to the ground as Avery took the last of the lights in hand. "She says 'my son' this and 'my son' that."

"She only had one child. And I know she's described him as compassionate, articulate..."

"Don't forget sweet," Jillian said. "And kind. She uses that word a lot."

Avery bit her lip. It couldn't be. Sweet, gentle Mrs. Franks could not be the mother of that huge, uncouth mountain man. "Didn't she say he was married?"

In the process of lifting one of her feet behind her head, Jillian whipped her head around so fast she stumbled. She quickly tucked her head to her stomach and did a summersault. She landed on her back on the wet, cold ground and blinked up at Avery.

"I'm not sure. Separated maybe? Odd question coming from the all-men-leave-for-younger-prettier-women-so-why-bother person."

Avery leaned against the steps of the ladder and looked down at Jillian. "See? He's separated." She ignored the part of her that eddied in disappointment. "He's already left his wife for someone younger and prettier."

"You don't know that."

"It's a safe bet."

"I disagree with you, but I'm also going to say we all have our little hang ups and that one's yours. That and your cat. Where is it by the way?"

"I left Miss Prissypants at home. Ever since she jumped out of her carrier when I was setting up the farm display for the Christmas celebration next week, I've been afraid I'd lose her, so I've not been carrying her off the farm."

"I'm telling you, she jumped out because she saw the dog catcher. Animals hate him." Jillian had tucked her elbows in and folded her legs and feet in such a way as to form her body in a ball. She rocked back and forth. "You mark my words. There's bones in his basement."

Avery snorted, but didn't argue. They'd already had this discussion. Ellie had said that McKoy Rodning was a genuine nice guy. A local fellow, well-liked in the community, and good at his job. But nothing anyone said would convince Jillian that he was anything but Jeffery Dahmer's evil twin. Jeffery being the good twin, of course.

Avery gave a silent sigh. Some people were just not meant to get along. "At any rate, Miss Prissypants is too valuable to risk losing her."

The screen door slapped as Avery stepped off the ladder. Mrs. Franks, bundled in a heavy coat, with a long scarf wrapped around her bare head and neck, stepped out onto the porch.

"I was about to come in and get you," Avery called, folding the ladder and carrying it to the porch where she leaned it against the railing. "We're ready for the initial lighting."

"I'm giving you the honor of flipping the switch, Avery."

"Are you sure? I thought you would want to."

"No. Tradition demands that the person who does the most work setting up the displays gets to flip the switch. Usually that's been my son, but this year, it was definitely you—you've been working for days on this. It was sweet of Jillian to come help you today."

A little bite of guilt pinched Avery. Jillian had manned the Christmas tree sales counter so she could spend extra time helping Mrs. Franks. She deserved to flip the switch.

Jillian waved her hands. "No. I'm good. I wouldn't have had the patience to replace all the burnt out lights and read the diagrams about where each piece of the display went in the yard. I can tell by your face that you think you owe me, but the little bit of untangling I did here today makes me want to go bury my frustrations in cheese fries and a chocolate milkshake."

"So, it's up to you." Mrs. Franks' smile was warm and sincere. She could not be Gator's mother. Not Gator of the woman-eating dogs.

Avery and Jillian stood at the switch with Mrs. Franks, whose expectant smile never faltered. Avery reached for the black knob and flicked it down with a snap. Immediately, the yard and surrounding acreage illuminated with brightly colored lights.

White lights and red ribbons had always been Avery's favorite Christmas decorations, but she had to admit the work had been worth it. The smile on Mrs. Franks' face rivaled the brightness of the decorations in her yard.

"It looks just like it did ten years ago when my son lit them for the last time," Mrs. Franks said breathlessly. Her cool, dry hand slid into Avery's. "Thank you so much."

"It was fun," Avery said and meant it.

"Both of you come inside for some hot cocoa. I have those pictures you asked for, too, Avery." Mrs. Franks slid her fingers out and turned toward the door.

Jillian moved toward the steps. "I can't. I promised Ellie I'd be back at the counter by dark to help with the crowds."

"But you can stay for a few minutes?" Mrs. Franks turned to Avery.

"Sure. I'm excited about those pictures. I really wanted to come up with some old pictures of the farm to copy and frame for Fink and Ellie for Christmas."

"I'll see you guys later," Jillian said as she walked on her hands down the porch stairs.

"Thanks for your help, honey," Mrs. Franks called to her before she gripped Avery's elbow and they turned and walked in the front door. Lights from the decorations in the yard twinkled in the glass. "I wish I could pay you."

"If you would have paid us, it would have been work." Avery patted Mrs. Franks' hand. "I'm glad we could do it."

Fifteen minutes later, they sat at the old oak table in Mrs. Franks' cozy kitchen, steaming mugs of hot chocolate in front of each of them and old pictures from the seventies and eighties spread out on the scarred wood surface.

"This is the courthouse where it sat on State Street before the flood of '72."

"State Street? In Love? There aren't any houses there. It's a park."

"That's right. They were all washed away. The remnants of Hurricane Agnes." She tapped the picture with a thin finger. "No one died. That's why we decided it was okay to make a park. I think it was the next year or the one after that when they built the levy and started having the Christmas celebration there."

"They've been having it for almost fifty years?"

"Yep. And every year it gets bigger." She tapped a picture that was almost all white. "There's the blizzard of '93. Three feet of snow. That's the school."

"The school? The same building the kids use today?"

"Yep. It was only about twenty or thirty years old in that picture.

You can't tell because the snow was so deep. That was a March storm. The whole town was shut down for almost a week. Roads were closed. Nothing could get through, not even the milk truck. Farmers' tanks overflowed, and they had to dump their milk down the drain." She tapped another picture and Avery's heart jumped. It was her barn. "There's Fink and Ellie's barn. Of course, at the time it belonged to Ellie's first husband's grandparents, Sam and Marge Bright."

It wasn't her barn. She knew that of course. She pushed aside the little ache in her heart and pointed to the picture. "They must have had the area where Harper's small apartment is now, planted in Christmas trees. I can see about a foot of the tops of the trees through the snow." Harper, Ellie's daughter, was now married and living in Chile.

Mrs. Franks laughed. "I do believe you're right." She considered the picture for another moment. Avery noted that there were no missing boards on the sides of the barn as there were now. The old milkhouse still stood in the picture, although it was half-buried in snow. All that was left of it now was the cement foundation and two feet of stone walls.

"Oh, my." Mrs. Franks fished a picture out of the pile and held it up slowly. "I haven't seen this one in years."

Something in Mrs. Franks' tone caused Avery to look at her face. Her top lip was pulled between her teeth and her eyes glistened with moisture. Avery glanced back at the picture in her hand. It was in full color and looked newer than the ones they had been looking at. In the photo, the women's hair was big, very big, with frizzy, permed curls. A few wore knee warmers. None of the men had sideburns or any facial hair. At least two older people wore timeless ugly Christmas sweaters. Lights glittered in the background, illuminating bales of straw...

"That's the inside of the barn! It's some kind of party that was held in Fink and Ellie's barn!" Avery tried to be dignified, but she knew her smile was big and sloppy and probably made her look like a five year old who had just met Santa Claus.

"Yes. It was." Mrs. Franks' voice seemed dreamy. Avery wondered if she even realized that she had spoken. She stroked the edge of the picture, then gently pushed aside the pile of photos.

"Here," she said, picking up a similar colored photo with a young couple standing, arms around each other, smiling at the camera. The man towered over the woman and her left hand lay on his chest possessively. A small diamond twinkled on her hand.

"I just saw that man," Avery whispered. His dogs had tried to eat her.

"That was the night Jake asked me to marry him." Her voice wobbled. "We look so happy."

They did. Despite the fact that a very disturbing thought had taken root in her brain, Avery couldn't look at the picture without smiling back at the couple. "You look like you're in love."

"We were. That was a magical night. What I wouldn't do to go back and relive it."

You can never go back, only forward. Avery thought of the old proverb, but didn't voice it aloud. Mrs. Franks' face had a healthy glow and a beautiful smile. Avery hadn't ever seen her this happy and alive. It was like the memories that swirled through her head had brought out the life that the cancer had tried to smother.

"He was killed not long after that picture was taken."

"You never married?"

"No."

"But..."

"I know. My last name is Franks. I changed it after he died. After his son, my son, came to live with me."

Avery blinked, trying to figure out the puzzle Mrs. Franks had presented.

Mrs. Franks gave a laugh. "I can see the wheels turning." She tapped the picture. "It's a long story, but Jake's first wife left him and their small son for another woman. He hired me to watch his boy, and well..." She shrugged. "We fell in love." Her gaze seemed to caress the picture again. "I raised her son as mine."

"Don't these memories make you sad?" Avery bit her tongue. Maybe she shouldn't have asked that question. There were a hundred other questions wanting to tumble out her mouth, the biggest and most pressing one being about the man, her husband, in the picture, who looked exactly like...

"I supposed they should. But I'm not sad anymore. It's been thirty years. Looking at those pictures, remembering that magical night...all those feelings come back. The newness of being in love and the happiness as I thought of our life together. The lights and friends and fun...great food, good times and the fairy tale of Christmas. No, there's no sadness. Maybe the faintest longing for what might have been."

"I see." Avery studied the grain of wood on the table, hesitating to ask the question that lay like a tremolo on her tongue. She took a breath. "What's your son's name?"

"I guess you haven't met him, have you?" Mrs. Franks lifted her head and looked at Avery, her eyes still sparkling. "Gator. His name is Gator. And I'll have to arrange for you two to meet. I think you'll like him."

No. Avery wanted Mrs. Franks to take an interest in life. She wanted to cheer her and take her mind off her sickness, but she didn't want to spend any more time in Gator's presence than absolutely necessary.

She struggled for diplomacy over the extreme rejection she wanted to issue. "That's sweet, but I've actually already met him. And his dogs. They were..." Avery paused, trying to find a word that wouldn't scare Mrs. Franks.

"Just the sweetest dogs you'll ever meet," Mrs. Franks finished for her. "I know. They were from the last litter that Grandpa ever bred. They mean the world to Gator, but they have to be getting up in years. He slept with them in high school and they went everywhere with him. They were the only thing he took with him when he married and moved west."

Gator was married. Of course, he was. Not separated. Not divorced. Just every time she saw him he was alone except for the dogs. Now that she knew for sure he was married, she would absolutely put him out of her mind.

"They don't have parties like that anymore." Mrs. Franks was looking at the photo again, tracing the edge with her finger. "That barn gave the party character."

"Yeah." And they were going to tear it down. *Gator* was going to tear it down. Not that she could say that to Mrs. Franks. Although, she bet he wouldn't destroy it if he knew how much it meant to his mother.

Or maybe he still would. It wasn't like Avery knew him or the way he thought or anything.

"I wonder if Fink and Ellie would consider hosting another party there?" Mrs. Franks mused aloud.

Avery bit her tongue.

"I never really thought about a bucket list; I've been content with my life. But, if there's one thing that I'd love to do again...I'd love to relive that night." She tapped the picture gently, then lifted her head. This time her eyes looked tired and older than the mid-fifties age that she must be. Cancer had a way of stealing a person's youth, along with their joy. "Do you think..." Her voice trailed off.

Avery's heart twisted. She wasn't here to be a do-gooder. She wasn't even here to help a neighbor in need, although she might have started out with that in mind. She was here today to put up Mrs. Franks' Christmas decorations because she had come to admire and respect her, and she wanted to ease her burden and give her a reason to smile.

That had to be why, even though she knew the barn was slated for demolition, she opened her mouth and said, "I bet Fink and Ellie would let us have a Christmas party there this year. In fact, I'm sure they would."

Mrs. Franks beamed.

Avery reached over and sorted through the pictures. "I can decorate for it. Do we have more pictures to give me a better idea?" She could make the decorations match exactly if she had good enough pictures.

Mrs. Franks almost seemed to bounce in her chair. "I have a ton of pictures in boxes in the attic. I'll have to have Gator bring them down for me."

Avery's stomach grated like an out of tune orchestra. She'd promised something she had no hope of delivering. Mrs. Franks might actually get sicker because of the disappointment if Avery couldn't convince Fink and Ellie. Quite possibly Avery had set in motion what could be her final disappointment.

She had to look on the bright side. It could work out. It wouldn't be a money-making proposition for anyone, but maybe she could frame it in such a way that it would appeal to Fink and Ellie's compassionate nature. They both helped and volunteered in the community and were always open for ways to give back. Just this week they were donating the Christmas trees for the town Christmas festival.

They had said the barn was too expensive to insure. They would need insurance to do the party.

She thought about the money that she had been saving to buy a better tuba. She'd wanted to buy it before she went to audition in Washington D.C. on the fifteenth of December, and she had all but a couple hundred dollars in her savings account. There might be enough money there to take out an insurance policy for a one-night party.

"Did you hear me, honey?" Mrs. Franks asked.

"Um, no?" She'd been way too deep in her thoughts. She'd not even realized that Mrs. Franks had spoken. "I'm sorry. What did you say?"

"I said parties like this one are a lot of work." Mrs. Franks put a hand on her shoulder. "I can't ask you to put that kind of time into a frivolous thing just to make me happy. It's a nice idea, but let's let it rest."

"You didn't ask. I offered. And I love planning and decorating. I want to recreate the decorations and the menu and the music. Well, maybe not the music. Was it '80s rock?"

Mrs. Franks chuckled. "It was all Christmas music performed by the school orchestra. In fact, if I recall correctly, that was their concert venue that year because the auditorium was closed since they were removing the asbestos tiles from the ceiling."

"I might not be able to recreate a school building renovation to cause the auditorium to be closed."

"That's okay. They had a set of twins who went on to play professionally and they sounded much better than most school orchestras, or so I'm told. You're the music expert."

Immediately, Avery wondered if the twins that had gone on to play professionally were the Humphry twins from the Philadelphia Waterfront Orchestra that she'd played with. They were the right age. She made a mental note to call them. They weren't exactly close friends, but she had a good professional relationship with them. As good as a brass player could have with someone from the string section, anyway.

"We'll figure something out." Avery nodded decisively. She'd thought that a new tuba with better resonation might give her a slight edge when she auditioned, but right now, she'd rather spend her money on insurance so Mrs. Franks could have her party than on a new tuba that probably wouldn't make any difference in her sound. After all, she got the position at the Philadelphia Waterfront Orchestra with her old tuba. She was kind of attached to it anyway and hadn't relished the idea of setting it aside for a new instrument. Felt too much like the way her dad had set aside his wife and daughter for a new, younger wife. Whether or not he had children with that woman, she couldn't say. She hadn't talked to him since he walked out when she was ten. The last thing he'd said to her was, "Why don't you put all that hot air to good use and learn to play an instrument?"

So she did. Take that, Dad.

"I'll talk to Ellie and Fink, and if they'll let me, I'll be back to get all the details. But I don't want to tire you out."

"Planning a party is fun." Mrs. Franks smiled as she said it, but Avery recognized the droop of her shoulders and the tightened lines around her mouth. There had been a lot going on for Mrs. Franks today with the decorations and now the party talk. Obviously, it had worn her out.

"Do you feel well enough to eat the chicken rice soup I brought? I'll warm it up."

"That would be wonderful."

"How about I help you onto the couch?"

They had walked back down the hall and reached the living room doorway when the door opened, and Gator stood outlined in the light from the Christmas lights.

Chapter Four

The dog-hater was standing with his mother.

Gator ground his teeth together. Just because she didn't like Gladys and Finch didn't mean that she wasn't good with anyone. Still, it annoyed him that she was here with his mom. Or maybe he was angry at himself because the sight of her had made his heart skip and the dark cloud that seemed to be following him lift.

"Hi, Gator. I wasn't expecting you so early." His mother sounded weak and tired. Fear caused his irritation to hitch up another notch.

His eyes snapped to the little blond. "You should know better than to have her outside working in her condition. She's exhausted. You need to know when to quit."

It was an unfair attack. Guilt choked Gator's throat. Avery's eyes opened wide as she eased his mother down on the couch. He hadn't considered decorating the house or yard for Christmas, but when he saw it, he knew someone had made the effort just to make his mother smile. It should have been him. He should have thought of it. He should have been here helping her all fall.

He rubbed the back of his neck. "I'm sorry. I'm more angry at myself. But she is tired." There. He'd seemed to get really good at apologizing for stuff he couldn't even say he'd done, and it still hadn't kept his ex happy. He had vowed to never apologize to a woman again. Still, it didn't take a brain surgeon to see that in this case, he needed to.

Avery squatted down at the foot of the couch and gently slipped off his mother's shoes. "It's okay. You're right. We were talking and I got excited about something and we should have stopped a long time ago."

His mom waved a hand. "Stop it, Gator. I like the company."

"You've tired yourself out." He grabbed the folded comforter from the back of the couch.

"Just because I have cancer doesn't mean that I'm not an adult that has been making her own decisions since before you were born. And I can continue to do so." His mother smiled to soften her words. "I was having fun. I think Avery was too."

Her last statement sounded uncertain and her eyes cut to Avery who had set the shoes aside and carefully placed his mother's feet on the couch. Gator's heart ached, and he thought of the ugly snowman in the hall. He opened his mouth to reassure his mother that she was still beautiful on the inside.

But Avery was already talking. "I was. I love looking at the old pictures and dreaming about other places and times. But Gator's right. We should have stopped before you were too tired to stand. You can't fight the cancer if your body is exhausted by doing things, even if they are fun."

As she spoke, she tucked the blanket in around his mom's feet. "Now, you'd better not say that I've worn you out too much and you're not hungry, or your scary-looking son might forget about feeding me to his dogs and eat me himself."

Gator pursed his lips to keep from grinning.

"I'll eat," his mother said, not bothering to hide her grin.

"That's what I want to hear. I'll go warm up that bowl of chicken rice soup." Avery walked out, not looking at him. Why would she? He'd basically yelled at her and insulted her, while all the time, it was obvious she cared from the careful way she handled his mother and spoke to her.

He waited until he heard sounds from the kitchen before he opened his mouth to voice the thought that was uppermost on his mind. "Isn't this what home nursing is supposed to do? Feed you. Help you up and around? What is she doing here?"

His mother's eyes stayed shut, but her chest compressed like she was letting out a long sigh. "Home nursing does a great job. And I loved Laura, my nurse this fall. But since she quit, the other nurses...they're very professional, and I'm not complaining, but they don't..." Her mouth trembled. Gator knelt and took her hand. "They don't love me. I'm just a job to them."

"And this Avery does?" He regretted the question as soon as it left his lips. "Never mind. Did you consider that maybe she's expecting you to die and thinks you'll sign the house and ground over to her?"

"Gator!"

"Mom, I don't know this person, and you really don't either. People do this kind of thing all the time. They prey on folks that are too old or sick to think straight." He didn't actually believe this of Avery, but once he'd started on the subject, it seemed like a good idea to continue. His mother didn't actually own the house—when his grandfather died, leaving it to her, she had signed it over to him, saying that it was rightfully his since she wasn't actually a "real" part of the family. In return, he had said that as long as she was alive, it was her house to live in.

"Gator, I raised you better." His mother still didn't open her eyes or raise her voice, but her words cut him, just the same. Because they were true.

"I'm sorry." He seemed to be unable to open his mouth today without saying something he needed to apologize for. "I feel guilty because she's doing the things that I should have thought of doing."

His mother draped an arm across her eyes like she had a headache. But her mouth ticked up some. "You're a man. I would be weirded out if you suggested decorating."

"Weirded out?"

"People say that on TV all the time. Why can't I?"

"Because you're my mom and my mom doesn't talk like that." And his mom wasn't bald and didn't have cancer and had always looked young and healthy. He couldn't stand it if her personality changed too.

As though she could read his thoughts, she patted his hand. "How was your trip?"

"It was great. I got the things I needed out of my apartment, and my boss said I could take as much time off as I needed to." He didn't add that he wouldn't be paying any more rent on his apartment, so everything he left was gone for good. And, he could take as much time off as he wanted. Without pay.

"That's wonderful. But really, you don't need to stay here with me. An occasional visit is fine and if you can't swing that, we can talk on the phone."

Before he could answer, Avery walked in carrying a bowl on a tray. "Here's your soup, Mrs. Franks." A glass and some pills along with silverware and a napkin were arranged beside a vase with one happy yellow rose. Maybe it was just a grocery store flower, but his mother's eye caught on its cheerful color and it made her smile.

Gator stared at the flower. Everything Avery did made him feel inadequate. His mother loved the flower. Just as she loved the knick knacks and the yard decorations. Why couldn't he think to do something that would make her smile?

Paying the deductibles and copays that lay stacked on her desk an inch thick ought to do it. The sooner he could get that old barn torn down, the sooner he could make his mother smile. Ease some of the worry lines from her forehead.

Avery set the tray down on the coffee table. "Can we prop some pillows behind you?"

Gator stood and took the pillows that Avery held. When she didn't let go, he looked down. Her eyes cracked like flint and her mouth didn't move when she gritted out, "I'd like to talk to you. Alone."

His heart beat faster. Drat the stupid thing.

Turning back to his mom, he said, "This soup's a little hot, and Avery has something in the kitchen she needs me to see."

His mother nodded slowly, not opening her eyes. "I've been telling you for days that the light over the stove needs fixed."

"Avery needs to show me." He didn't wait for his mother's answer, and stepped away from the couch. He didn't touch Avery as he brushed by her, but for some reason he couldn't explain, he grabbed her hand. He tugged on her hand and she moved to follow him, not speaking. Not pulling away, either.

When they got to the kitchen, he was so focused on how he could unobtrusively keep holding her hand, that he had forgotten she was angry. He turned to face her, freezing at the look on her face.

"If you honestly think that I'm here to take your mother's house or money or anything else that is your mother's, I want to tell you now—"

"I don't."

A few more words came out of her mouth before his two penetrated. Her mouth stopped, open half-way. Her brows lifted. She took in a deep breath, then exhaled.

There was only a short distance between them, a few inches separating their bodies, and the air around them seemed to settle as the charge dissipated.

"That's not what you said," Avery breathed out. Just as quiet, but these words were without heat.

"I know. I'm stupid sometimes."

Wrinkles appeared in her forehead and her lips pursed.

He took the offensive. "Mom doesn't even own the house. I do."

"I don't care."

"I know."

"So, you...don't want your mother to like or trust me?"

"I told you. I'm stupid sometimes. I want to protect her when I'm not around and it seemed like a good idea, since I was on the subject anyway, that I warn her about strangers taking advantage. I knew as I was saying it that you weren't a threat."

"How did you know?"

"I saw the way you handled her. I saw you waving your overgrown trumpet around. You climb light poles for fun."

"I most certainly do not." Her hand twitched in his and he realized that he hadn't ever let go. He'd be darned if he was going to now. It felt way too good in his. There was no harm in holding someone's hand.

"Fink and Ellie wouldn't trust you if you weren't trustworthy. Honestly, I look at everything you've done to make her smile, and I realize that I should be doing those things."

Avery's expression had changed. Her eyes pleaded with him to understand. "I really like your mom. She's like the mom I wish I had. Not that my mom wasn't a good mom. She did her best. But Mrs. Franks is so...nurturing. I know it's good to help people, and I enjoy doing that for the sake of being a good person, but I'm here with your mom because I truly enjoy her company."

Her lips formed and "O" before she yanked her hand out of his. "But maybe you could help her with her soup? I really need to go." And, without waiting for an answer, she turned and was down the hall and through the front door so fast, Gator actually looked behind him to make sure the stove wasn't on fire. He had no idea what caused her to fly away. But his hand felt warm and it tingled along with his heart as he stood in the kitchen with a bemused smile on his face.

Chapter Five

W hat had she done?

Avery blew into her tuba, not even thinking about the music as she hammered out the bass line of the Tuba Polka. She'd memorized it years ago and didn't have to give the notes a thought. Which was good because she was so busy castigating herself for holding a married man's hand.

She hated cheaters. Those people who made promises that meant less than broken glass and rotten fish. People like her dad. Someone younger. Someone prettier. Someone who didn't have a loud, obnoxious daughter who never stopped talking.

Then that loud, obnoxious daughter grows up and manages to find a man exactly like her dad, dates him, and almost marries him. Would have married him if the guy had waited to cheat on her until after the second ring was on her finger.

Now, she was just like them. Those women.

"Maybe you're being a little dramatic."

Avery jerked her head up at Jillian's voice. She hadn't even realized that she'd come to the end of the music. She lowered her tuba away from her mouth and looked across the old barn floor as Jillian closed the wooden door behind her.

"Dramatic?" Had Jillian found out? How? She hadn't breathed a word. Surely, Gator wouldn't have...

"You told Ellie that having this Christmas party could save a neighbor's life." Jillian gracefully jumped up on the knee-railing that divided the barn floor in half.

Relief made her exhale deeply. So, maybe that was a little dramatic. "Research has shown that a positive attitude is invaluable in overcoming a sickness like cancer. You have no idea how much this will cheer her up. If we get it right."

"Dog owners are more likely to survive cancer than cat owners." Jillian did a perfect backbend on the knee-wall.

"You made that up." Avery set her tuba down in its case. She pressed the mouthpiece into its velvet holder.

"If anyone ever does a study on it, that's what they'll find."

If anyone did a study on girls whose fathers cheated on their mothers, what would they find? Was she messed up in a conventional way, or was she abnormal all the way around? Because normal women did not go around holding hands with married men. Especially married men that they didn't even like. Because she didn't like Gator. Much. Honestly, she might have been a little attracted to him before she found out that he was married, despite the dog issue, but now that she knew, she was not going to give him another thought.

She stood up, brushing off her knees, and looked around.

Jillian had disappeared, and Avery knew what that meant.

"I'm up here."

"I figured you'd found something to climb."

Miss Prissypants padded over from where she had been grooming herself. She rubbed against Avery's leg, then looked up, blinking her green eyes.

"Just a minute, Miss." Avery picked up the slightly altered baby carrier and fitted it over her shoulders, clicking the fastenings. Then swooped down and deposited Miss Prissypants in it. She stroked her head and searched the ceiling for Jillian, finally spotting her on the top beam over the large, open barn floor.

"I can see the big picture up here. The thing needs cleaned. First."

Avery gave Miss Prissypants one last pat, then pulled her phone from her pocket and pulled up the Notes app. After creating a document, she put a number one, then typed "clean."

Something banged against the outside wall.

"What was that?" Jillian called.

It had sounded like someone hammered against the wall. "I'll check."

A gap from a few missing boards seemed to be close to where the noise came from. Avery walked cautiously along the old floor—not only were there boards missing from the walls, but the floor, which was covered in places with old hay and straw, had a few holes in it as well. She wasn't going to think about what that said about the safety of her idea of having a party in less than three weeks. The floor could be patched. She stuck her head out the hole.

"What are you doing?"

Gator stood halfway up a ladder perched against the side of the barn. A tool belt hung from his waist.

A huff caused Avery to glance to the left and freeze. His ferocious man-eating canines lay in the brown grass, their teeth sparkling in the weak December sun. Noticing her mistress's distress, as cats were naturally attuned to their human's moods, Miss Prissypants opened one eye and studied the creatures with more intelligence than both of their brains combined contained.

Avery moved her hand slowly and stroked Miss Prissypants's head. "Don't worry, honey. They'll have to eat me before they can get to you." Maybe that wasn't the most reassuring thing she could have said, but most of her brainpower was involved in trying to figure out if the hole she was looking through was big enough for the dogs to squeeze in. It was a toss-up.

"Avery." Jillian placed her hand on Avery's shoulder.

She jumped and turned, smacking her head on the barn board before jerking herself out of the hole.

"Ellie texted me, and I need to take over at the shop for a while."

"Oh, sure. Fine." Avery had worked all morning and, although it was the busiest time of year for Christmas trees, it had been pretty slow, even for a Tuesday. Things always picked up in the afternoon.

"Gator's here, and I'm going to find out what's going on." She

45

could only think of one reason why he and his woman-hating dogs would be here. "Ellie said they'd hold off on tearing the barn down until after Christmas." Obviously, he couldn't wait.

Jillian grinned and held a hand out, palm down in a *calm down* gesture. "I know. I know. Maybe he's here to replace a few of the missing boards."

Avery didn't really think so, but she didn't disagree. She nodded skeptically, and with a raised brow, Jillian left.

How could she confront that confounded man without getting eaten? Her stomach twisted when she glanced back out the opening. The dogs still stared at her. A silvery rope of drool hung out of the brown one's mouth. Avery swallowed the tightness in her throat. She would brave the dogs for Mrs. Franks. If that's what it took to keep Gator from tearing her barn down.

Plus, she wasn't the slightest bit afraid of facing him after holding his hand. He's the one that should be ashamed, since he knew his marital status. She had forgotten he was married. It was a mistake anyone could make. He could bet the farm, or the barn, that she wouldn't make it again.

After peeking back out of the opening, she looked around the interior. Through the cracks in the barn wall, she could see where Gator's ladder leaned up against the side. Blessing Jillian for teaching her climbing techniques—this was the second time in the last few days that she had utilized them—she patted Miss Prissypants's head. "I'm sorry, little girl, but I have to set you down. I know I can climb up there, but I can't do it with you in your carrier. Plus, if I fall, I don't want you to get hurt. It's not your fault I'm terrified of dogs and have to avoid them at all costs."

Miss Prissypants seemed to understand—she always did. Avery gently set her on a small pile of old, musty straw bales. "Stay here until I get back."

After looking around, switching her tail and sniffing the straw, Miss Prissypants settled her bottom end regally on the stiff bales.

"It's not going to take me long. I'm simply going to inform him that Ellie, who owns this barn, said that it stands until after my party." It wasn't Avery's barn, and she wasn't going to allow herself to be sad about its ultimate destruction. She would ignore the ache in her chest, and she would most certainly not think about how much rich history resided in these old beams and timbers.

Finding hand holds in the old wood was easy. Remembering the technique that Jillian had taught her, she twisted her knees out and flattened herself against the wall. Jillian could go faster, but Avery had never been athletic, so the very fact that she could even get herself up a wall seemed like a great accomplishment. However, she didn't take the time to congratulate herself on her achievement. There was an obtuse, obstinate man who needed to be reminded who, exactly, owned this barn.

Angling her climb so that her head popped up in the open space caused by a missing board, Avery pulled herself up one last foot and, clinging to the wall with both hands and feet, stuck her head out the hole directly beside the ladder and Gator's large left foot.

"What are you doing?" She wasn't going to beat around the bush.

For one terrifying second, she was afraid that he was going to fall off the ladder. He jumped and swung his head around.

"Holy crap, lady."

"My name is Avery," she snapped, instantly remorseful. Her eyes dropped. "I'm sorry. It wasn't my intention to scare you. However, I must inform you that you need to stop tearing this barn down immediately. I have express permission from Ellie Finkenbinder to use it for my Christmas party. That's not for three weeks. Obviously, it needs to be standing, intact at that time. Anything that you—"

"Stop. Be quiet for a second."

Avery clamped her mouth shut.

"First of all, I'm not tearing the barn down. I wanted to see the condition of the roof and do some measuring. Secondly, I spoke with Fink Finkenbinder. Who, apparently, owns the other half of this barn. And he said I could begin demolition today. I'm bonded and insured, and I have a signed contract. With Fink." Gator lifted a brow. "You have a contract?"

"Of course not. Not for a party."

"You're insured."

Avery looked down. Way down. Her stomach wobbled, and her vision wavered. "Not yet."

"Then I'm not sure what the issue is."

"This is obviously a misunderstanding between Fink and Ellie. And, as much as I don't like to get between married persons—" Guilt hit her hard between the shoulder blades as she remembered Gator holding her hand, and worse, that she had liked it. "But in this case, it's obvious that we need to say something to them." She took a breath to go on, but Gator interrupted.

"I don't see the need. I've got a contract. I've got a buyer, and I don't have time to mess around."

"You can't wait until after the party? It's only three weeks." Something that felt close to panic balled in Avery's chest. It wasn't that big of a deal if she couldn't have the party for Mrs. Franks. She told herself that, but somehow, it felt huge.

"Look, I wish I could." He opened his mouth to say more, but then closed it like he changed his mind. He pulled his tape measure off his belt and began to pull the tape out, sliding it up the slope of the roof.

His jaw set, his posture dismissive. Avery considered telling him about how the party would cheer his mother and possibly help her fight the cancer, but she dismissed the idea. If he had such little regard for his wife and such little respect for his mother that he would stand in her kitchen holding the hand of a woman he wasn't married to, then trying to appeal to his compassionate nature was futile.

Avery began to descend. She needed to get this stopped before it was too late. Ellie had agreed to allow her to have the party and to fix a few holes in the floor, but she wasn't going to be interested in paying to have the sides put back on the barn.

When she reached the bottom, she checked Miss Prissypants, who was sleeping soundly. Typically, Avery took her almost everywhere, but she was in a bit of a hurry and knew the cat would be fine. She wanted to get this settled. The party was not going to "cure" Mrs. Franks of her cancer, but in her heart, Avery knew that recreating the evening when she got engaged and enabling her to relive those memories would encourage her and lift her spirits through the difficult cancer treatments.

Avery hurried out of the barn towards the Christmas tree shop, feeling like a five-year-old going to tattle on her little brother. But since the barn wasn't hers, there really wasn't another way to solve the problem. Hopefully, Ellie wasn't busy with a customer and they could get this fixed fast. She wasn't trying to keep Gator from tearing the barn down eventually, as much as she wished she could stop it; she just needed it to stay up for another few weeks until after her party.

Chapter Six

Gator watched the confounded woman stalk across the yard and up past the house. It didn't take a rocket scientist to figure out what she was doing—tattling.

The tape spooled in and snapped as it hit the end. He hooked it over his belt. He'd better go make sure Ellie didn't change Fink's mind. Three weeks wasn't very long, but Christmas wasn't going to be very merry at his house if he didn't get the money for doing this job before the big day. The stack of bills from the hospital and doctors and the list of things the insurance company wasn't covering seemed to grow every day.

This morning when he'd come in from feeding the dogs, his mother had been sitting at the desk, deep creases in her forehead and her lips between her teeth. He wasn't a health nut, but he did know that stress wasn't good under ideal circumstances. It couldn't be beneficial to a woman with cancer.

Stomping down the ladder, he bade his dogs "stay" before striding up the yard behind that impossible woman. She did have a big heart. And soft hands. He shoved the thought of that hand, and how good it had felt in his, out of his mind. Although, he couldn't stop his heart from doing a little skip and jump.

His mother loved her, that was for sure. She'd been tired last night after Avery had gone home, but when her eyes were open, they were looking out the window at the front yard and the decorations that Avery had set up and lit. No small job. He ought to know, he'd done it throughout his high school and college years as he made new decorations to add to the old ones.

There were a few cars in the tree farm lot as he made his way over the stones to the small trailer that served as office and shop. Bells above the door jingled happily as he opened it and stepped inside to the almost suffocating warmth. Two heads—a light one and a dark one—turned in his direction. He shut the door with a decisive click and faced Avery and her dark-haired friend as "I'll be Home for Christmas" played softly in the background.

Avery's chin went up. Despite the fact that he towered over her, she somehow managed to give the impression that she was looking down her nose at him. "Ellie and Fink aren't here."

"I see," he said, not allowing his lips to turn up. The place was one room and an office, the door of which was wide open. He could see that they were the only ones in the room. Maybe Avery said the obvious because she felt as juvenile as he did.

The brunette shifted some papers on the counter. "Their son broke his leg. It's a pretty bad break."

Gator scrunched up his face. That sounded painful. "Ouch."

"Yeah. The ambulance just left. The whole family is headed to Pittsburgh."

He'd missed it since he had been working on the far side of the barn. "Hmm. So, you weren't able to tattle on me after all?"

"I wasn't tattling! I told you, Ellie told me the barn would stand for three weeks."

"And I told you, Fink said I could start demolition today."

"Would it hurt for you to wait?"

He didn't want to get into his money issues which involved his ex, nor his mother's unpaid insurance deductibles and copays. "I need to get this job done before my leave of absence is up and I have to go back to my real job in Montana."

The bell jingled over the door as it opened and Mayor Higham, tall and with slightly stooped shoulders, and who hadn't changed a bit in the last ten years, walked in holding a clipboard, with his face permanently wrinkled in the worried expression of a bloodhound under his bald head and bushy brows.

"Mr. Higham." Gator nodded at the mayor, who was as tall as he, and shook his hand.

After a few pleasantries, the mayor's expression grew serious again. "I have one more booth to fill for the town celebration on Saturday. It's actually the biggest draw every year. Sometimes we make almost a quarter of our profit on it. I should fill it first, but every year I think we should skip it, since it's the hardest booth to work. Anyway, I was hoping that I could offer a little free advertising for the farm and entice Fink or Ellie to man it for me."

"They just left..." Avery began, but the mayor was already nodding.

"I heard." The mayor's normally sour face stretched into a semblance of a grin. "So, Jillian, what are you doing Saturday?"

An expression, maybe like disappointment, flashed across Avery's face, and it occurred to Gator that the mayor hadn't really looked at her. His first impression of her was that she was a bit of an airhead, and she hadn't even had the cat strapped to her then. Granted, she was up a light pole. But maybe the town had assumed the same thing.

"I'm sorry, Mayor. I just promised Fink and Ellie that if they weren't back by Saturday, I'd man the farm's booth at the festival. Ellie has a ton of Christmas wreaths and decorations made, plus they have apples and cider. Wish I could." Her expression said she wished anything but.

"Gator?" The mayor turned toward him. "I know you don't have a business to advertise, so I can't give any incentive there, but maybe you'd devote some time for a good cause? We're splitting the money fifty-fifty between putting in new sidewalks in the downtown and sending Christmas sweaters to the mothers of active duty servicemen."

"Love to, Mayor, but I'm entered in the lumberjack competition. Plus, I'll be helping my mom."

"Oh, yes. I forgot about her. You'll be busy."

"I can do it, Mayor," Avery said in a small voice. She fingered her large, bell-shaped earring.

The mayor turned doubtful eyes on Avery. "This would involve taking people's money and counting it. Making change. That type of thing. Aren't you hauling that big horn around and marching in the parade?"

"The parade's at eight. I'm in it, yes. But I can open the booth immediately after."

The mayor looked around the office skeptically. He narrowed his eyes and raised a brow. "The cat stays home."

Avery hesitated. Her hand dropped from her earring and skimmed down her fuzzy, soft-looking oversized sweater which was cinched at her waist by a large, wide belt. "Okay," she said softly.

The mayor stared at her.

Avery met his gaze without blinking.

Gator watched the exchange, wanting, for some reason, to defend Avery. The mayor hadn't exactly made any accusations, either of stupidity or theft, but he'd implied something.

"My mother loves Avery." No one had a better reputation in town than his mother. Gator leaned a hip against the small table and crossed his arms over his chest, trying to appear casual. Like he defended women every day.

"Oh? She does?" The mayor's bushy brows floated up toward his forehead.

Gator hid his smug satisfaction. The mayor glanced back at Avery with fresh appreciation. Gator's estimation of Avery rose. Apparently, she hadn't been running around town bragging about how she was helping her sick neighbor.

"Well, then." The mayor lifted his clipboard. "I'll put you down for booth 342. Be there as soon as the parade is over and it's your responsibility until twelve."

"You've got it," Avery said.

The mayor flipped through a few pages. "I guess I'd better take Fink and Ellie off of the Christmas tree trimming contest. That's a shame. Their farm has not only donated the trees for it every year since Ellie and Fink married, but they've decorated under the farm banner, and if I'm not mistaken, they've won every year, except the year Ellie hired Mr.

Herschel, the chemistry teacher, to create changing colors of lights with chemical concoctions."

"That actually sounds like a great idea," Jillian said.

"It would have been, if the tree hadn't exploded." The mayor scratched his head. "I think that might have been the year after Mr. Herschel exploded the school's parade float."

"Oh, my," Avery said. "Mr. Herschel sounds like he might be a little dangerous."

"Yeah. Last I heard, he'd gotten a job in West Virginia in the coal mines, where they expect people to be blowing things up."

They all looked at each other and nodded silently. Sounded like that man had finally found his niche.

Avery cleared her throat. "When is the tree trimming contest scheduled?"

"Two o'clock," the mayor answered.

"I can do it." Avery tugged on her sweater sleeves.

"That would be fine," the mayor said. "Except, it takes two people."

"I can't help," Jillian said. "I'm at the booth all day."

"I'll do it." Gator wanted to take his lips off and examine them. Where did those words come from? He was already doing the Lumberjack competition. Plus, it would put him in contact with Avery.

The mayor nodded. "Well then. That's fine." He scribbled on his clipboard. "Do you want to decorate as a couple, or under the farm banner?"

"No!" Avery almost shouted.

Gator crossed his arms over his chest. What was that about?

Jillian gave her an odd look too.

"No?" The mayor's pen hovered over his clipboard. "You've changed your mind?"

"Uh, no." Avery's eyes slid to Gator's, then skittered away. "Under the farm. We'll do it for the farm."

He didn't have much use for women. Except his mother. After what his ex had done to him, he had no interest in relationships or any kind of acquaintance with a woman where she might be able to try to fleece him, or show him how his money, or lack of it, was more important than any promises they made or vows they spoke. But he had to admit,

Avery's quick and adamant denial—like she wanted to make sure that no one thought they were in any kind of relationship—shocked him. If he were honest, he was a little offended. Not hurt. Just offended.

"Okay then." The mayor scribbled the last letter with a flourish, then looked up with his lips pinched together. "Thank you all so kindly for your help. I'll see you Saturday." The bells jingled as he walked out.

There were a few beats of silence after the door closed. Gator still couldn't quite believe he'd volunteered to decorate a Christmas tree with Avery. He'd never even bothered to watch the contest before. Did people plan this? Did they bring their own decorations? He had no idea. After Avery's quick and strong denial of any kind of relationship, he didn't even want to discuss it with her. But he'd never catered to his wants before.

He cleared his throat. "So, how do we do the Christmas tree decorating contest?"

"I don't know. I just moved here this summer."

"Me too," Jillian chimed in as the bell rang and a customer Gator didn't recognize entered.

He nodded to the man, woman, and the two small children. They greeted him back, and after making sure he wasn't in line, walked to the counter and started talking about wrapping a tree with Jillian.

Gator caught Avery's eye. "I'm going back to the barn." He didn't have time to stand around and wonder about a tree trimming contest.

Her eyes got big. Almost like she was panicking, and he remembered she didn't want him tearing the precious barn down because she wanted to have some kind of fluffy little party.

Women. Seriously.

She didn't say anything as she walked past him as he held the door.

He closed it carefully behind them, wondering if she would turn and start yelling at him about how he couldn't destroy the barn. Either that, or freeze him out until she got her way. Or maybe yell at him first, then lapse into the silent treatment. Yeah. That last one was the most likely.

Avery walked beside him, taking two steps to his every one. Her head was bent like she needed to watch her step carefully. Her brown leather boots looked expensive to him and hardened his resolve.

She was likely giving him the silent treatment and was only walking beside him so he knew it. Well, he wasn't going to say anything and give her the chance to snub him.

"I'll call Ellie later tonight after things have calmed down for her and ask her about the contest," Avery said.

Gator stumbled. So, he wasn't getting the silent treatment. "Great. I'll talk to mom. Maybe she has some ideas."

"She probably has pictures of the winning trees from years past. She has pictures of everything else."

He shouldn't be surprised that Avery knew that about his mom. "She probably does."

Avery shoved her hands on the back of her hips, her head still down. "I'll get my stuff out of the barn. How soon do you think you're going to start demolition?"

This time Gator stumbled and almost fell. Avery stopped and turned immediately. "Are you okay?"

"Uh. Yeah." Surprised at how much he wanted to come back with an offer to hold off demo until she had her party, he slowly straightened. Surely, there wouldn't be any harm in waiting another three weeks. Except the money. He really needed the money. Not for himself, but for his mother.

Avery closed the short distance between them. "Did you sprain your ankle? It seems like you're in pain." She took a breath like she was going to say more, but then snapped her mouth shut. He almost wished she'd talk a little longer. It would give him time to gather his thoughts.

"No. My ankle is fine." His phone buzzed in its belt holder. He unlatched his device and glanced at the screen.

From Bret Shuff, his best friend from high school.

> Still looking for a short job over the holidays?

The heavy weight that seemed to push on his chest lifted. It might be nothing, but he was going to go with his gut.

"When were you planning your party?"

Her eyes widened as she jerked her head up, like she was wondering if she had heard him right.

"Between Christmas and New Year's."
He typed on his phone.

> Yes.

"Could you do it the week before Christmas?" he asked.
"Yes," she said without hesitation.
"Then I'll hold off on demolition until then."
His phone buzzed again.

> I've got a rush job. Needs finished by next
> Saturday. Pays good.

"That's perfect." Avery's face fell. "Except, I originally wanted it before Christmas, but the guy who was coming to patch the barn floor couldn't do it until the 23rd."

"See if he can change it." He looked down at his phone and typed.

> I'm in.

She shook her head, her lips flat. "He can't. I already tried."
"Gator."

Avery and he turned together, although he knew just by the sound of the voice who it was. The familiar tension bubbled in his stomach. It had been two years since he signed her papers. He thought he'd forgotten that feeling.

He hesitated, wishing Avery would walk away. He wasn't sure why he didn't want to have to introduce them, but Avery didn't move.

Kristen hadn't changed at all. Still thin and tall. Athletic. Dark hair and tanned. He bit the bullet. "Avery, this is Kristen. Kristen, Avery." He gave a small gesture between the two women. Maybe it would be enough.

"I'm Gator's wife."

He should have known it wouldn't be. "Ex," he ground out. Then he waited. If there was one thing he had learned, it was that she would talk when she wanted.

"So nice to meet you, Avery." Kristen held out a slender, but well-muscled hand.

"I didn't realize Gator was divorced." Avery shook Kristen's hand. Kristen made Avery seem extra small and curvy.

Kristen ignored Avery, turning instead to him. "I'm only in town for a couple of days, Gator. I was hoping to talk to you."

"Maybe later. I'm busy right now."

Kristen gave Avery a thoughtful glance. Gator knew she wasn't seeing what she thought she should. In her long boho-type skirt and thick corded sweater, Avery was obviously not an outdoorsy type. Her cheeks were pink, but her skin was white and delicate. Her loopy earrings and long pink fingernails would look out of place holding a rifle or scaling a fish. Things Kristen and he had done all the time. He had thought their shared interests made them perfect for each other.

He'd been wrong.

"Gator." Kristen didn't pout, and she absolutely didn't bat her lashes. His name was a firm word from the lips of a woman who was used to fighting for what she wanted.

"Not now." Taking a huge gamble, Gator grabbed Avery's hand. Maybe if he were honest with himself, he'd admit he'd been looking for an excuse to hold it again. It seemed to fit so perfectly in his. Still did. That frisson of feeling traveled up his arm again, hitting him straight in the heart. He told himself it was because they were so different. After all, the few times Kristen had allowed him to hold her hand, there had been no heat.

He tugged. Avery came with no resistance, making him doubly glad he'd offered to wait to start on the barn.

"I'll catch you at your mom's later," Kristen called to their backs.

As much as he wanted to completely ignore her, he made himself wave his hand in acknowledgement. He didn't turn around.

They were almost to the barn, and Gator was enjoying the walk and the feel of the woman beside him. The occasional brush of her arm against his. Funny, since he wasn't sure he even liked Avery. But, with the tingles that still buzzed up his arm and sizzled in his heart, there could be no question about the attraction he felt. If there was a woman more different than him in the entire world, he had yet to meet her. Why was it this one that made his blood warm and his heart thump?

"Kristen looks like the kind of woman who could give you a run for the money in the lumberjack competition."

"Yeah. She will. She shoots better than I do, too." He hesitated. "I'm faster. She has better aim."

"She fishes and hunts and cooks over an open fire..."

"Yeah. It's that obvious?" He had no idea women could read each other so easily.

Avery snorted. "I was actually being a little sarcastic."

"Oh. Well, it was all true."

"Seems like you're perfect for each other."

"I'd thought that too."

Avery took a breath and let it out. Then she took another. "What happened?" Her voice sounded hesitant.

"She found another guy just like me, only he had money." Gator pulled his hand away to open the barn door. He missed the warmth of hers, especially with the depressing subject matter. Avery didn't seem to judge, though it still rankled him that he hadn't been enough, had enough, to keep his wife. "She wanted to buy a big game preserve, and that's what we were working toward and saving for. Jace had the money, and if she went with him, she didn't have to wait."

"In my experience, it's the man who leaves," Avery said softly. She shook her head, and her blond hair twisted in the light. Gator fisted his hand, too tempted to touch her to trust himself.

She cleared her throat. "I think I'll run over and see if your mother is up. Maybe she can give us some pointers on what we need or can do for the tree trimming competition. After all, he said the tree farm has won every year except one. I feel pressure."

"That's fine. She can probably help you with your other booth, too."

Avery laughed. Maybe Christmas had gone to his head, because her laugh sounded like tinkling bells to him. A sweet sound he wouldn't mind hearing again.

"I don't even know what that booth is, to tell the truth. If the mayor said, I didn't hear."

"Me either." He looked down at this cheerful, funny woman. It seemed that everything she did was exactly what he wanted to see, which was odd, since they were so very different.

"I'll get Miss Prissypants and her carrier and head over to see your mom."

He couldn't take his eyes off her. "I won't start demo, but I still need to get some measurements and make some estimates."

She smiled at him and he found himself wanting to step closer.

He shoved his hands in his pockets and backed out of the barn.

Chapter Seven

Gator wasn't married.

Avery stepped into the cool, dim barn interior. She closed the door and leaned against it. Her hand, still tingling, rested on her chest where her heart threatened to escape.

She had to get a grip on her emotions. Men leave. It was a fact. She knew it. Actually, Gator made no bones about the fact that he was, indeed, leaving. Going back out west to his ranger job. What exactly he did, she wasn't sure, but she was sure it happened in the "great outdoors."

As her eyes adjusted to the dim interior, she looked on the old hay bale where she'd left Miss Prissypants. The cat wasn't there.

This farm interlude had been fun for her, but her plan had always been to go back to the city. Whatever city had an orchestra where she could earn her chair in the brass section. She wasn't an outdoorsy person and never would be.

She'd forgotten that for a while between the shop and here. Forgotten that men always leave, and that Gator wasn't a man who would work for her anyway. All she had to do was look at his ex—tanned and toned and looking like she could wrestle a grizzly. Or at least stand and shoot it, with her hiking boots and confident stride. Her fearless gaze made Avery feel like something soft and weak and helpless.

Kneeling to look behind the hay bale, she called her cat. Nothing.

Seeing that woman, who was the perfect match to Gator's athletic outdoorsmanship, had been depressing. Until Gator had grabbed her hand. Then all sane thoughts had fled.

Avery straightened up. It was perfectly normal to be attracted to a man. Just because it wasn't something that happened to her every day, well, ever...

And now she knew Gator wasn't married, which she was sure made her subconsciously more susceptible to her feelings.

Time to get back to work. Ellie and Fink needed Jillian and her to step up while they were gone with their son.

She sent a quick text to Ellie, saying that she hoped everything was okay and to not worry about anything, while she walked around the perimeter of the barn floor. Miss Prissypants never wandered off. Hardly ever.

Gator and she would do an amazing job on the tree trimming and win the contest for the farm. With that thought, she remembered she didn't have Gator's phone number.

She had heard him go up the ladder. Her eyes narrowed as she looked at the hole in the wall. It was possible the dogs were still there, but at least now she was pretty sure Gator wasn't going to let them maul her on purpose.

Miss Prissypants often found a comfortable place to wait, so Avery kept an eye out for her, but she wanted to get Gator's number before she forgot.

Reaching the place in the wall where the board was missing, she stuck her head out. Her heart lurched. The two ferocious dogs lay in the same spot they had been in earlier. Miss Prissypants lay curled between them. Sleeping.

Avery gripped the sides of the opening. She didn't want to do anything to disturb the dogs. Maybe they hadn't realized her cat had curled between them, and if she woke them up, they would eat her.

"Yeah. I thought it was kinda cute, too." Gator's voice came from above her on the right.

Cute? It wasn't cute. Miss Prissypants' life was in danger.

Breathe.

Avery sucked a breath in, blew it out. Trying not to hyperventilate. Another.

"Will they hurt her?" she whispered.

"What'd you say?" he asked in a loud voice that caused the brown dog to open its eyes and perk up its ears.

Avery gripped the barn walls tighter. If that dog made one threatening move toward Miss Prissypants, she would force her body out the hole and rescue her cat. Or die trying.

"Will they hurt her?" she said louder.

Gator grunted. "They haven't yet."

"I'm not reassured."

Gator leaned down and waited until she looked at him.

She forced herself to hold his gaze.

"Gladys, the black dog, is thirteen years old. She's supposed to be a hunting dog, but she's never been any good at it. She'd rather sleep." He glanced back toward the dogs. "Finch, the one that's looking at us, is fifteen. She had one litter of pups. They all died except for Gladys. The only time she refuses to listen to me is when some little kid has her by the ear. Or tail. Or whatever. She is the happy servant of any person shorter than three feet tall and forgets that I even exist."

"Not to be smart," Avery said in a low, calm tone. "But how was that supposed to make me believe they won't eat my cat?" She paused. "Or me? I'm taller than three feet."

Gator studied her for a moment. Then he shook his head and backed down the ladder, went over to the dogs and picked up Miss Prissypants. He walked over to Avery, stroking the cat's head, and handed her through the hole.

Avery grasped her pet, ignoring her awareness of where Gator's hand had touched her own. Her hand smoothed over the soft fur while relief cooled her chest. "Thank you."

"You are not faking that fear, are you?"

Avery pressed her face into her cat's warm fur. She rubbed her cheek against it, enjoying the soft, comforting sensation. "I was bitten when I was little."

Gator nodded. He reached a hand up and leaned against the outside wall. "You ever thought of facing that fear?" His tone was conversational, not probing too deep. Which was probably why Avery felt she could be honest.

She studied the black thumbnail on his hand. "No. It's easier to avoid dogs. Most people keep them on a leash, and I don't exactly frequent areas where dogs might be."

"Well, I'm not a big fan of cats. Not because I was bitten, but because they seem snotty." He dropped his hand. "But yours seems like a decent one."

She opened her mouth to say thank you.

He grinned. "She's got good taste. She likes my dogs. Maybe we'll have her over for dinner and a movie sometime."

Avery stared at Gator, coming to grips with this new side she hadn't seen. He was joking. Right?

"You could come too, I guess. Be dessert."

Her mouth dropped.

He slapped the side of the barn and strode off.

GATOR PARKED his truck in the house lot and jumped out, keeping the door open until his dogs climbed out after him. It had been warm so far for December and the ground wasn't frozen, so he didn't want to drive through the grass to get to the barn.

The muted sounds of Avery practicing her overweight trumpet carried over the early morning air and made him smile.

The door to the house slammed and he looked over. Avery's dark-haired friend with the exotic eyes waved.

He returned the gesture. Jillian, he thought her name was. Gladys and Finch trotted over to her and he stopped, ready to call them back if she had the same reaction as Avery. She didn't. Instead, she knelt while his dogs sniffed then licked her, then rolled over on their backs, legs in the air for her to scratch their bellies. The big babies.

"Nice dogs," she said as she stood back up.

"Thanks. Avery doesn't think too much of them."

She laughed. "She'll come around."

He didn't think so, but he just shrugged. "Might."

"Yeah, she will. She's got a good heart." She gestured at the dogs. "Better make sure you've got the paperwork up to date on these cuties. The tree customers are saying the dog catcher's a real jerk, and he's been making the rounds."

McKoy Rodning, a good friend of Gator's from high school, used to be the animal control officer. But that was years ago. He must have moved on, because he definitely wasn't a jerk.

"I'll keep it in mind." A particularly loud note tore through the morning mist. Gator's face scrunched up.

"I see that face."

"I'm not an expert in music, but that note had to be wrong."

"I'm no expert either, but Avery actually is. The tuba isn't exactly known for its beautiful tones, but it is known as a man's instrument."

"A man's instrument?"

"Yeah. Avery was one of only two professional women tubists in the country. It's a pretty big deal that she's so good. Women can't usually play the tuba professionally. They don't have a big enough lung capacity."

"I didn't know there was an orchestra around here."

"There's not."

"Thought you said..."

"She lost her chair last spring. That's part of the reason she came out here. Fink was laid up over the summer, and she was at loose ends because of losing her chair."

"Is that a full-time job?" Gator was having trouble imagining that it would take up much time. Did they play every weekend or something? He'd never been to an orchestra concert.

"No. She had a teaching position too. I think she gave it up when she lost her chair, but I'm not sure. She never really talks about it."

"I see." He wondered how hard it really was to play the tuba.

"I'd better get up and open the shop." She gave the dogs one last pat on the head and did some kind of flip off the porch with her hands tucked into her sides.

Gator snapped his fingers and his dogs fell in beside him. The tuba music was still loud and strong as he opened the barn door.

"Sit. Stay." His dogs dropped to the floor. Avery really was terrified of them, for good reason, he supposed. The considerate thing to do was to keep them away from her. It's not like this odd attraction he felt for her could take them anywhere—she'd never have to learn to like his dogs. He wasn't going to force them on her.

Avery, walking while she played, had her back to him. The music had become something that it was hard to not tap his toe to, but he didn't recognize it. Of course not. He'd never listened to any music except whatever tunes were on the radio. Just one more difference between him and the woman across the barn floor.

Her blond hair swished around her narrow shoulders. She wore some kind of flowing, ruffled top that reached past her hips and tight jeans or leggings disappeared into high boots. Her feet marched in time to the music. His heart seized. She headed directly toward one of the many holes in the barn floor. As involved in the music as she was, he felt sure she didn't see it. Three steps away, then two.

He shot over, grabbing her arm as her body tilted and started to fall. But the big instrument she carried had her more off-center than he'd anticipated and, in a tangle of legs and arms and brass, they ended up on the floor together. Somehow, he managed to twist at the last minute and have her land on top of him. Pain thumped in his elbow and the bell end of her tuba pushed into his hip, but her hair flowed across his chest and some type of sweet scent with enough tang to be sassy wafted across his nose.

His hands rested on either side of her rib cage. He didn't remember letting go of her arm. Under his callouses her body curved, and he had to grit his teeth to keep from moving his hands down and back up. One of her legs were caught between his. Her other foot was still in the hole on the floor.

"Did you twist your ankle?"

She tugged at her leg. He swallowed a groan as her body moved over his. "No. My leg doesn't hurt at all, but my boot is stuck." She moved around, sliding her tuba away and releasing his hip from the pressure.

Her hair brushed his chin and he clenched his jaw against the urge to run his hands through it. He settled for another deep breath through his nose, memorizing that scent. The most alluring thing he'd ever smelled.

"Let me see." He sat up and she slid down his chest. Curving his arm around her waist to keep her from falling off of him and onto the floor, he reached across their tangled legs and gently twisted her boot, popping it out of the hole. "There."

She didn't get up right away. "I'm sorry. You'd think I'd learn after I'd fallen like this at least five times, but no. I always get so caught up in the music, I completely forget."

He couldn't imagine getting so caught up in something that he forgot where he was or to look where he was stepping, but he'd just witnessed that very thing happening to Avery.

"You don't need to apologize."

"Sure I do. You're here on the floor...are you hurt?" she added, like the thought had just occurred to her.

"No." His elbow didn't count enough for him to mention it. And, honestly, there for a few seconds when she was wiggling on top of him, he'd forgotten about it completely.

"Thanks for catching me. It hurts a lot less to fall on top of you than it does to fall on the barn floor." She moved to get up.

"For you." He couldn't help it. He grinned.

Her lips pressed together in mock outrage, but her eyes twinkled and met his for a happy minute. His hand moved without his permission, taking a strand of her hair between his fingers, moving down the shiny velvet before his hand slid into the softness.

Her head tilted into his hand. Their eyes held. Her lips parted, her lower one glistened pink as her breath came in little pants. His chest couldn't expand big enough or deep enough and he felt like he was falling again. The air around them was charged, but distant, and he had nowhere to hold onto to stop himself. Nowhere except her.

His other hand flexed on her waist. Her hands gripped his shoulders, her fingers tightened.

His brain didn't seem to be thinking at all, but a million thoughts were ripping through it at the same time. What was he doing? Was he really going to act on this crazy attraction between them? Maybe she felt it too. But it couldn't go anywhere. She had her music career, whatever she was doing with it. She wasn't going out west. There were no orchestras, or even music teaching positions for her where he was going.

But maybe they could have a short affair.

As soon as that thought hit his brain, he dismissed it. He wouldn't be one of those guys. Using her for the physical aspect. It wouldn't matter how many meals he paid for or how many trinkets he bought, it wouldn't even matter if the desire was mutual. He couldn't get upset about a woman only wanting money if all he wanted was sex. And that was all he wanted, he told himself. But as he looked into her eyes for the seconds that felt like years, he suspected that if he spent much time around her, he was going to want more. Much more. And Avery, used to her city life and her upscale music and whatever else that entailed, would need money to keep her in the style she was used to. He'd already been dumped because he didn't have enough. He wasn't going to offer the opportunity to anyone else.

But his hands didn't want to let go.

"Gator." Her lips moved slowly, and his gaze left hers to watch them. His name coming off her lips. The hard case around his heart started to melt. Just a little.

And it scared the crap out of him.

He jumped up. Having only the presence of mind to grab her arm to keep her from plopping on the floor.

"Can you stand?" he asked, his voice sounding more gravelly than he'd ever heard it. Like he'd spent the night with her instead of two minutes on the floor.

"Yes." If she were confused or upset about his abruptness, he couldn't tell. Her eyes were downcast. She bent to her instrument.

"Is it okay?" He scanned the shiny gold of the tuba. She might be scaring him, but he still cared about her. That had happened sometime in the last few days. Maybe when she'd cared enough about his mother to spend days decorating her home.

"I think so. It's survived me falling before. It is expensive, though. And it's my livelihood."

"I've never played an instrument." He'd never been interested. Until this very moment.

Avery smiled and held her tuba out to him.

He looked at her. Blinked.

"Take it. I'll show you."

"I don't really think I'm an instrument playing kind of guy." He looked at the tuba. Better than a cat. Maybe.

"People change."

"Not that drastically." But he took the instrument from her.

She flipped it around for him and showed him where to place his hands.

He lifted it up, surprised at how heavy it was. "Just blow into here," he said, but it was really a question.

She grinned, but didn't say anything.

He put his lips to the mouthpiece and blew. He'd expected a horribly bad sound to emerge. But there was no sound at all. He glanced at her; she was still grinning. He remembered what Jillian had said about chest size and capacity and took another, deeper breath. He blew into the mouth piece.

Nothing.

"Because you're grinning, I'm going to assume it didn't break when you dropped it just now."

"Nah. I was worried about dents, but not about breaking it."

"So, there's a trick to this?"

She laughed. "When I first started, I couldn't believe my instructor when he told me how you actually make a note."

"You're saying you wanted me to see what didn't work, so I'd believe you when you told me what did."

"Yeah, basically." Her teeth flashed, before her face became more serious. "Without going into a whole bunch of embouchure, basically you keep your teeth apart, press your lips together and blow out, making a buzzing sound." Then she proceeded to do so.

Just because she looked so cute doing it, or maybe because he loved the excuse to stare at her lips, Gator said, "Show me that again?"

She did. Then she lifted a brow in challenge.

He couldn't resist the challenge. If it had been anyone but Avery watching, or maybe if she hadn't thrown down the gauntlet, he would have felt like a fool. But he pressed his lips together.

Her hand came up and touched the skin right next to his mouth. "Keep your teeth open."

He gave her a long look, wondering what she'd do if he opened his teeth and took her finger between them. Maybe his eyes showed his thoughts, because her lips opened into an *O* and she dropped her hand. Her eyes, however, never left his. He allowed himself a wolfish grin, pleased that she wasn't immune to him after all.

He shook off the feeling. He had no business flirting, if that's what this was—it wasn't like he flirted on a regular basis, or ever, actually— with someone he had no intention of developing a relationship with.

He pressed his lips together and blew. After a few seconds and a couple of adjustments, he was making the same buzzing noise she had. She nodded eagerly. He didn't tell her that little boys were programmed at birth to make noises like that. From the sound of things, she might be a little sensitive to men's innate ability to play the tuba easier than women.

"That's right." She beamed at him like he'd done something really hard. "Now put the tuba to your mouth and do that exact thing into the mouthpiece."

The same mouthpiece where her lips had just been. He castigated himself for that junior high thought.

Lifting the tuba and putting his mouth on it, he repeated the technique and a sound—note—came out of the end of the tuba. He held it out for a moment before lowering the instrument.

"Nice!" Avery beamed.

"I admit. It was a little more complicated than I'd thought." He handed the instrument back to Avery.

"It's not that hard. But, like anything else, to be good, you have to practice."

"So, you play in an orchestra?" He didn't really want to admit he'd been talking about her to Jillian, even if he hadn't brought the subject up with her friend.

She looked down, twisting the mouthpiece off, before answering. "I lost my chair early last summer." She shrugged her shoulders like it didn't matter and gave him a fake smile. "I'm excited to work with a different orchestra, and I actually have an audition next week in Washington D.C."

"You driving down?" He followed her back to where her case lay on the floor.

"Yeah. Why?"

"Just wondering. I heard there was going to be snow next week, but it'll probably be nothing. This far out, meteorologists are just guessing."

"I'll keep an eye on the weather. Thank you." She knelt in front of the blue velvet and nested her instrument lovingly in the cozy interior.

She wasn't staying here. Of course. He wasn't either, but somehow the knowledge from her mouth that she was moving on set him on edge. "So, you audition and find out after Christmas? Then you'll move to D.C. in the spring?"

"Right after Christmas. They need a tubist for the spring concert season. I've already gotten an offer from a small private school to be the music instructor for their regular teacher who is taking the semester off. I have ten days to let them know."

A feeling like quicksand sucked at his insides. It didn't matter. Not at all. Once he'd seen his mother through her treatments and into remission, he'd be going back out west to his ranger job. He wouldn't be here anyway.

A part of him admitted that he'd been considering giving his job up and coming back permanently to stay with his mom. But normal men didn't leave the careers they went to college for to come back and take care of their mothers. He could hardly be a forest ranger here, and the only openings for game wardens were in the eastern part of the state. He'd checked. The doctors his mother had here were good and, most importantly, she liked them, so he didn't want to move her.

"I hope you get it." He sincerely wanted the best for her.

"Me too. That's what all this practicing is for. Fink and Ellie would hate me if I played this much in their house."

"It's chaotic enough in there."

"Yeah." She laughed. "Did your mom talk to you last night about the tree trimming?"

"She said you didn't mind coming up with the materials and ideas, and that I could be the brawn that hung the stuff up high."

"You sure you don't want to be part of the planning?"

"Yep."

"You did such a beautiful job on those decorations you made for her yard."

"I made those because I loved working with wood. Not because I loved decorating."

"Oh. I see."

He took out his phone. "I'm going to patch these holes in the barn floor. You can't have a party with that kind of danger."

"I thought I'd put orange cones around them."

He glanced up. She was smiling. His lips turned up in response.

She shrugged. "Fink was going to patch them for me, but their son is scheduled for surgery tomorrow. I'm not sure when they'll get back."

"I've got it. I'll measure them, put the numbers in my phone, and I've got some plyboard that won't look the greatest, but will keep your guests from breaking any legs. Or disappearing into the cow pens down there.""They'd have to be pretty skinny. But they are a danger to small children," Avery said. "I'm not sure how many people will come, let alone if anyone will bring their kids, but I really appreciate you fixing them for me."

"It's a public service." Gator snapped the measuring tape off of his belt. "You sending out invitations and that kind of stuff?"

"I just posted it on Facebook."

"The easy way."

"Yeah. I don't really have time to do more. I want to focus on getting the decorations just right."

He gave her a look.

"I know. You aren't into decorations. I got it. I promise I won't ask for help with that."

❧

IF ONLY SHE had someone to help her.

Avery had spent the afternoon and evening selling Christmas

wreathes and decorations with Jillian. Things had slowed down now and Jillian was handling the few remaining stragglers for the last two hours until closing.

Avery sat at the big table in the farmhouse kitchen. Craft pieces, glue, and glitter interspersed with pictures of Mrs. Franks's party. She'd already taken notes and managed to figure out what was imperative to duplicate, and what she could get away with changing, either a little or a lot.

The tablecloths she could do. Also, the ruffles around the top beams and the party favors shaped like two candy canes intertwined around a Christmas tree wouldn't be that hard, just time-consuming. She was working on them now. It was going to take forever; she half-suspected that for the party in the pictures, women had gathered and spent evenings making the crazy things together. Today, especially at this time of year, people were too busy to take a whole evening and make decorations. Mrs. Franks would help, but she had been especially tired today and had gone to bed early.

She put the last dab of glue on the candy canes and attached the tree. While that one dried, she gathered up the pictures, which she should have done earlier. She didn't want anything to happen to them. Placing them safely on the top of the fridge, she opened the green paint to do another Christmas tree.

Her mind puzzled over how to do the snowflake lights in the picture. Plastic would melt, paper would burn...she needed little squares of glass and wood-cutouts. There was no way she could do that herself. And the lights were in every single picture. She wasn't going to be able to do without them.

Jillian would help her with the food. But still...the lights were central to the party's theme.

At least Gator was fixing the floor.

Gator.

She sighed. Not a good sign.

Men leave. How many times did she have to live it to learn it? Her dad, her fiancé.

Gator was handsome, funny, and he was back to take care of his mom, but he'd leave too.

Plus, she had seen his first wife. Beautiful. And as opposite from Avery as she could be. He wouldn't have to get tired of her to leave. He'd never be interested in the first place. Of course, he wanted a woman who could keep up with all his outdoor pursuits. Avery wasn't outdoorsy, and never would be. Gator was probably looking for a clone of his first wife. Only younger, if Avery knew anything about men.

Still, that didn't mean they couldn't be friends. Until she left for D.C., anyway. If she got the chair. She had to think positively. She was going to get the chair. They would be friends, nothing more, until she left. This time, she would be the one leaving.

Setting the tree down to dry, she tried to concentrate. Thankfully, Ellie had called her back about the tree trimming contest and had made some suggestions. All she had to do tomorrow was march in the parade at 8:00. Then man the booth—whatever it was—for the mayor until twelve, then trim the tree with Gator.

Deciding that she needed to keep working, otherwise she'd never get done with the decorations, Avery sat back down at the table and picked up the glue bottle.

She'd been working for another thirty minutes when a knock on the kitchen door startled her. It opened before she could get up. Although common sense told her a thief or murderer wouldn't knock first, Avery still slid her chair back, ready to grab Miss Prissypants and run.

"Hello the house." Gator called out the traditional local greeting.

Avery's heart jumped and kicked. "I'm right here," she said. "Is your mom okay?"

"Hey. I talked to the nurse that comes before bed. She was fine and in bed a few hours ago. Just finished helping setting up things for the celebration tomorrow and I saw your light on down here."

"Yeah. Tomorrow's going to be a big day, but I need to get these party favors done."

Gator stepped farther into the kitchen and leaned over the table, studying her decorations. "Party favors?"

"For the Christmas party at the barn."

"I see." He pulled a lip back.

"Go ahead. You can say it. You think it's a waste of time."

"I think it's a waste of time."

"That hurts."

"You told me to say it."

"I didn't actually mean for you to say it."

"Then don't say to."

"Well, that is what you were thinking."

"Not gonna lie." He touched the one picture that she had left on the table. The one that looked like the picture had been snapped accidentally, because it was a close-up of the glass-snowflake lights.

"You making those next?"

"I wish." Avery put the glue down and leaned over to look at the picture too. The fresh scent of the outdoors and Gator's own unique rugged scent reached her. She inhaled. "I can't figure out how."

"Glass and wood."

"I know that much. But I can't cut wood, and I have no idea where I could find glass that shape and size."

"What size do you think they are?"

"Maybe four by four and six inches high?" Avery went to the fridge and pulled down the pile of pictures, sorting through until she found one with a person standing near the light. Looking at this..."

"Is that Fink and Ellie's barn?" Gator asked.

"Yeah." Avery didn't want Gator to know she was doing this party for his mom. It might not work. It might not help her at all. It could even make her worse, if she got nostalgic or depressed about the past, rather than being cheered and encouraged, like Avery hoped. Gator might even think it was a dumb idea, like the decorations. She didn't want to try to defend an idea she had been sure was brilliant a week ago, but now she wasn't sure what she'd been thinking.

"Looks like before my time."

Miss Prissypants strutted over and rubbed against Gator's leg.

"Right around your time, I think."

"I see. I think you're right about the lights. Four-by-four-by-six."

"Do you know where I could get pieces of glass that size?"

"No. But I'll look into it." He bent down and scooped her cat up. Miss Prissypants lolled in his arms like she had no bones at all.

"Really?" she said before she could close her mouth around that word. "Thanks." Her cat acted like Gator picked her up all the time.

"Miss Prissypants is not a mean cat, but she never lets anyone but me hold her like that."

"Cats aren't loyal like dogs are."

Avery blinked. "Are you sure about that?"

"Yeah. I'm sure. My dogs will let you pet them, but there's never any question that they like me best. They won't listen to you."

"I see. So, when they try to take bites out of me and I tell them to stop, they'll eat me anyway?"

Gator looked at her from under his brows. He continued to stroke Miss Prissypants who was purring so loud Avery could hear her over the refrigerator condenser.

"You don't really believe that my dogs are going to eat you?"

"Maybe not eat me, but I'm not convinced they won't bite me."

He continued to stroke Miss Prissypants. "I'm not a big cat guy, but I like your cat." He looked up and smiled, the same smile that he'd used at the barn when she'd touched his face. It was a smile that said if she kept her fingers near his mouth, he'd be capturing and chewing on them. She let out a shaky breath. There was nothing scary about Gator chewing on her fingers.

She stared at his lips. Swallowing, she looked away. She had lost the thread of the conversation, and from the heated look in his eye, he knew it. Who would have known that a man holding her cat would be irresistibly sexy?

Right away, she knew it wasn't just any man. Gator. Gator holding her cat was totally doing it for her. For some odd reason, that made her think that maybe, possibly, she could, if not make friends, at least call a truce with his dogs.

"Are you sure I won't get bitten?"

"No." Gator said.

"Then I'm not taking a chance."

"Maybe you should walk on the wild side."

"Maybe not." She had thought they were talking about Gator's dogs. But something in his expression—the way his eyes darkened and his brows drew together—suggested that maybe she had said the wrong thing.

"I think you're right. It's not a good idea at all." He set Miss

Prissypants down. "I'll see you tomorrow at our booth." He gave a short laugh. "I found out what booth you're at tomorrow. Did anyone tell you?"

"No. I've been busy and haven't asked."

"It's the dunking booth."

Chapter Eight

She had volunteered to man the dunking booth.

In December.

What kind of fiendish town had a dunking booth at their Christmas celebration? One that was really twisted, if the long, long line of people at her booth was any indication.

Avery sat, shivering, on the end of the plank. So far, the first three patrons who had put quarters in the slot—eight quarters for one ball, at least they weren't going cheap—had not been able to throw the ball with enough force to push in the lever that dropped the plank, which would dunk her into the water. One little boy had hit the lever, but it hadn't been enough to drop her. It was just a matter of time.

She wasn't even wet, and she was shivering.

Had the mayor done this on purpose? She knew the town thought her odd because of the cat carrier, and possibly the tuba too. And maybe because she planted corn with full make-up and inch long nails. Possibly because she hung out with Jillian, who was regarded with just as much suspicion. Probably, though, she had ended up perched on the plank because she was new to town and as gullible as a two-year-old being offered candy.

The town probably thought her parents had kept her in a cage. It wasn't really true, but she had been cooped up in her room most of her high school years practicing the tuba. Mediocracy didn't land a woman a chair in a prestigious orchestra. Even at fifteen, she had known that. But now, at twenty-seven, she hadn't enough street smarts to know when she was being bamboozled by a small-town mayor.

He'd acted all innocent about it, and if she recalled correctly, hadn't even asked her outright. Just goaded her into offering by making her feel bad about the poor town and their great need for help. And insulting her intelligence by hinting that she couldn't make change. The man was good.

They could at least heat the water.

"Why aren't you wearing a bikini?" the teenaged boy who was next in line asked.

Because she'd thought she was going to be picking up rings from bottles and handing out teddy bears with pretty red Christmas ribbons on them. Not to mention, it was only forty degrees out. She'd have worn a wet suit if she'd have known, and if she'd had one. But, hey, she could be a good sport. Plus, she needed to distract him. He was the first one who looked like he had the brawn to get enough power under the ball to push the lever in.

"Your mother was bringing me hers."

The kid behind him guffawed and smacked him on the shoulder just as he threw the ball. It went wide. Avery breathed a sigh of relief. Only two hours and fifty-five minutes of this torture left. It was not going to get better. Avery pulled her legs up to her chest and held her cold toes in her hand. Surely, this was illegal.

The next kid in line started to put his quarters in.

"Hold up."

Avery jerked her head up as her heart sank. Gator. He had the power to slam the lever in. His aim was probably dead on too.

"Aw, man. It's my turn," the kid whined.

"You'll get your turn, bud. I'm going out on the board."

"You are?" Avery gasped.

"Unless you have some kind of weird cold-water fetish."

"I don't," she said immediately.

He grinned. "Didn't think so."

She let go of her legs.

He nodded to his side. "You'll have to hold my dogs."

Her eyes went to the animals sitting calmly at his side. "You can just tell them to stay. They listen pretty good."

Gator shrugged and started to turn away.

No! He couldn't leave. "Um, Gator?" she called out.

"Yeah?" He glanced over his shoulder.

"Where are you going?"

"I wanted to help you out, but I can't let my dogs roam wild. Someone told me it was illegal. Plus, I've also heard that the dog-catcher is a real jerk."

Avery wilted on the board. The cold water inches from her feet mocked her.

She lifted her head as Gator started to walk away again. "Okay. I'll hold them."

He turned. One corner of his mouth lifted. "You don't have to. I just wanted to see if you would."

"You mean you're not coming up here?"

"Stay," he said to the dogs. He ducked under the rope and walked around the side of the tank. "I am. Hop down."

She licked her dry lips as he dropped his jeans, revealing a black wet suit. "You really are helping me."

"I figured you didn't have a wet suit."

"No."

"It's what everyone does. Doesn't keep you warm, exactly, but it helps."

"I'll keep that in mind for next year."

"They probably won't ask you next year. Typically, they get a newcomer to town. Newbies will do anything to fit in, and, trust me, the town takes advantage of that big-time. I'd kind of forgotten that the night the mayor came in the office. The man's good. I'll give him that."

"I see."

"But usually, they have enough time to get themselves a suit. I knew last night you didn't."

"I've got one she can borrow. It's in the attic at your mother's house, honey." Kristen stood at the edge of the rope.

Gator stiffened at the sound of her voice. "Slide back, Avery. I'll help you down."

"Don't get off. You're not even wet." Kristen held a ball in her hand.

Avery hadn't seen her put quarters in, not to mention she'd cut in line. She scooted back faster, hoping she didn't end up with splinters in her butt. Splinters in her butt was preferable to being submerged in ice water. If they were going to make people be in a dunking booth in December, they really should give them a nicer place to sit.

Sliding her feet around behind her, Avery reached for the rungs with cold toes that felt more like blocks of wood than her normal, supple appendages. She had no idea how she'd ever get herself down the ladder.

What if she'd actually been dunked? When her tongue was no longer frozen to the roof of her mouth, she'd have to ask if anyone had ever died at the dunking booth. She was guessing not, but one could never be certain. Maybe the mayor was also the town lawyer.

Strong fingers gripped her foot and guided it to the ladder, holding it steady as she backed down. Her knees shook so hard, she wasn't sure she would stay on. She held the sides of the ladder as tightly as her frozen fingers would allow.

Large hands gripped her waist, pulling, and she let go with relief, allowing Gator to ease her body down his. His big arms wrapped around her from behind, pulling her into his warmth, although she was shaking so hard he had to press to hold her against him.

"You stay there and warm her up. I'll sit on the plank for a while." Kristen brushed past them, saying something about a wimp and climbed the ladder.

Avery watched, a little stunned. She turned her head up and asked against Gator's chin, "She has a wet suit on? Is there something about this whole Christmas celebration that I've missed?"

"Nah. She's probably doing the lumberjack competition."

"You need a wet suit for that?"

"Not really. But there is a part where you walk across logs on the water. You can still win if you fall in, but even with all the exercise, you get cold." He ran his hands up and down her arms. He probably thought she was a huge baby, shivering and cold, too much of a wimp to sit on that plank any longer. She supposed she should have insisted on sitting there until hell froze over, which wasn't going to take long. And of course, it had to be Kristen that showed her up. Hard to figure it was anything but purposeful.

"You warming up?" Gator's voice, soft and low and right beside her ear, caused her to shiver. "Guess not," he said and she could hear the smile in his voice.

"I'm better. I'm kicking myself for not being stronger." She eyed his dogs as they came around the tank, but at Gator's command they stopped and lay down a few feet off.

"I'm not an expert, but I think one of the things that men like about women is that every once in a while, we get to rescue them. It makes us feel manly and needed."

Avery stood still, his arms around her. Was he insulting Kristen? "Are you saying I make you feel 'manly and needed'?" The idea that a tough guy like Gator would need her to make him feel good would make her laugh if her teeth weren't chattering so hard.

But after a few seconds of silence, his answer was low and sincere. "Yeah."

Her entire body heated with the warm, comfortable, and unfamiliar feeling of being taken care of. She loved the idea that she was making him feel good too.

After a moment of that, though, the modern woman in her bristled at the implication. "You like it when women are bumbling and incompetent because it makes you feel like a jock?"

She felt, more than heard, him sigh. Like she'd let him down. Maybe she'd jumped to the easy conclusion. After all, she liked it when Gator looked at her like she was good enough to eat, but she didn't want to be regarded as a sex object. That didn't really make sense. She could hardly expect him to be totally reasonable when, Lord knew, she wasn't.

A shout and a splash interrupted her musings. To her shame, knowing how cold the water was, she grinned anyway. Bigly.

Gator's voice contained a smile when he whispered in her ear, "Sounds like Kristen got wet."

She snuggled deeper in his arms. Her mind might say that she needed to be strong, but the rest of her was enjoying every second of having this man's solid arms around her, taking care of her.

"That should have been me." She sighed.

The dogs lifted their heads at the noise, but didn't get up.

"It was going to be me. She volunteered." He paused. "I might have to donate a few dollars to the cause."

"Is that passive-aggressive behavior toward your ex?"

"Nope. It's pure aggressive. Not pretending anything else."

"You two have a complicated relationship." Water splashed behind them as Kristen got out of the water.

"Not really. We don't have a relationship at all. This is the first I've seen her in years."

"Does she have family in town?" The dogs didn't look as ferocious when they were sleeping. Avery relaxed even more into Gator's heat.

"No. Unless you count my mother. But Kristen never really warmed up to her."

"I don't get that. Your mother is the nicest person I know." Gator's arms around her had warmed her up enough her teeth had stopped chattering.

"Kristen is pretty focused on getting what she wants and isn't too interested in people."

"But you married her anyway."

"We were pretty much the same. But I think I might have grown up some, and she just got greedier. That's my side of the story, anyway. Maybe she has a different one." Gator's shoulders moved against hers in a shrug.

"So, you have no idea why she's in town."

"I'm guessing she wants something. I don't have any idea what it could be, and I'm not interested in finding out. Was hoping if I avoid her, she'll have to leave before she corners me long enough to tell me."

Avery snorted. "I see. You're not a little curious?"

"No."

She shut her mouth. Talking too much was a fault she'd been working hard on overcoming. That and prying into other peoples' lives. Both of which she was doing just now.

"Thanks for rescuing me."

"Thanks for needing rescued." The dimple beside his lip appeared as his lips turned up, and she couldn't help but grin back. She still couldn't believe that the man needed reassurance that he was strong and capable. It was odd to think of a man—men—as insecure, but maybe that had something to do with the men she knew running off with younger women. They needed that reassurance that they were still desirable or something. But that only confirmed her decision that she shouldn't have anything to do with Gator. After all, if he were constantly looking for reassurance, he'd be leaving with another woman before she knew it.

She stepped away and his hands slid off her shoulders. "I think I'll go get your mom and walk around with her, if you've got a handle on the dunking booth."

"She's here. That's why I was a little late rescuing you."

"Oh?"

"I left her with Jillian. Mom is pretty well respected in town, and I thought Jillian and she got along well."

Avery tilted her head and narrowed her eyes. Gator had seen that Jillian wasn't considered "normal" by the townspeople and had dropped his mother off to help Jillian integrate. She could hardly believe that's what he was saying.

But as she met his gaze, she had no trouble reading his expression. He knew Jillian didn't fit in and he knew his mother could help her.

"Close your mouth, Avery."

She slapped her mouth shut.

Gator glanced back at the dunking booth where a wet, shivering Kristen sat on the dunking board. "I'd better go relieve Kristen."

"If you think your mom is okay, I'll stand and keep the unruly hoards in line." She eyed his dogs, then gathered up her nerve. "And I'll watch your dogs too. Keep them from leaving you for the little people."

He laughed and they split up—him to the back of the tank, she to the front where a small boy wearing a Santa hat had just put eight quarters in the slot.

Kristen didn't hesitate to climb down, and Gator sat on the board in his wet suit.

Avery took a moment to admire him. It emphasized his broad shoulders and narrow waist and defined his muscular arms and legs.

Stepping back to give the miniature Santa room to throw, Avery checked the time. Two hours until the booth closed.

"Have you and Gator known each other long?" Kristen's voice came over Avery's shoulder as the little boy threw his ball. It missed, she noted with satisfaction, dropping in the chute and rolling to the queue with all the other balls.

"No." She smiled at Kristen. No reason not to, just because they were different. "I think they were selling hot chocolate with cinnamon sticks over by the court house if you need to warm up."

Kristen's lips were blue around the corners, although she wasn't shivering. Possibly because she had her jaw clenched.

"I saw coffee down the block." Kristen waved her hand.

"Coffee works too." Avery smiled at the next person in line—another little boy. A few teenaged girls had gathered at the end, and she figured seeing Gator is what had drawn them to the booth.

"I thought it was kind of weird that he took your place up there." She nodded to the dunking booth. "And I thought it was really odd that you let him."

That was not a veiled insult, Avery told herself. "Why wouldn't I?"

"You don't want a man, any man, to think that you can't do something. It makes the entire gender of women look weak." Kristen shook out her towel and rubbed it over her hair.

Avery kept her smile firmly in place, even if the gratitude she'd felt toward Kristen had been misplaced, seeing how Kristen had only been trying to keep her gender from looking weak. "I didn't have a wet suit. Even if I did, I have no desire to get dunked into a tank of cold water. Seems to me I'd have been stupid to turn him, or you, down."

"Well, I gave our gender a good showing, at least." Kristen ran a hand through her short, dark hair.

Avery shrugged, not really caring. It wasn't a competition between men and women. At least not to her.

Although, as Kristen walked away, Avery wondered if it kind of was. After all, she had lumped all men in the 'leaving for a younger, prettier woman' category. Then she'd promptly quit the game. Not that she considered dating and marriage a game, but she'd quit, none the less.

The next little boy's ball went way wide and Avery ducked under the tape to pick it up plus get a few others that had missed the chute.

"Isn't Kristen sharing her suit?" Gator asked from the board.

"I'm sure she would. I never thought to ask."

"Smart girl."

At that, a ball whizzed by and smacked the lever dead-on. With his lips in an *O* and his brows raised, Gator dropped into the tank. Water splashed out the sides. He popped back up quickly, a big smile on his face.

"You play baseball?" he called to the grinning teen.

"Pitcher."

Gator rolled his eyes and asked, "Can we ban people?"

Avery chuckled. "I don't think so."

"It's okay. I promised my girl I'd win her a teddy bear on the bottle ring game. But I wanted to dunk this guy first."

Gator surged out of the water and onto the board. The play of his muscles fascinated Avery, and she forgot to breathe. Heat curled in her stomach.

He shook the water out of his hair before he said, "I'll put a word in with the mayor that you'd like to be in the tank next year."

"You do that, mister. My mom would never let me do anything like this."

They laughed and he ran off, holding the hand of a dark-haired girl. Avery watched them go. Gator had been young and cocky once, she was sure. And she'd been young and innocent like that girl. Life had a way of robbing your cockiness and your innocence.

She glanced back at Gator, who was joking with the next ball thrower before her eyes rested on his calmly sleeping dogs.

Life replaced the things it stole with other things. Like wisdom. Compassion. Forgiveness. Maybe she needed to forgive. Her dad and her ex-fiancé. Maybe. It was possible that all men weren't the jerks she'd labeled them as.

But backing away from that label meant opening herself up to the possibility of hurt again. The risk wasn't worth it.

One dog stretched out on its side, its head coming within inches of Avery's foot.

She backed away.

Chapter Nine

Gator lined up for the lumberjack competition beside Kristen, facing the huge poles they'd have to climb and the temporary pools of water created exclusively for this day. They competed by twos since the course was only big enough for two at a time. He'd say she was his partner, as fate would have it, but it wasn't fate. With twelve other competitors, she had either requested him, or Grady Hanson, Gator's friend who was running the competition, had thought it would be funny to put them together.

It was a timed competition, with the three judges who made sure the contestants made it to the top of the climbing pole, and that their logs were chopped the whole way through and that they didn't cut any corners, but thankfully there really wasn't any specialized knowledge that the judges needed to know. Which was good, since Mrs. Baker, who retired from the post office before Gator graduated from high school, and who was even now proudly wearing her blue ribbon for best Christmas cookies—which was actually a pretty big deal since the competition for the Christmas cookies was cutthroat—didn't have any particular knowledge of anything lumberjack.

Neither did Larry Fountaine, who owned a computer repair shop across the street from the bakery. The third judge was Bradford

Jennings, the attorney who had handled Gator's divorce. From the amused smile on his face, Gator assumed he hadn't missed the irony of Kristen and him competing together. Grady leaned down, maybe to give the table of judges some last-minute instruction, but more likely to remind them to watch the competition and not to focus on the animosity between the contestants.

Dr. Chandra Hamer, the family doctor whose shingle hung two doors down from Larry's, held the starting gun pointed in the air, waiting for Grady's signal to start.

Gator scanned the crowd lining the area. The single set of portable bleachers the town owned had been set up. No other competition or booth drew such immense interest. Gator was used to the attention. In high school, he and McKoy Rodning had spent a lot of summer evenings at Fink and Ellie's pond, which had been the Bright's pond back then, practicing standing on a floating log and chopping through another one. It was the hardest skill in the competition to master. McKoy and he had gotten pretty good at it, and since they began entering, no one had ever beaten them.

McKoy had gone earlier and posted a really good time. Gator hadn't seen him since he'd come back to town, and hoped he'd get a chance to catch up later. Right now, he didn't really care about winning the competition necessarily. He only wanted to beat his ex. He supposed that made him a small, petty person.

Again, he scanned the crowd. This time he saw her. Standing at the end of the bleachers beside his mother, her cat strapped to her chest, his dogs at their feet, even if Avery kept his mother's chair between her and them. It was closer than she'd have been not long ago.

It did something funny to his heart to see her there now. Pretty sure she wasn't standing there to see Kristen.

She smiled when she saw him looking and bent down, whispering to his mother, who looked over and waved. Gator nodded, but continued looking at Avery for a moment. Studying. He half expected that when she found out she'd signed up for the dunking booth that she'd have refused. He hadn't been in a huge rush to get there, and he'd been flummoxed when she was already sitting on the board. It wasn't the first time the fancy-looking woman had surprised him. That would have been when she climbed that light pole.

He looked away before he allowed himself a smile. His eyes met Kristen's.

She closed the short distance between them, bumping him playfully. "Ha. Usually you're pretty serious before this. You'd better quit smiling or I'll think you're happy to see me."

He turned his body away, facing down the course. He couldn't think of an answer that wasn't rude or nasty, and he'd never been a trash-talker. Not before a competition. Not before a divorce. And not after.

"Now you're going all big, silent type on me."

"Where's my replacement?" If all he wanted to do was look at Avery, eating her up, surely Kristen should want to make googly eyes at her husband. He almost laughed out loud at the idea of Kristen making googly eyes. That wouldn't fit her image of a tough woman, either.

"He's judging the tree-trimming contest and is at the meeting right now, getting the fact sheets and guidelines. Since it's next."

That might make it a little hard to win. It was supposed to be a blind competition, but he didn't know how closely the rules were followed. The town celebration was serious business, but they were also serious about having fun. Hard to tell which way the tree trimming would lean.

He glanced over at Avery again, pulled by some invisible attraction between them. She had her eyes glued on him, absently stroking her little cat's head. Her lips turned up, but this time she didn't bend over to his mother.

"Are you ready?" Grady called through the hand-held loudspeaker.

Gator gave a thumbs up.

"Ladies and gentlemen, our last two contestants. Gator and Kristen Franks."

Gator bit down hard on his lip to keep from smirking. Kristen had never taken his name, even when they were married. He had no idea if she'd changed it for husband number two.

"It's Pandifino, Grady. Get it right," she yelled above the crowd. Laughter rumbled.

"Sorry, folks. This is an interesting pairing since Gator and Kristen used to be married. I'm sure there's no hard feelings or any extra competitiveness involved today. However, the lady has corrected me that her name is no longer Franks."

"It never was, you moron. You know that." Kristen gestured like she was going to give him the finger, but kept her hand in a fist instead.

The crowd "ooh'd."

"Sorry folks. The lady corrected me again." Everyone laughed. "Kristen Pandifino and Gator Franks are the last contestants. The judges have confirmed the points of all prior contestants. Currently in the lead, we have McKoy Rodning."

The crowd cheered.

"Contestants, take your marks."

Gator adjusted his safety belt and stepped behind the line.

Kristen stepped beside him.

"Good luck, Gator. I hope you come in second."

He ignored Kristen. Sawdust littered the path ahead from the previous runs. Gator's old high school chemistry teacher stood on a ladder ready to dump a bucket of sawdust in front of the running fan while they climbed the telephone poles that had been set up first on the course. The sawdust obscured the climber's vision, causing them to rely on feel to get to the top and grab the star and bag of hot dog buns that had been placed there. They'd be used for the bonfire later. The town organizers believed in frugality.

"Ready?"

"Go!" Grady yelled and Dr. Hamer shot the gun with a little 'pop' and a lot of smoke.

Gator took off running. Kristen was lighter and quicker on her feet. She might beat him up the pole. He'd catch up with the parts of the course that demanded strength—the log chopping and the hand saw. They'd be even with the chainsaw. He'd beat her in the burling—spinning a log in water and balancing on top of it. On this course, they had to do it for twenty seconds without falling in.

He was halfway up the pole and could see through the sawdust out of the corner of his eye that he was higher than Kristen when the image of Avery climbing that light pole the first time he met her entered his head. Avery had scooted up, somewhat clumsily, with strength born of fear. Gator grinned at the image. His concentration gone, his feet slipped and he slid about ten feet before he caught himself.

The gasp of the crowd and the silence that followed made him cringe. He'd never entered a competition and not done his best. He shoved the image of Avery out of his mind and knuckled down, climbing with a single-minded purpose. Sawdust blew past his face as he reached the top, grabbing the star and hot dog buns in his right hand. There were points off for crushing the buns and if he recalled correctly, Mrs. Baker was quite strict about it.

Wrapping his right arm around the pole, he slid as fast as he could, seeing that Kristen had already reached the bottom and had just thrown the star and rolls on the judges' table. He could see from here that her rolls were smashed.

A few seconds later his feet hit the ground and he raced to the table, taking care to set the rolls and stars down gently. Aside from the time, judging was subjective, and he couldn't help but think that he might get a half a brownie point or two for being polite rather than ignominious.

Kristen was already on her log, spinning it in the water when he stooped to put the special cleats on his shoes. Over the years, as the competition had grown, the coordinators had added stations and designed accessories to accommodate the additions. The cleats were one of the additions.

They didn't take long to strap on. He grabbed the hatchet and jumped. In his haste, Gator almost overshot the log which was floating in the four-foot-deep tank. The judges had stopwatches, but the contestants had to time the curling in their heads. Once they'd done it for twenty seconds, they used the hatchet to stop the log, then chop through it. If they underestimated the time, they were docked.

It was close to impossible to stay on the log the entire time, hence the wetsuits, but this is what Gator had practiced with McKoy in Fink's pond years ago. In all his years doing the competition, he'd only fallen once. So when his body started to tilt, maybe confidence didn't allow him to correct as quickly as he should have. He lost more time as he pulled himself out of the cold water and climbed back up on his log.

The rhythmic chopping from the other tank was a sure sign that Kristen wasn't having any of his problems.

He ignored the cold and started chopping again. The scent of fresh wood filled the air. A splash indicated that Kristen had made it through her log. Despite his fall, he'd made up a little time since he was stronger and chopped through the log faster. His log broke in two a few seconds later. With the perfect balance he hadn't had earlier, he pivoted to one log and hopped out of the tank. His feet felt like cold lead blocks. Falling in the water would make the rest of the course more challenging because of the cold. But the race was still winnable.

He sprinted over to where Kristen had her chainsaw running, slicing through the logs. She was slightly tentative. Other people might not be able to tell, but he knew that Kristen was afraid of the chainsaw. It was her least favorite part. Like most men, he was happier with a power tool in his hand. The fact that it was destructive and dangerous was an added bonus.

He made up a few seconds with the first cut. As the circular piece of wood dropped down to the ground and he started on the second of three cuts, he saw a blond head moving out of his peripheral vision.

He didn't look to see if it was Avery, but the flash of blond made him think of how her pink nails would look against the bright yellow of the chainsaw. The image of her in safety glasses gripping a chain saw floated through his brain. She'd probably wear a stylish shirt and maybe leggings and have that infernal cat strapped to her chest. In his head, he moved behind her, wrapping his arms around her and showing her how to hold her thumb so if the chain snapped back it didn't break and how to tilt the saw to get the most aggressive use of the blade width and the perfect amount of pressure to keep the saw cutting but not snagging in the wood. He could smell her sassy-sweet perfume.

Beside him Kristen dropped the last piece of wood and dropped her saw, sprinting off to the last station.

Gator shook his head, trying to get the tempting images of Avery out of his brain. He never had this much trouble concentrating. He hadn't made up any time at all. In fact, he might have lost a second.

By the time he finished his cut, Kristen was already up the last pole with her hatchet and had about a quarter of the pole chopped through.

Grabbing his hatchet, Gator climbed easily and began chopping, taking out his frustration on his lack of focus on the pole. Whatever infatuation he had with Avery had to be overcome. He couldn't live his life daydreaming about a woman. He'd never been plagued like that before, and he certainly wasn't going to ruin his life with it now.

Almost in the next breath, he wondered if she'd be disappointed that Kristen had beaten him as his ex-wife's pole top fell to the ground. She whooped and slid down the pole, smacking the bell at the bottom with her hatchet to signal to the judges to stop her time.

Three more hard chops and Gator's pole top fell. He slid down and smacked the bell himself. Immediately, his gaze found Avery.

His mother had her arm around Avery's waist. Avery's smile burned up the distance between them. She clapped with abandon. Her eyes never left his. He found himself grinning at her and shrugging. He should have known she wouldn't give a flip about winning. For some reason it didn't really bother him, either. Even the fact that Kristen beat him didn't matter.

"Getting slow, old man." Kristen slapped him on the shoulder breaking the spell that had woven itself around Avery and him. He looked away from the pretty blond standing beside his mother, and over at his ex.

"I guess. Congrats to you. McKoy is the only one who might have beaten you."

Kristen's hair sparkled with the remnants of the saw dust. "That old lady judge always docks me points for the stupidest things. If it were just a matter of time, I'd be the winner."

The judges sat with their heads together. It usually took them five or so minutes before they all agreed on points and deductions.

"Maybe." Gator shrugged. He wasn't going to win this year, and he supposed he should be more upset, but he just wasn't.

Bending over he picked up the pieces of cut wood. They'd be used for the bonfire where people would roast hot dogs and marshmallows and socialize until late in the night.

"Gator?"

He straightened, his arms full of wood pieces. "Yeah?"

Kristen put her hands on her hips. "You know I'm in town because I need to talk to you."

"So you said." He picked up more wood. Maybe if he ignored her, she'd go away.

"I have a proposition."

As he recalled, she was the one who had asked him to marry her. In fact, he thought she'd mentioned a proposition that night too. She said they'd be good together. What she'd failed to mention was that marriage and being good together wasn't a permanent thing for her.

"Not interested." Gator took a few steps and threw the wood into a pile.

"It's going to pay you." Kristen paused, then emphasized the last two words. "Big time."

He paused, just for a fraction of a second, not long enough for most people to notice, but Kristen could see a weak spot from the next hill over.

Her lips pursed and she smiled knowingly. "I thought money might be more meaningful to you than it used to be."

"It's not." But he thought of his mother and the medical bills. He turned to go for more wood.

She grabbed his bicep. "You haven't heard what I'm offering."

Gator glanced over at the judges. They were still huddled behind the table. He pulled away from her grip. "You have two minutes. I'm gonna say no. Then I don't want to see you or hear about it again."

"Relax. Your caveman persona doesn't scare me. Remember? It's Kristen. Not some little blond bimbo."

His eyes shot to hers, which were narrowed and calculating.

Her lips curved in a triumphant smile.

He didn't smile back, but he didn't say anything either. He couldn't acknowledge that she'd scored a point. It had been a while, but he hadn't forgotten how the game was played. Everything was a competition, and Kristen kept score.

She waited a few more seconds as though waiting to see if he would acknowledge her point. After a minute she said, "The big-game hunting preserve that Jace and I bought needs a manager. Someone to supervise the animals, and someone to lead the hunting parties. I want you."

94

That had been Kristen's dream. To have a hunting preserve. Part of the reason she'd married him and said they were so good together. He had the education and the skills to help her get what she wanted. He'd been lacking one thing. Money. Kristen thought he'd sell the house out from under his mother to get it. She'd been mistaken.

"Jace has the money, but not the skills." It was a statement and Kristen didn't argue with him. He laughed. "Sucks for you, doesn't it?"

"Shut up."

Gator didn't need to be told twice. It wasn't like he wanted to be talking to her.

"Don't you want to know how much I'm offering?"

"No." He'd never had a taste for trophy hunting. Meat for the table, yes. Bragging rights? It just didn't interest him. Same as teaming up with Kristen didn't interest him. If she'd ditch him after saying vows in front of a church, she wasn't the kind of woman he wanted to do business with. Not that he was bitter about the dissolution of their marriage. It was probably for the best. But he would have stuck it out, just because he gave his word. She was the one that needed the divorce. She couldn't have Jace's money while she was married to Gator.

"You forget, Gator, that we were married once."

He snorted. But he looked her in the eye. "A marriage isn't something that slips a guy's mind."

She rolled her eyes. "I know your mother didn't have the best insurance. I bet she's got some pretty big bills to pay." Kristen tapped him on the arm. "And I know you. You're not going to let those bills go to collections. You're worrying yourself to death trying to figure out a way to pay them. Right now. You're worried. Remember that tough guy exterior doesn't fool me."

"It fools me." Let her chew on that for a while. She'd accused him of being weak plenty of times when he didn't do what she wanted. Maybe she'd wonder if he actually was faking the whole tough guy thing. He tossed the last of the wood on the pile. He didn't care what she thought.

Over at the judges' table, Mrs. Baker had gathered all the papers together and was shuffling through them.

Kristen's chin jutted out. "You don't have to get smart."

"I'm not interested." Gator made his way over to his mother, nodding at people who complimented him or just said hi, but he didn't stop to chat. His mother, who had sat back down, was breathing a little hard, and Avery had knelt beside her and spoke softly to her with her hand on her knee. He caught the last part of what she was saying. "I can take you home if you want."

"No. I want to watch you and Gator trim the tree! What's the point of living if I miss all the fun stuff?"

Avery glanced up at him, her brows drawn together and her lip caught between her teeth.

His eyes caught on that. A swirl of heat tightened his abs before he met her gaze.

Mrs. Baker took the loudspeaker. "Ladies and Gentlemen. We have a decision for the last two contestants and a final standing to report." The crowd cheered. "Kristen Franks won this round with 342 points."

"Kristen Pandifino," Kristen yelled, but no one paid attention.

"Gator Franks had 311 points. That is good enough for third place in the contest."

The crowd cheered. Someone whistled.

"And of course, the score to beat was McKoy Rodning's 359. It stands as our winning score, with Kristen Franks in second place. Congratulations to all of our contestants. Let's give them a nice round of applause."

After the clapping stopped, Mrs. Baker reminded everyone about the bonfire, like anyone had forgotten, and then announced that the tree trimming competition would start in thirty minutes.

Avery smiled but didn't say anything, as though waiting to gage his reaction to being beaten by his ex. He looked away without giving her any clue. After all, he could hardly say that out on the course the only thing he could think of was her. That he couldn't concentrate, and he sure as heck didn't care about Kristen or whether or not she won.

"Let's find you a comfortable place to sit, then, before it starts." Avery put a hand on his mother's shoulder.

"Gator. You looked great out there." His mother started to rise, but he scrunched down beside her, his hand on her other knee.

She stroked his head, like she used to do when he was a boy. "You know it doesn't matter to me whether or not you win."

"It didn't matter to me today, either."

His mother's eyes narrowed a fraction, and her gaze became thoughtful, but she didn't say anything.

"It was hard to root against Kristen, because she did sit at the dunking booth for me for a while, but I cheered with your mother."

He raised a brow and wondered if she knew Gladys had her nose on her shoe. He doubted it. "I could have let you borrow my suit if your loyalty is so easily bought."

She snorted. "Kristen and I both could fit into yours."

"Better to have none, then."

"I thought you didn't care if she beat you?"

"I don't. But I wouldn't want to be stuck in a wet suit with her, either."

Laughter bubbled up. "I see."

"Are you ready to move, Mom?" Gator stood up.

She nodded and Gator placed a hand under her elbow and helped her to stand.

Avery slipped an arm around her waist and said, "Jillian said she would set up a chair near our tree and put a reserved sign on it. I haven't been over to see where it is."

"I saw the farm sign right in the middle of the line." There was a double line of about twenty trees. The Sweet Haven Farm sign sat right in the middle. "That must be her chair," he said. He was grateful it was a low-slung lawn chair with a blanket folded neatly on the seat under the "Reserved" sign.

"Let's get you tucked in here, Mrs. Franks." Avery lifted the blanket and the sign and bustled around, getting his mother settled. She reached up to tuck some fly-away strands of hair behind her head.

"I've got this," Gator said. "You go take a few minutes for yourself."

"I'll check on Jillian, then. Be right back," Avery said and hurried off.

Chapter Ten

A very paid for her hot chocolate and picked up the cup carrier, feeling almost naked without Miss Prissypants, who was in her carrier with Jillian.

Avery had bought a hot chocolate for Gator, as well as for his mother, but she didn't know if the guy even drank the stuff. Was it unmanly to drink hot chocolate? Belatedly, she remembered that Kristen was going to get coffee. Maybe Gator was a coffee drinker too. She supposed it didn't matter. If he didn't like it, he didn't have to drink it.

People milled about around the trees, lugging boxes and bags of decorations. She said hi to the few she knew, nodded to the ones who nodded to her, and stole surreptitious looks at the decorations they were unpacking. Lots of sparkly, glittery items with plenty of color and lights. Her stomach knotted. It wasn't what they had planned at all. But Mrs. Franks had given her the decorations, and Ellie had given her suggestions of what to do. She hoped they knew what they were doing.

When she reached the chair where she'd left them, Gator had his mother tucked into the chair, the blanket bundled around her. His coat was around her shoulders, and she wore a beanie hat that Avery hadn't seen before.

"You look cozy."

"Gator insisted. He said I looked cold."

Avery hunched down. "It was your shivering that gave you away."

"It's the medicine. It makes me shiver."

Avery exchanged a look with Gator. If her medicine made her shiver, this was the first she had heard about it.

"I brought you some hot chocolate." She held out the holder.

Mrs. Franks beamed. "Perfect. Thank you."

"And one for you." She lifted it back up and offered it to Gator.

One side of his mouth quirked up. "Good choice." He tilted the cup and took a sip.

Her heart flipped.

She shook off her reaction and looked around at the supplies. There were two big boxes and one smaller one. Gator had taken the lids off and set them by the tree that had been assigned to them.

He followed her gaze. "There was a bare spot on the tree. I shifted it around so it pointed in."

"Oh, great. Thanks. I hadn't even noticed."

"You would have," he said with confidence.

"That bad?"

"Yep."

A voice on the loudspeaker came on, announcing five minutes until the competition started. The speaker ran down the rules, which were basically anything goes on your own tree, but you couldn't touch anyone else's tree or have anyone but the two team members touch yours. Thirty-minute time limit. No cutting or altering the branches on the tree.

By the time he was done with the instructions and announcing and thanking the sponsors, it was time to begin.

Avery stood by the yellow caution tape, Gator at her side. She could feel his heat at her side. His size and strength radiated out. Again, she wondered why he'd let Kristen win. It had been obvious to her that Gator had not been trying very hard. Actually, he'd try for a while, then let up, like he needed to slow down to keep her ahead of him.

Maybe Kristen was holding something over his head, but Avery felt like it might be more like Gator had seen Kristen and had remembered what had drawn them together to begin with. So, he'd let her beat him to make her feel good and to make her happy with him. Avery wouldn't have pegged Gator for that kind of man, but what other explanation was there?

"Competitors take your mark."

Gator shifted slightly beside her.

"Go."

He lifted the yellow tape and she stepped under it, reaching in the box and pulling out the wooden Christmas shaped decorations that Mrs. Franks had allowed her to borrow. Gator had made them in high school. They were simple and rustic, decorated with twine and a few red berries.

They went onto the tree with hooks and more twine.

Gator pulled one out.

"You'll have to tell me where this goes." He held the decoration up in his hand.

"Okay. That will work." She'd wondered how she and Gator were going to get along. Whether he'd be throwing things on the tree and she'd come along after him, fixing them. Of if he'd stand and watch her until she asked for help.

"Let's start at the top. I think she said there were thirty of these."

"Yes, ma'am," Gator said, not a little sarcastically.

"Watch it, mister."

He held the decoration up and she instructed him where to place it, keeping in mind that these were the easier of the two kinds of ornaments that would be on the tree. As he brushed by, she caught a hint of his scent, rough maleness mixed with sharp pine. The calls and conversations around them faded as her awareness of the man beside her rose. The rustle of his plaid shirt, the cords of his neck, the strength of his legs as he bent and stretched. She became fascinated with the gentle way his large hands held the rustic ornaments. Calloused, long, capable, they had been running a chain saw with ease not that long ago. Now they cradled fragile wooden pieces, attaching them to the tree with agility. They said so much about the man, but at the same time made her more curious.

She handed him a cutout and pointed to where she thought it

would look best. "So, I assume you work outside, but not trimming trees? You probably shoot a lot of things."

He laughed, but shook his head while he hung the bulb. "No. I do more watching and observing than shooting."

"That's your job? To watch animals?" She had been curious, and she told herself it was a neutral topic. Just because she wasn't that interested in any other man to try to find out what, exactly, they did at their job, really didn't factor into anything.

"Not exactly. I do actually do a lot of observing of wildlife. If there seems to be extra skinny deer or a lot of mange, or if animals seem to be dying at a higher than usual rate, or natural or unnatural causes of death. There is also keeping an eye on the flora and fauna, invasive plants, and I do a lot of interacting with people too. Hikers and people who are just interested in learning about our country's natural resources."

"You love your job?" It seemed like he didn't.

He hesitated. "Yes."

"That pause said a lot."

"I'm good at carpentry work. More than tearing down old barns."

She handed him more cutouts. Every second the attraction to him grew and she couldn't help but feel how homey it was to be decorating a tree with a man. She'd never done it before. Her dad had certainly never helped before he'd run off, and she hadn't even considered asking Ralph to help her decorate the tiny tree she'd had in her apartment the few Christmases they'd been together.

"You must be thinking hard about where to put these."

She blinked. She hadn't been thinking about it at all. The expression on his face, part concern, part question, said he knew it.

"I'm sorry." She studied the tree. "Are there two more?"

"Yes." He held up one in each hand.

She quickly found them spots and checked the time. Ten minutes had slipped by.

His hand put warm pressure on her shoulder, and she turned to face him. His fingers moved slightly. A caress or reassurance. "Are you okay?"

She opened her eyes wide and nodded quickly, trying to look sincere. "Of course."

His fingers tightened for a moment, and she thought she felt his thumb brush the corner of her jaw just below her ear. She shivered, but resisted the urge to wrap her arms around herself.

"I thought maybe this was bringing back bad memories or something."

"No. Not at all." Her cursed feminine heart was trying to make new ones. With him, who was totally unsuspecting that she basically had a ring on his finger and him in her living room for the next fifty years. What a time for her mind to go all domestic. She'd spent most of her life telling herself that men couldn't be counted on, that they'd leave and that she didn't need a man anyway, and now, now, her whole body was going to rebel. Wonderful.

"Yep. I'm sure." Her answer sounded breathy and fake. His forehead wrinkled. Seconds ticked by as they stared at each other.

She pushed past him to where the boxes sat. His hand dropped, making her shoulder feel cold, and her heart colder.

She cleared her throat, praying her voice came out sounding normal. "Let's get these other ones out. We're running out of time."

He turned with her and they opened the second of the larger boxes. Light brown, square, wooden candle holders filled it. Gator lifted two out carefully.

Avery refused to look at his hands. She definitely couldn't allow herself to wish them back on her shoulders. She eyed the decorations, then considered the time. They had to have them hung and lit before the bell rang.

She put a finger to her lips and tapped. "How about you help me place the upper ones that I can't reach, then I'll take over while you insert the candles and light them?"

"You're the expert." His back was toward her and she couldn't see his face, but he sounded sincere.

She showed him where she wanted to place the first one. He secured the heavier ornament with the wire attached to the back. They were ingenious if she did say so. It was hard to believe a high schooler came up with the idea, although Mrs. Franks said they'd only used them one year because of the risk of fire.

"On that branch." She pointed to a stronger-looking branch than the one she had indicated previously. The symmetry was still good. She actually liked her decorations to look more natural, but she'd assume the judges would prefer balance and proportion.

He stretched and reached the branch she indicated while she admired the ripple of his shirt and how it stretched over his shoulders.

This was crazy. The poor man couldn't even spend the day with her without her acting like a love-starved kid. Maybe she was love-starved. Maybe that's why she didn't have a problem walking away from her home in Philly and spending the summer and fall here, in limbo as she waited for her life to patch itself up. Living with Ellie and Fink and sharing the closeness of a family. Working with them to make the farm profitable. Having fun while they did it. She had to admit, she loved being part of a family and a business. It was icing that she was able to use her love of decorating to directly help.

But as much as she loved it, Fink and Ellie deserved to have their home and family back to themselves. She didn't want to overstay and make them wish she was gone. It was time to move on. Hopefully, she'd get the gig in D.C. Even if she didn't, she had the teaching position that she'd been offered. She just had to let them know that she was taking it.

She handed another candle holder decoration to Gator. His fingers brushed hers. Deliberately. Her breath caught and her eyes flew to his. A sparkle of humor lurked there, but also something deeper, something she wasn't quite sure about. Her hand went to her chest before she purposely turned away and pulled another holder from the box.

She couldn't believe he had made all these decorations. She held one up. "You enjoy carpentry work."

"Yeah. Bigger things even more. Cabinets. Kitchens. Sheds. Chairs. I made a couple of chicken coops for people out west. Stuff like that."

"So why don't you do that?"

"Because I'm a big boy who knows that I'm lucky to have a job I enjoy. Not everyone gets to make a living doing what they love. Plus, I know a guy who used to love fly fishing. He started a tour guide company where he leads people on fishing expeditions. Basically, he fishes all day and gets paid for it. You know, it's just a job now."

"You think if you became a carpenter, it'd stop being something you love and become just a job?"

"Yeah."

"I disagree," she said as she handed him another holder.

"You know me better than I know myself?"

"No. I think it has everything to do with your attitude."

"So, I have a bad attitude." He stretched above his head and used both hands to secure the holder.

She snorted. "I didn't say that."

"Okay?"

"I love playing the tuba. And I got to do it for a living when I played in the symphony and taught at college. I still love playing the tuba." After pushing in the candle, she waited for him to take the next holder from her.

"You're not making a living from it anymore."

A pang hit her heart. "No. But I'm trying. And I still love it. I just think anything becomes a job if you let it."

He seemed to consider her words. "So, attitude is everything. Anyone can learn to love anything?"

"Not exactly. I think you're a better fit for some jobs than others. But, for example, I think I could be happy as an interior decorator, except I don't want to go back to school and get the degrees I'd need." She laughed. "I'd still play my tuba, though. For fun. Maybe give lessons. I can't imagine life without it."

"It'd be quieter," he said with a flash of his dimple.

She lifted her brows at him. "Funny guy."

"Yeah. I can't imagine a job where I was chained to a desk."

"I can't imagine you in a job like that, either."

He lifted another holder from her and met her gaze. "Really? That obvious, huh?"

She rolled her eyes. "It's kind of hard for me to picture you making the intricate cuts that those decorations require, though, too."

After taking a quick glance at the other competitors to make sure that they weren't falling behind, Avery grabbed another candle and holder.

Gator carefully attached the holder to the tree. "Making these things does take patience. And exacting measure. I enjoy doing it. I made these in the evenings after school. Then, to relax and get out of that headspace, I'd take my dogs coon hunting."

"And go to school the next day?"

"I was always in by three or four in the morning." He grimaced. "Almost always."

"And you were coon hunting?" She stopped and put a hand on her hip. "Really?"

He looked at her with a baffled expression. "Yeah. What'd you think? I was really street racing my truck on the highway?"

"Um, no? I figured you were out with a girl."

"Nah. I wasn't really interested in girls."

"That's weird," Avery said before she could stop herself.

He shrugged, but kept working. "Yeah. It was, actually. I mean, I liked them okay. I just didn't understand them and preferred to be with my dogs."

"Wow. That's bad."

"They're nice dogs."

"Until Kristen came along."

"I thought, since she loved the things I did, that we'd get along just fine. Actually, we do get along just fine."

"I saw that." Avery tried to keep any rancor out of her voice. It was obvious he and Kristen got along. "So, is it prying to ask what happened?"

"She wanted more than I had." He stated it simply and lifted a shoulder, like it didn't matter.

She wasn't fooled by his casual manner. The pinched look around his eyes and the slight tightening of his mouth gave him away.

"More time? More stuff?" she asked.

After he'd finished the top tier of the tree that she couldn't reach, she took over attaching the wooden boxes while he began to light the candles.

"More money. We both loved the outdoors and being active. Hunting and shooting. It's a great pastime and hobby for both of us. But she wanted to turn it into something bigger. That was gonna take more money than I'd ever have."

"Didn't she know that when she married you?"

He clicked the lighter on and touched it to the candle. "I think she thought I'd sell my mother's house. Not a chance."

"What's this bigger thing?"

"She wanted to purchase a hunting preserve."

"Did she?"

"Yep, she did."

"How'd she get the money?"

He shut the light off with a snap. "Married it."

Avery laughed. "What's she doing here if she has the big hunting preserve she always wanted?"

One side of Gator's mouth kicked up in an ironic half-smile. "She wants me to manage it for her."

Avery's stomach dropped. She knew he was leaving, but somehow him leaving to work for Kristen was much worse than him going back to his old job. She studied the decoration in her hand. "Isn't that a little twisted?"

"What?"

"Her getting her ex to manage the preserve she bought with her current husband's money?"

He shook his head and lit another candle. "Maybe. I guess. I don't know."

"You're interested?" Avery asked softly, glad her voice didn't tremble. Her whole body had turned to ice at the thought, and she recognized the feeling for what it was: jealousy, made worse by the fact that she didn't want him to leave at all.

Maybe he didn't hear her because he never answered.

It was close to five, and winter twilight had stolen over the celebration grounds. As he lit the candles, the tree started to glow, almost becoming life-like as the flames bounced and flickered. Thankfully there was no wind.

Gator had caught up to her, and as she knelt on the ground, fastening the last candle holder to the tree, he knelt beside her, waiting with the lighter.

She leaned back as he secured the white candle in the holder before he touched the lighter to the wick and the last flame flickered to life.

He leaned back beside her, almost as though he knew exactly where she was without looking. Or maybe she was just pushing her own awareness onto him. Whatever it was, she didn't move and allowed their sleeves to brush as he settled back and they stared at the tree.

The other groups were winding down as well, although a few frantically rushed to finish before the bell. The crowd was silent, as though awed by the magic of the beauty of lights and decorations before them. Soft Christmas music still played from speakers somewhere and drifted on the evening air. Random flakes of snow meandered down, catching and reflecting the lights of the pretty trees.

Avery leaned her head back and watched the flakes coming down, envying them their complete unconcern about where they landed or even which other flakes fell with them. Wouldn't that be nice, to go through life unconcerned with where you lived or who lived with you? She wouldn't harbor any resentment for a dad who preferred a woman other than her mom and a fiancé who felt the same way about her.

She wouldn't be wishing this time with Gator would never end.

She turned her head, meaning to study him, but found him watching her. Normally, she might think a man who looked at her like that might be interested, but she hadn't fixed her hair or makeup all day, and she'd just spent the last half-hour bossing him around. Plus, she'd seen his ex. Avery wasn't going to lie to herself. A man who was interested in a woman like Kristen would never be interested in her.

"I think you should be smiling. Your tree looks pretty darn good." Gator spoke low, almost intimately, and the low rumble of his voice made her shiver.

She blinked as a snowflake hit her eyelash and turned her head back to the sky.

Gator shifted, but she didn't look at him. "What's the matter, Avery? You've been pretty chatty this whole time. Now all the sudden nothing but Christmas music. It's like you're somewhere else."

She could hardly believe that he hadn't noticed that she was hyper-aware of him and totally attracted. That was the problem. Wouldn't he just flip if he knew?

What if she told him?

Avery's eyes opened wide, even as her brain automatically screamed *no way.* He would laugh, and she'd be embarrassed. Plus, talk about opening oneself up to hurt and ridicule.

But she was leaving, and Gator was going back out west, so it wasn't like it was going to make the rest of her life awkward or anything. And, for once, she could be honest. If she read his earlier look correctly and he felt an attraction toward her, they could have a little fling together. She'd never done anything like that, but that didn't mean she couldn't try it. Once.

She allowed the words to come out of her mouth before reason took back over. "I enjoyed working with you."

His look was skeptical, which prompted more, even worse, uncensored words to erupt from her mouth. "But you're right. I do want to be somewhere else. After all, I can't hardly take your shirt off here."

Gator looked at her, his mouth slightly ajar.

Her courage and sass evaporated like a drop of water on a hot skillet, and she scrambled to get up.

He grabbed her arm. "No. No, you don't get to say something like that, then run away."

Her arm heated where he touched it, and his eyes smoldered into hers. She hadn't anticipated that she might need to explain her comment. Or defend it.

The sharp ringing of a bell pierced the air.

Gator's lips tightened, but his eyes never left hers.

"The time is up." After the quiet of the past minutes, the voice from the loudspeaker seemed unnaturally loud. "Please take any unused decorations and surplus boxes and bags and exit the decorating area. Stay outside the yellow tape. The judges will be around. A winner will be announced at the bonfire area in forty-five minutes."

Avery tore her eyes away and struggled to stand. Gator's hand loosened on her arm, moving to cup her elbow and help her up. She turned away, feeling like a coward, and he let her go. Part of her wanted badly to flirt a little, see where things might lead. But she'd spent her life building walls to protect herself from any pain associated with getting close to a man. Even with her fiancé, their relationship had been built on shared interests rather than shared attraction.

Mrs. Franks was slouched in her chair, bundled in her blankets, sleeping. Avery didn't even have that as a distraction.

The idea of letting go a little and having a fun little relationship with Gator was appealing, but she knew where that road led. She'd managed to avoid it all her life. Just because a man had come along to whom she was attracted and who also happened to be nice and fun to work with, didn't mean that the rules, or the outcome, had changed.

Determined, she turned to Gator. "I'm sorry. That was a stupid, juvenile thing to say. I needed to concentrate on getting the decorations just right. That's why I seemed so far away." She brushed her hands down her legs and nodded at the tree. "I think we did a great job."

The energy that had shown from his eyes had dimmed. "I never thought I'd have fun trimming a tree."

Relief that he wasn't going to press her about her asinine comment flowed through her. She indicated his mother. "Should we wake her?"

Chapter Eleven

G ator tried to meet Avery's gaze, but she wouldn't look at him. The comment about his shirt had probably just slipped out, and had obviously embarrassed her. She didn't need to know how it completely shifted his world. He'd had such a good time with Avery, but it was this attraction that he couldn't shake that had him bothered. His heart and body had jumped on the idea that she might feel it too.

From the way she was looking at anything besides him, apparently not.

Gator's dogs were stretched out under his mother's chair. "I think I have time before they announce the winners to take her home and get her settled there."

"I'll help you," Avery turned and started toward his mother's chair.

"You haven't seen the whole celebration—I know you haven't had time to walk around today. Go, see some things."

"I'll help you with your mom, first," Avery insisted. "Unless you want to do it all yourself?"

It would be easier with help. He could feed the dogs while she took care of getting his mom in the house and ready for home nursing to come. "People come from all over to see this festival. It's a big deal."

She shook his mother awake gently. "I think I saw the most

important things," she said. Then her attention focused on helping his mom sit up.

"If you come with me, I'll walk you around when we get back." He could tell himself he offered because he felt he owed her for helping, but he knew that wasn't it.

"Deal."

While Avery took care of his mom, Gator loaded the dogs and brought his pickup as close to the tree area as possible. It helped that the security guard knew him and let him pull through one closed street, so his mom only had to walk a half of a block.

Gator carried the chair in one hand. His other hand went around his mother's back, overlapping Avery's slender arm.

He'd never had this much fun at the festival. Usually, he'd done the lumberjack competition and left.

They didn't talk much on the way home. He helped Avery get his mom in the door. By the time he fed his dogs and bedded them down for the night, she had his mom changed and on the couch.

"I have a treatment tomorrow in Pittsburgh." Her voice sounded scratchy, maybe from the cold air.

Avery propped pillows behind her as she spoke.

"Gator is taking you to it?"

"Yes."

Gator stopped in the doorway, unnoticed, as his mother grabbed Avery's wrist.

"Did you ask him about what I said earlier?"

Avery patted his mother's hand and shook her head.

Gator almost interrupted them to ask what she had said earlier, but he held himself still.

"If he brings it up, I'll say something, but it's not something that interests him."

"Honey, you interest him."

An automatic denial sprang to his lips, but he swallowed it and stood still. His mother was right. Avery did interest him. She attracted him. She amused him. She pulled him out of his little bubble and helped him see the world with new eyes. Maybe that was why opposites attracted.

His mother reached a hand up and patted Avery's cheek. "You do."

"I don't know about that. But he's quite interesting too."

Gator's chest expanded. He'd take interesting.

"He needs a good woman in his life."

"You're not going anywhere, so no hinting about that."

Gator was surprised that she felt comfortable enough with his mother to be so blunt. His mother wasn't a beat around the bush type of lady and Avery had her figured out.

"Oh, I wasn't hinting anything of the kind. Plus, I wasn't suggesting you take my place as his mother."

Avery tucked her feet in. "Yeah, he's a little big to be sitting on my lap."

"Mine too," his mother said with a wry grin. "He's a good man."

"Mom, I'm standing right here. Would you please stop?"

"Didn't hear you, son."

"That would be the first time in my life you didn't hear me walk in the house without taking my boots off."

His mother closed her eyes and raised her brows.

A look he was familiar with from childhood. "That look does not make you look innocent."

"I actually thought it did," Avery said.

"After you've been around her for a while, it doesn't fool you anymore."

"Hey, people. I'm right here." His mother waved a hand without opening her eyes.

Before he could say anything, there was a knock at the door. He let the home nurse in, and after chatting for a few minutes, Avery and he left.

All the close spots were taken when they got back to the town square, and he ended up parking along the road about a half mile away.

"I hope you don't mind walking a while," he said as he reached for the door handle.

"I don't think we have a choice. I would have guessed that things would have thinned out by now." Avery got out. He met her at the front of the truck and they started walking.

"Maybe at other places, Christmas festivals die down after dark, but here the bonfire is the most popular activity. I hadn't heard anything this year, but in years past, they often have fireworks too."

"I love fireworks!" Avery said. "But I just can't believe people are out in this cold." Since the sun went down, the temperature must have dropped twenty degrees. She folded her arms over her chest and shivered.

Gator didn't question his instinct. He slid his arm around her shoulders and pulled her to him. She tucked very nicely right under his arm. It was a new feeling and he liked it. "I don't think you ever warmed up from being on that plank."

"You got wet and I didn't, but I think you're right. I'll welcome hot chocolate."

He relaxed. She was actually going to allow him to walk with his arm around her. And not only that, but she nestled in closer. It was a good feeling.

Her sweet and sassy scent drifted to his nose and he pulled her in tighter. "I'll have to make sure you get some."

"You don't owe me anything."

Her hip brushed his thigh. Feeling that sweet caress for the rest of their walk might be the definition of torture, but he didn't move away. Although, he did try to focus his mind. He couldn't deny the heat that raced through his body, but Avery was a beautiful person on the inside and he enjoyed talking to her.

"I do owe you. I've been meaning to thank you for what you've been doing for my mom."

"You don't have to thank me. I believe she's a friend. I know she's older than me, but I've never chosen my friends based on their age. It's more about how connected I feel. I just really feel at ease around her. I like her. And I enjoy helping her."

"I'll still get you a hot chocolate."

She chuckled. "I guess I'll let you."

He took a deep breath, not entirely sure he was not making a huge mistake, but he couldn't get her words from earlier about his shirt out of his mind. "What are you doing next Friday?"

"I have that audition I told you about in Washington D.C."

He'd forgotten. "There's supposed to be a snow storm next week."

"The weather never does what it's supposed to do. If the weather people say it's going to snow, I'm placing bets on it being seventy-five and sunny."

"You're one of those people who wouldn't evacuate for a hurricane. I wouldn't have guessed it by looking at you."

Her shoulders drooped a little. "I suppose I am kind of stubborn."

"Kind of?"

"A little?"

"The barn is still standing, Avery. And that is solely because of you and your determination to keep it up, even though there are a hundred other places more suitable for a Christmas party around here."

She took a breath like she was going to say something, but she exhaled and stayed silent.

They passed the first streetlight. A few clusters of people, mostly teens, laughed and talked as they walked by.

"All the booths will be closed except for the ones in the square, probably."

"I would have loved to see the crafts."

"Maybe next year you can have your own booth."

"I'm not very good at making stuff. I'm better at decorating."

"I see." He was good at making stuff. It was an example of how their differences complimented each other. Maybe, when he looked at Kristen and saw all their similarities, he hadn't realized how being the same might get boring. Or worse, how it fostered competition between them. Mostly on her end, though, to be honest. He wasn't a real competitive guy, but she hated it when he won or was right.

"Are you getting warmer?" he asked. Not because he wanted to let her go, but more because he didn't want her sweating to death beside him. He also figured it would give her the opportunity to get rid of his arm without having to say she didn't want it.

"I am."

His heart fell a little.

"I must have left my gloves at your house, though." She held up her bare hand.

He looked at it, then at her face. Her mouth curved in a small smile. Her eyes held a question.

Without breaking their gaze, he slid his hand up her wrist. Their palms brushed against each other with a sizzle before his fingers slipped between hers. They stood like that for a moment, hands pressed against each other, eyes meeting. Gator's heart pumped hard and heavy in his chest.

Little fogs of breath puffed out of Avery's mouth and swirled between them. Her eyes darkened and her lips trembled. Gator brought his other hand up and slid it along her cheek, touching the corner of her mouth with his thumb.

The snow began falling more earnestly. From somewhere far away, bells chimed and Christmas music floated on the air.

"I'll keep it warm," he said, surprised that he had a voice at all, even if it was low and gravelly and sounded like he'd just woken up.

She bent her fingers over his hand and looked at their entwined digits. "I trust you to do that." She said it slowly, with wonder in her voice.

He got the feeling trust wasn't something easy for her to say or admit.

"What happened that trust is so hard for you?"

She looked away and their hands dropped between.

Gator kicked himself for breaking the spell that had them cocooned in their own world. He should have known that anything that had destroyed her trust in people would be a sore subject. It's just that he wanted to know everything about her. He wanted to protect her from those hurts. He wanted... He closed his eyes against all the impossible things he wanted. He didn't know everything, but he'd learned in the last ten years that life wasn't about getting what he wanted.

"That bad?" he prompted when she still didn't answer. He tugged on her hand. Maybe it would be easier for her to tell him if they were walking.

She fell in easily beside him, as she always did. He enjoyed it. "No," she said slowly. "It's not that I've been treated so horribly, I guess. But," her hand tightened in his, "my dad left my mom for another woman. My fiancé left me for someone else." She threw up her other hand. "The woman was a flutist. Seriously? A flutist!" She laughed and he joined in.

"Right. Note to self—don't date flutists."

"Seriously. I've seen it over and over, and I've experienced it twice. Men don't stick around. Most men." She bumped his arm with her shoulder. "I already know you're not staying."

"I didn't leave Kristen." He felt like he needed to defend himself.

"I know," she said softly.

But he couldn't suspend reality. "I do have a job in Montana that I have to go back to eventually."

"I know."

"Have you ever thought about living anywhere but here, in the East?" he asked casually.

"I have a job offer in Washington D.C."

"But you haven't accepted it yet?"

"I'm going to."

"I see." He leaned his head back and watched the flakes of snow swirl down. What was he doing? Following up on an attraction he'd never felt before, which felt too strong to ignore, and chasing a woman who planned to live a continent away from him. He looked back down. The top of her red beanie hat was white with snow. "Well, we can have a good time tonight, can't we?"

"I'm planning on it."

"Great. Let me get you that hot chocolate."

They dove into the outskirts of the milling crowd, many of whom carried plates loaded with hotdogs and roasted marshmallows, Christmas cookies, and gingerbread men. At the perimeter of the fire, folks roasted their food over the open flames. Long lines curled like tree ribbons at all three hot chocolate vendors.

Gator noticed a few raised eyebrows when they saw the woman at his side and their entwined hands. There were a few smiles, but more dropped jaws, which made him grin. He wasn't the only person in the world who thought Avery and he were complete opposites.

They walked by the long line of tables laden with the entries of the gingerbread house competition and several areas where children had made decorations and iced cookies.

"I'd like to check out the farm booth, if you don't mind," Avery said.

He adjusted his steps and headed toward where Jillian stood behind the counter of a booth in the center of everything.

"I have flyers there for the Christmas party. And I should make sure she doesn't need anything."

"That's fine. I'll get us a couple cups of hot chocolate and come back around."

Her hand slipped out of his. He let go reluctantly and watched her walk away with a bemused smile on his face. A tiny little powerhouse full of kindness and creativity, Avery had surprised him in a lot of different ways since he first saw her at the top of the light pole.

He turned and headed toward the hot chocolate vendor with the shortest line. If he was only getting tonight with her, he was going to make it count as much as possible.

He got a drink for Jillian too and had just paid when McKoy Rodning walked up. "Gator, where you been? You missed the announcement of the tree trimming winners."

Gator couldn't believe he'd forgotten about that. "I took my mom home. Getting out like this wore her out."

"Oh, yeah. I heard about her cancer. How's she doing?" McKoy took one of the cups of chocolate and walked alongside of Gator.

"Good. Tired. It's hard, but she's got a great sense of humor and she's always been happy."

"Yeah. She's the type of person it's hard to keep down."

Gator nodded. His mother had always been a positive, happy person. He'd been blessed to have her. It was easy to see that now.

"So, Gator, we've known each other a long time..." McKoy started.

Gator immediately tensed. "Yeah?"

"Your ex beat you in the lumberjack competition."

Gator snorted and relaxed. "Yeah."

McKoy waved the cup as he searched for words. "And you're not upset about that?"

"Not really."

"Okay. That would be one thing. You came in third by the way. I beat the ex for you. You can throw cash later. Anyway," he continued with a grin, "you didn't win the lumberjack competition, which you always win, and correct me if I'm wrong, but you won the *tree decorating contest?*" He said "tree decorating contest" the way he might have said "pig guts eating contest."

Gator couldn't keep the triumphant smile off his face. "We won? That's great!"

McKoy looked at him with one raised brow. "Did she mess you up that bad?"

"Avery? No way, man."

"I meant Kristen. Who's Avery?" McKoy stopped walking and faced Gator.

"Kristen didn't mess me up. Not really."

"She left you, dude."

Gator pressed his lips together and stared at his friend. "Seriously?"

"Sorry. Didn't mean to rub it in, but come on. You and Kristen were perfect. I mean, she was into everything you were, man. And now, you lose the lumberjack for the first time in my life, and you win some decorating contest? And, no offense, but the people around town are saying that little blond chick you have on your arm isn't all together there, if you know what I mean." McKoy pointed to his head and made circle motions.

Gator's forehead thumped and his fingers tightened on the hot chocolate cup.

He loosened his fingers deliberately. "Since when does nice equal crazy?"

"I don't know about nice, but she hangs out with that circus performer. People have seen them doing really weird stuff, like swallowing swords, hanging from their hair, and walking ridgelines. She has some kind of massive instrument that she plays incessantly, and she never goes anywhere without a cat strapped to her like a baby."

Gator reminded himself that all those things were probably true. "You've actually missed a few things." He'd seen her climb a light pole, and what kind of crazy person hung out with an old lady who had cancer? For fun. And decorated the woman's house and yard.

"So you know what I mean? And she's always wearing weird clothes."

"Gator." Kristen pushed between them. "Congratulations, McKoy.

You two must be talking about that blond you've been hanging out with, Gator. It's the weird clothes comment that gave it away."

"Her name's Avery." He wanted to add an insult about Kristen's clothing choices, but his mother had always told him to take the high road. Plus, as much as he'd like to defend Avery, he didn't think it would make her happy to have him insulting people for her.

Kristen ignored him. "McKoy, did Gator tell you about the huge game preserve that I bought out in Oregon? He's coming out to run it and lead hunting parties for me."

Gator opened his mouth to argue, but a gasp made him look to his left. Avery stood about three feet away. She'd stopped in mid-stride and her hand was over her mouth, the other on her stomach.

Gator's stomach sank like a lead ball in a bucket of water.

Chapter Twelve

Avery didn't really believe that Gator cared about her choice of clothes. And the first time he'd seen her, she'd been up that light pole. He acted like he liked Miss Prissypants too. So, even though she and Jillian could hear the whole thing from where they stood at the farm's booth just feet away, she hadn't really been bothered much.

However, for some reason, the announcement that Gator was going to work for Kristen... Well, it was more that Gator hadn't told her that he was going to work for Kristen. He'd just described his job out west and said that he was going to back to it and had also mentioned that Kristen had offered him a job. But he hadn't answered her when she asked if he was going to take it. Guess she knew the answer now.

"Avery." Gator's cheeks flushed a guilty red around his natural dark skin and tan.

"Why, Avery. We didn't see you standing there." Kristen pulled her lips in, like she was trying to contain a smirk.

"I assumed that was my hot chocolate? It's getting cold." Avery held out her hand with a smile that she hoped said there were no hard feelings. None at all. Since she and Gator were not a couple or in a relationship, there couldn't be. She had no rights.

"Yeah." Gator gave a little cough. "This is McKoy Rodning. He won the lumberjack competition."

"Nice to meet you." Avery held her hand out, wishing she'd put gloves on instead of being stupid and thinking that Gator might hold her hand again.

He shook her hand. "Here," McKoy said to Gator. "This is yours."

"Thanks," Avery held her hand out. "It's actually Jillian's. Don't let me interrupt you. Jillian can use help at the stand."

"We were done." Gator dipped his head at the other two in a farewell, and moved to Avery's side with his back to them.

"Jillian can use the help. Really. The spiced hot apple cider is selling better than hot chocolate right now." She wasn't trying to avoid being with him, exactly. But it sure seemed like she'd been duped. Or at least misled.

He took her shoulders and bent until she met his gaze. "I'm not working for Kristen. I'm not doing anything with Kristen."

"She lied?" Avery hated the weakness in her that believed him. Had she learned nothing from the other men in her life? Plus, he was entitled to work with whomever he wanted, wherever he wanted.

"It's not the first time." His face pinched, and compassion welled inside her. He'd been hurt too. It wasn't just about her.

"Thanks for the hot chocolate." She tilted her head, wondering if he'd accept her words as a peace offering.

His dimple appeared. "I can help with the stand."

"I'm sure Jillian won't turn us down. Maybe she can take a break."

His finger touched her cheek, slowly sliding down. "Send her home or wherever. We can handle it until closing. I don't think she's had a break all day."

"I think you're right."

By eight o'clock, the farm booth was sold out of everything except a few odds and ends decorations.

Gator took the cash box to his pickup.

Avery watched him walk away, her hands still on the plastic table cover she was folding. He'd surprised her so much today. From taking her place on the dunking booth to being a great help trimming the tree to working the booth with her tonight. Was he hoping to get something? Or was he just being nice? Or, and this thought made her heart go from *adagio* to *allegro*, did he actually like her?

She finished folding the orange table cover and reached for the other one. What did it matter if he did? Sure, she was attracted to him, and after today, she liked and respected him too. But even if he wasn't working for Kristen, he was still headed west, while she was going to D.C. Unless she didn't get the place in the orchestra. If that happened, she still had a teaching job offer, but she could stay on the farm. Except she'd already decided that she wasn't going to impose on Ellie and Fink any longer. After the Christmas rush, things would slow down for them, and they deserved to take a break and have family time. They had spent so much time away with Kent's broken leg and surgery that they were probably looking forward to having their lives, and their house, back.

Her heart whispered it wouldn't hurt to enjoy an evening or even a week with a kind, respectful man that she was attracted to. Her brain shouted that even considering the idea was the height of stupidity.

"Hey, Avery. You gotten too attached to that covering to pack it up, or what?" Jillian strolled up to the other side of the table.

Avery startled. "Whoa. I was way out there."

"Yeah. I noticed." Jillian took the covering from her and began folding it. "And before you panic, I'm just warning you that some kind of scruffy dog started following me around. It's kind of shy, and everyone I've asked has said it's a stray that the dog catcher has been trying to round up and take to the pound for weeks."

"Oh. That's sad." She might be terrified of dogs, but she didn't want to see them put in cages and killed, either.

"Yeah. So, anyway, I've been leaving pieces of hotdog out for it, and gonna see what I can do for it. I didn't want you going crazy when you saw it."

"Thanks. I've been working on my dog fear, anyway." Avery met Jillian's emerald eyes. Jillian had been a true friend to her since they'd both come to the farm this past summer. Maybe the first true friend she'd ever had.

"Really? I didn't know. Where? Whose?"

Avery laughed as she laid the table on its side to put the legs down. "Gator has dogs."

"The elderly dogs that you insisted wanted to eat you?"

"Did I sound that dumb?"

Jillian bit her lips and raised her brows.

Avery slapped a leg down against the underside of the table. "I think that's a yes."

"I'm kidding. Getting bitten as a child would cause anyone to be afraid of dogs."

"Well, you were right. Gator's dogs are nice. Although, I don't think I'd want to be around them if he weren't there."

"Shh." Jillian froze.

Avery did too, looking around without moving her head.

Gesturing slowly with one finger, Jillian indicated the corner of the next booth over. A black nose poked out not very far from the ground.

"This dog reminds me of the ones I trained in the circus in Mexico. It looks like a part mini-poodle. I bet it's smart." Jillian spoke low without moving her lips. She jerked her head. "I laid a piece of hot dog down. It smells it."

They watched, not moving, as the dog sniffed around, grabbed the tiny chunk of hotdog and bounded back between the booths.

"I think I can get it."

Avery wasn't so sure. The dog looked starved, abused, and way too fast to catch, but she wasn't going to discourage her friend. "You've got a way with animals. That's for sure." Miss Prissypants loved Jillian almost as much as she loved Gator. The only two humans aside from Avery that Miss Prissypants would allow to touch her unless she was in Avery's carrier.

Jillian grinned. Triumphant. "So, what's up with you and Gator? I saw you guys walking around together. I was kind of surprised because the last time I heard anything, you hated his dogs and didn't sound like you thought too much of him."

"I don't know what to do." Avery bent the legs in on the second table.

"He seems to like you."

"Yeah. That's weird, isn't it?"

Jillian snorted. "Stop it. Although, you two do look kind of odd together. He's wearing camo and has a knife strapped to his belt. You're usually gussied up to the gills with makeup and hairspray and wearing some kind of flowing, hippy skirt." Jillian tilted her head at Avery. "Today being the exception. Is it an off day, or have you started a new look?"

"It's an off day. I still have these." She wiggled her long, bright pink fingernails in the air.

"Ah, yes. The Dolly Parton nails."

Avery grinned and looked down. "Yeah, because nothing else on me looks like Dolly Parton."

"True, there's no boobs to speak of, but you do have the blond hair."

"Yeah, well, boobs or no boobs, Gator and I don't exactly look like people who would get together. Not that it matters because he's leaving going west and I'm going to D. C."

"So what's the problem?"

Avery brushed her shirt off and looked down. Stalling. "I'm afraid if we spend more time together, it's going to hurt when he leaves."

Jillian paused as she held the one wreath that didn't sell. "Of course it's going to hurt when he leaves. That's life."

"But the less I know and like him, the less it will hurt." Avery grabbed a box for the wreath from behind the booth.

"You can't live your life avoiding anything that's going to cause you pain." Jillian stopped abruptly and put a finger up. The dog was back. Avery took the wreath while Jillian took a chunk of hotdog out of her pocket and tossed it so the dog would have to come a little closer than the last time to get it.

They waited silently. Finally, after sniffing and crouching and sneaking forward, it lunged, grabbed the treat, and ran off.

"But I guess I understand being cautious. Especially since you've been hurt before," Jillian said after a moment, continuing their earlier conversation. "Still. Don't let fear keep you from experiencing something wonderful."

Avery wasn't convinced. "Even if it's just a week or two?"

Jillian's head jerked down in a quick nod. "I think it's worth it."

Avery considered that. She also considered that Jillian hadn't shown any interest in any men since coming to Pennsylvania in the fall. But that could be because the whole town thought she was crazy with her contortions and different manner of acting and speaking that she'd developed in the circus atmosphere.

"You're probably right. Maybe I should relax a little and move out of my comfort zone." She stacked the closed box on top of the others. "But I'm not going to get Dolly boobs."

"Dolly boobs?" Gator took the table out of her hands. "Is this something you're discussing with people, or is the decision already made?"

Avery's face heated, but she said, "It's made. As in, not happening."

Gator smirked. "I think that's a good decision."

Avery thought maybe the tips of his ears were red. Maybe.

"Where do the tables go?" he asked.

"They belong in the courthouse basement." Jillian pointed to the large building across the street.

Gator hefted the tables. "Anything else need to go? I can handle a little more."

They gave him the poles for the booth and a bag with the coverings.

"Mrs. Baker should be there showing everyone where to set things," Avery said.

"Okay. I'll be back."

Jillian left to look for her dog, and Avery walked over to the old oak at the edge of the big expanse of grass, out of the lights, but she was still able to see while she waited for Gator. Other folks were finishing packing their things up. Some had left their booths up to take down the next day, so the place looked partially finished.

Jillian was probably right. It wouldn't hurt anything to enjoy the next few days. Make some memories. The only thing that might happen was that things could get a little awkward between her and Mrs. Franks. Maybe she could say something to Gator to try to keep that from happening.

"Deep thoughts?" Gator's voice rumbled beside her.

"I was just thinking I want to enjoy being with you tonight."

He put a hand on her neck, behind her hair. "Hmm. That's funny. I don't have to make an effort to have fun when I'm with you. It's been a great day for me. Thanks."

His rough skin on the sensitive part of her neck sent shivers down her spine. Definitely the right decision was to spend some time with him.

She tried to focus so she could speak. "I've had a wonderful time, too. You know that's not what I meant. I have a tendency to overthink things. I don't want to do that with you."

"I was thinking..." He moved closer. Slowly, as though giving her the chance to get away.

But getting away wasn't even on her radar. She wanted to be closer. "Dangerous," she murmured, and he laughed.

"I'm trying to be serious here." But his face still held the grin.

She focused on the dimple at the corner of his mouth. A man as big as he was should look out of place with a cute dimple. But it fit him perfectly. Before she realized what she was doing, her finger had come up and touched it, tracing the dip in his skin, feeling the roughness of his stubble.

"If you're trying to get me to stop thinking, that was brilliant." He closed his eyes. His breath fanned out, warm over her face. He pressed lightly into her finger.

A heady sense of power surged through Avery. The feeling that this man, so much bigger and stronger than she, would close his eyes and sigh at her touch. That she had control. The heady feeling warred with humbleness. She didn't want to get hurt, but instinctively, she knew that by being here with her, allowing her to be close to him, he was giving her the power to hurt him as well. She had no desire to damage or weaken the man in front of her. On the contrary, with the power he'd handed her, she became aware of a feeling of great protectiveness and a desire to help him.

If she wasn't careful, those feelings could swirl and mix, and it would no longer be about her and what she wanted, but about them, and what they could do together. The idea frightened her.

"That's not a good look," Gator said softly from above her.

His eyes were open again.

"I'm scared." Typically, it wasn't easy to admit weakness, but the words were out before she thought about them.

His fingers moved on her neck. "Of me?"

Her lips tilted up. "No. Of course not."

"Good. Because that scared me."

"That I might be afraid of you?"

"Yeah. I'm just saying we're not close enough right now, and if you were afraid of me, that would have meant that I couldn't do this." He slid his other hand around her back and pulled her body to his, pressing her against him. "And, man, I've wanted this all day."

Her arms went around his waist and she lay her head on his chest. She couldn't remember anyone ever saying they wanted to hold her, let alone saying it with the longing and emotion that had been in Gator's voice.

His heart beat strong and fast against her cheek. His masculine scent filled her senses. His strong arms cocooned her and made her feel safe and cared for. She didn't ever want to move.

"We should go find a spot to watch the fireworks."

She didn't care about the fireworks. Not the town's fireworks anyway.

He didn't move to release her, and she didn't pull away, enjoying instead the novelty of holding and being held.

Finally, Gator's voice floated softly above her. "I know you're leaving, and so am I. I can't ask you to give up anything for me, and my job isn't transferrable." His chest lifted and fell in a big way under her cheek. "I guess I'm saying I know there is no future for us, but I'd like to spend time with you for the next two weeks anyway."

"Yes," Avery whispered against his chest, with no hesitation.

He moved back and lowered his head, looking into her eyes. She had trouble keeping them open. His lips almost brushed hers as he asked, "Yes, there's no future, or yes, you want to spend time with me?"

She remembered what she'd thought earlier about hurting him. She didn't want to get hurt, because men always left—he was even admitting he was going to leave. But for the first time in her life, she was more concerned about the pain he might feel. People and relationships might not be her area of expertise, but she knew Gator wasn't the kind of guy who shared his life and feelings easily. This type of arrangement could hurt him as much as her. More, maybe.

His hard, hot body felt wonderful and safe under her arms.

Snuggled in close to him was like being home. And his thumb softly stroking at the nape of her neck sent delicious zaps of tingles all through her body, with warmth pooling at the bottom of her stomach. She wanted to move her own hands, explore the width of his back and the breadth of his shoulders. If she looked up and stood on tiptoe, she could kiss the hard angle of his rough jaw and taste the column of his throat.

But for what? A momentary pleasure that would only turn into acute pain when he left. And to be fair, when she left too.

She pulled away and stepped back. "Yes, to both. Yes, I would like to spend time with you, but unfortunately that's not possible, since, yes, there's no future." She stuck her chin out, but pulled her bottom lip in, chewing on it. *Spiegel im Spiegel* played softly, sadly in her head, even as the faint strains of happier Christmas music drifted in the background.

He nodded his head. His throat tightened several times. "I can see how you might think the pleasure isn't worth the pain."

"Actually, for the first time in my life, I think it might be. It was the thought that something I might do could hurt you that made me decide it wasn't worth it."

She expected him to smile, maybe even laugh that she was concerned about hurting him, as big as he was next to her. But he didn't. He sighed and his lips flattened.

"That's part of what I find so attractive in you. It doesn't surprise me that you'd put me ahead of yourself. You did it with my mother. And Fink and Ellie. Heck, it's the reason you were at the dunking booth this morning. I guess it was selfish of me to want you for only a little while."

"No! I'm the one that has spent my life being selfish. Always concerned about a little hurt or about being uncomfortable or about getting ahead. Whatever. It's always been about me. I spend time with your mom because I like her. I was at the dunking booth because it benefits me to advertise for the farm. This decision, the decision to walk away from you, right now, is the first decision I've made in my life solely to benefit someone else." Her throat was dry, but she tried to swallow anyway. Her eyes stung. "Thanks for a really great day." It was the best day she could ever remember having. This decision to walk away from

Gator, for Gator, showed how much she cared about him. But it didn't matter.

He hadn't moved, hadn't reached for her. Had only watched as she struggled and spoke. Already there was pain in his eyes, in the tightness of his face, in the clench of his fist. How much worse would it be, for both of them, after two more weeks of wonderful days like today?

A muscle worked in his jaw and his eyelids dropped a little. "To me...the pain is worth every second." He spoke low and her heart trembled along with the tympanic vibrations in his voice.

Maybe that was his way of begging her to stay, to reconsider. Maybe she should...

"Gator! I've been looking everywhere for you." Kristen, dressed in a cute, fur-lined vest and khaki pants, strode up to them looking slim and graceful. Even her hiking boots looked feminine next to Gator's much larger, chunkier footwear.

She was the perfect foil for Gator, and they would be in the same quadrant of the country. They liked the same things and they already had a shared history. Plus, Kristen had things Avery would never have. She looked one more time at the thin, willowy shape that somehow made her rugged outdoorsy clothes look tough, yet feminine. Avery would look as out of place in those clothes as an elephant in a tutu. But those trappings defined Gator's life. Even if she were to give up her teaching position in Washington and go west with Gator, she would never fit in or belong.

Avery moved to turn, planning to walk away.

"Don't go," Gator begged softly. "Please. Stay with me."

Chapter Thirteen

Gator hated the words even as they left his mouth. He didn't beg. And he accepted someone's no. Except, apparently, when that "no" came from Avery telling him she didn't want to hurt him. Heck, when was the last time a woman was concerned about hurting him? Ever? Other than his mother.

She hesitated when he spoke. Both lips drew in and her eyes shimmered before she spun and walked quickly away. He watched the straightness of her spine, the flow of her golden hair brushing her shoulders, the curve of her waist and the sway of her hips. His hands still burned. His chest felt cold and empty. His heart ached.

What if he quit his job and moved back home?

"Hello? Gator? I don't think you heard a word I said."

"I didn't." His eyes didn't leave Avery's retreating figure until she disappeared around the corner of a building. Gator shifted his gaze to Kristen.

Her lips were set in a straight line and her hands were planted on her slim hips. "I think the lady doesn't want you. She didn't seem to be moved by your groveling."

Irritation flashed hot in his chest. Of all the people in the world he really didn't want to see him beg, Kristen would have been numbers one through twenty. At least. But he had been begging for Avery, and he'd do it again.

"She has good taste. I was just trying to get her to lower her standards."

"To get to Avery's standards, you'd have to dig a hole," Kristen said with disdain. "If you'd have begged me like that, I would never have let you go."

He wasn't going to fight with Kristen, again, over whose fault it was that their marriage collapsed. He wasn't the one who cheated, and he wasn't the one who left. "Did you want something?"

"Yeah, they're going to give the lumberjack awards for first, second and third place before the fireworks start. You need to get down there."

He'd forgotten about the ceremony the town always had before the fireworks. Everyone who won a competition would get a ribbon. He and Avery would get a prize for their tree too. But it looked like she was leaving. Then he remembered, she couldn't leave. She'd come with him. Unless she hitched a ride with someone else.

"Thanks for the reminder," he said to Kristen before he took off at a jog in the direction Avery had gone.

He turned the corner just in time to see a short, curvy blond get in the passenger side of a pickup. A man, who looked very much like his suddenly *ex*-friend, McKoy, closed the door behind her and walked around to the driver's side.

Gator sped up, until he was almost full-on sprinting, but he was still a block away when the pickup pulled away from the curb.

McKoy did a three-point turn in the quiet street. As he backed up for the last time, Gator could see Avery's cheek shine in the streetlamp. Pain shot through his chest like a mountain lion had dragged a claw from his breastbone to his abdomen.

Just as the truck started forward, she looked up. Her eyes widened and her hand swiped at her cheek.

He stopped in the middle of the street with his hands on his hips, his chest heaving. He'd already begged her to stay, now he'd just chased after her.

Tell him to stop, he begged silently. But although her head twisted, keeping him in her sight until the truck had pulled away, her mouth stayed closed. At the last second, he saw her fingertips on the window as though she was reaching out for him, but the truck kept moving.

He considered going back, but he didn't feel like celebrating. He certainly didn't want to be around people, especially Kristen. Plus, he hadn't had time to consider the question that had popped up in his mind earlier: what if he quit his job and moved back home?

～

AVERY BRUSHED HER HANDS TOGETHER. Dust flew off of them and pooled in the sunlight that shone through the cracks in the barn.

"Too bad you have tickets to see that concert with Mrs. Franks tonight. I think we could have finished clearing off the barn floor today," Jillian said, dangling from a barn beam while attaching a string of lights.

"It doesn't really matter. It's not like we can scrub it down. Water on these old boards will just rot them out. I wish there was something we could do about all this dust, though."

"We've swept it a hundred times. The dust comes with the territory."

"I guess." Avery looked around. This would be a perfect place for wedding receptions and family reunions. But people wouldn't put up with the dirt. It would need a thorough renovation before anyone would even consider renting it. Hopefully folks would overlook it for one Christmas party.

Jillian finished tacking the string of lights to the horizontal beam. "You can tell me this is none of my business, but I kind of thought that Gator might be around to help us this week. After seeing you two looking so cozy at the Christmas celebration..." She hopped the last three feet to the floor and landed with a soft thump.

"Of course you can ask. We've been through enough this fall with Harper and Wyatt's wedding and leaving for Chile and the farm's being shorthanded—you've covered for me many times. And you've certainly earned the right to pry into my personal life, such that it is."

"And you have deftly sidestepped my question," Jillian said with a slender brow arched high above her right eye. She placed a graceful hand on her slim hip. "Well?"

Avery shrugged and looked at her nails. Sparkly red and green. Happy colors she chose specifically to try to mitigate the black cloud that had hung on over the weekend and through the first few days of this week.

"His job is in Montana. I'm planning on moving to D.C. Tell me how that's going to work. I think we're a little old to pretend that a Skype relationship is going to lead anywhere." She gave Miss Prissypants a pat as she walked to the pile of greenery.

"Don't people play the tuba in Montana or listen to music?"

Avery picked up several pine boughs and arranged them in a swag long enough to go over the door, tying them with twine. "You're saying I should run to Montana, chasing after some guy who's probably just going to leave me anyway, once someone better comes along."

"Really? That's how you see Gator?" Jillian asked. Her head tilted to the side before she swung another string of lights over her shoulder and shimmied up the barn beam.

"He's a man." Miss Prissypants rubbed against Avery's leg. She cut the twine with a snap of her scissors before picking the cat up and petting her.

"Men are the enemy?"

"They leave."

"That's funny. Gator looks like a guy who wants to put down roots. Deep roots."

"He's already been married and divorced once." That wasn't fair. None of what she was saying was. Gator was so much better than she was making him sound.

"You know the details? Was it because he left? Really? I saw the ex. She looks like a gold digger."

Avery was slightly amazed at how well Jillian had pegged Kristen. She seemed to be confident in her assessment of Gator too. "How can you tell these things about people?"

"Maybe after working with animals so much in the circus, I'm better at reading non-verbal cues. I could be wrong."

"You're right about Kristen. According to Gator, anyway."

Jillian clung to the overhead beam as she tacked the light string up.

"I don't have to live with your choices. Only you do. I just think you might be a little wrong about Gator."

"He never said anything about long term. And honestly, life is messier with a man in it. I don't need one." But she wanted one. It was some kind of internal desire that she couldn't shake. But only for one specific man.

"Your choice."

"Seems to be yours too." Avery set her cat down and picked up two more pine boughs.

"My life is going to be dedicated to making the world a better place for animals." Jillian tossed a treat. It landed on the floor about ten feet away. Her dog came out from under the old hay mow and snatched it before going back to its makeshift cave.

"You'll be great at that." Avery didn't even flinch from the dog. Thanks to Gator. "The nice thing about having a barn floor you can't scrub is that you can do things like that and it doesn't matter a bit."

Jillian laughed. "It's perfect for dogs and men."

"And kids."

"So basically, only women won't appreciate it." Jillian jumped down, landing lightly on the barn floor.

Avery set her things aside.

Jillian unplugged the lights and walked out the door in front of Avery.

"Yeah. And, I think with the right ambience, women will love it too." At least she hoped so.

Ninety minutes later, Avery pulled up to the Franks' drive. She hadn't seen Gator since she practically ran away from him at the Christmas celebration. Thankfully, she'd run into McKoy, who was also leaving before the presentations and fireworks and he'd been happy to give her a ride home. He'd been upset that Gator had brought her and left her, so she'd had to explain that it was all her fault.

She paused for a moment before she got out of her car. Maybe Gator wasn't home. Maybe she wouldn't run into him. Maybe the cramping in her stomach was indigestion and not nerves caused by the possibility of seeing him again.

Definitely nerves, she reasoned, as the front door opened, and he stepped out wearing dark blue jeans, a bright green plaid button up, and scuffed brown cowboy boots, and her lungs froze. Her heart, on the other hand, tried to jump out of her throat. Presumably to try to get closer to the man it beat for. Drat the stupid thing.

Well, she could hardly drive away, and she was only making herself look stupid by sitting there, so she yanked on her door handle and stepped out of the car.

"Hey," Gator said as he walked down the walk toward her. The lights from the Christmas decorations emphasized the rugged lines of his face, but his eyes were shadowed. His shirt made his shoulders look wider and she allowed herself a couple of seconds to admire them before she forced herself to look away.

She'd never seen him dressed this nicely, not even at the Christmas celebration, so he must be going out. Maybe with Kristen. The thought stung, and she pushed it away.

"Hey. Your mom and I are going to a concert together. I'm here to pick her up. I'll just walk in myself. Looks like you're headed out, so I don't want to hold you up or anything."

He had tilted his head and let her ramble, but he didn't move out of her way.

She ended up stopped in front of him and forced herself to stop rambling.

"Mom had a pretty crappy day. She's sleeping now, but before she laid down she asked me to take her place." His feet were planted apart and his hands hung down at his sides like a gunslinger at high noon, waiting on her response.

"What's wrong? Is it just the treatments?"

"Yeah. Each time she goes, it hits her a little harder. This has been the worst week so far. Thankfully, there's just one more."

"Yeah. Then hopefully nothing but good reports. I wish she'd have said something when I spoke with her on the phone yesterday."

"She told me she knows you're busy with the barn and didn't want you to take time away from that for her."

"I see." Avery fingered her Christmas tree earrings.

A couple of beats of silence ticked by.

"If you don't want to go with me, I understand," Gator finally said.

Avery pushed the worry over Mrs. Franks aside. Suddenly, she felt young and carefree. Every time she'd been with Gator, she'd had fun, and tonight would be no different. She batted her eyes, "You're tall, handsome, and you took third place in the lumberjack competition. Of course, I want to go with you."

His jaw sagged before he said, "You're going to hold that third place finish over my head for the next hundred years, aren't you?"

"Nope. I'll take an artistic man over big muscles any day."

"Well, I don't have an artistic cell in my body. Are you sure you don't want to rethink your choice of a date for this evening?"

"You have artistic cells. I'll help you find them. We're going to the college orchestra concert after all."

Gator stopped in the act of opening her door for her. "Orchestra concert?"

"Yes. And you are not allowed to say anything nice about the tubist."

"That won't be hard." Gator smirked at her. "What's a tuba?"

"Whoa. Stop right there, mister. I don't require my dates to be able to play an instrument, but they at least have to be able to identify the brass section."

He closed her door and walked around the car. After he sat, he glanced over. "I can pick out the harp, I think. Is there a harp in the orchestra?"

"Humph. A harpist would rather be sharp than out of tune. And I hope you aren't ticklish." Avery waved her fingers in the air imitating a harpist's hand movements.

"Oh, boy." Gator's expression was mock-horrified. "I'm definitely ticklish. But only on my feet. Might work if I don't take my boots off."

"Guess a foot massage is out of the question."

"But you're not a harpist." Gator winked at her.

Avery wiggled her fingers in the air again. "I can give a good imitation.".

Gator laughed. Which was a better sound than the entire orchestra, including the harp, playing a perfect chord.

"Did you really not know that we were going to see the orchestra?"

"Nope. Just got in twenty minutes before you got there. She'd mentioned at lunch she didn't feel well, but it wasn't until I walked in tonight that she asked me to take her place. Until I was done with my shower, she was sound asleep on the couch." He looked over at her. "I made sure home nursing would send someone at the normal time."

"Oh, good." Avery signaled, then turned right. "You don't have to suffer through this if you hate it. I know it's not for everyone."

"I might be able to force myself to sit through it if you hold my hand."

"That's it? That's all it takes?"

"Yeah. That's all it takes."

With a little twist in her chest, she took her hand off the steering wheel and placed it between them, palm up. "I'm a big believer in practicing."

"I just converted." He slid his hand into hers. The same sweet sensations from before slipped like a slow melody up her arm, wrapping around and squeezing her heart. Her lungs stumbled before she stiffened and forced air into them.

His thumb rubbed over her super-sensitized skin. She kept her eyes on the road. How was it that just holding this man's hand threatened to derail her entire concentration?

"I thought about this a lot this week," Gator said softly.

"Me too." After his raw honesty, she was unable to be anything but the same.

The only sound was the muted hum of the car motor. Lights blinked in the interior as they passed street lights and decorations.

"What are we going to listen to tonight? Holiday music?"

"Not exactly." She launched into an explanation of the music being performed tonight and why they were playing it close to Christmas.

Gator seemed interested and asked pertinent questions, which surprised and pleased her.

When they arrived, he hopped out and opened her car door, then took her hand again. "Is this odd for you?"

"What? Holding a man's hand?" She shrugged. "Actually, yes. I haven't done it much."

"I was actually talking about going to a concert to watch and not play."

"Oh." She laughed. "Yes. I guess that's kind of not the norm. But over the years, I've enjoyed live music in which I've not been playing." She hadn't really thought of it, but she really hadn't been to a full orchestra concert simply to listen and enjoy for years. "Hopefully, this will be the last one. I'm going to audition the day after tomorrow."

"That's great," Gator said, and she believed he meant it. "What about the storm that's coming? Will they reschedule?"

"No. I actually have the very last spot on the audition schedule. The announcement will be made Monday and rehearsals start after the New Year."

"You're going down early?"

"To avoid the snow? I can't. Jillian and I need every second left to get the barn fixed. I've driven in snow before. I'll be fine."

Gator didn't answer, but his lips set in a disapproving line.

They arrived at the door to the auditorium. Avery handed their tickets to the usher, who directed them to their seats.

The familiar scent of music cases and rosin mingled with the palpable excitement and nervousness of a live performance. Avery squeezed Gator's hand as regret and eagerness along with anticipation and desire swirled through her.

He squeezed back. "You're okay?"

"Yes." Her body hummed with emotions set on edge by the man beside her.

"Where's this tuba player that I have to hate."

"You don't have to hate him."

"I know." He shifted, putting his arm around the back of her seat. His fingers rested lightly on her shoulder. At that moment, she would rather have been in the audience than on the biggest stage in the world. As long as Gator was beside her, it wouldn't matter.

Her brain froze. Was that true? As long as Gator was beside her, it wouldn't matter where she was or what she did? She examined her mind, trying to determine if she really believed that.

Before she had enough time to think, he asked her about the music listed in the program, and they talked until the lights dimmed.

Chapter Fourteen

With his fingers on her shoulder, Gator could feel the music pulse through Avery. Even if he weren't touching her, her enjoyment was obvious on her face and he admired it openly. It wasn't like he needed to be looking at the stage in order to hear the music, which, to his surprise, he hadn't hated.

But he liked Avery's expressive face far more than the music. Idly, he wondered if this was music one could dance to. Ballroom dancing, maybe? He'd never been even the slightest bit interested, but for the chance to hold Avery while she closed her eyes and enjoyed something so thoroughly, he'd suddenly developed a very, very strong interest.

The music got louder, seeming to build the excitement in the room, just as the feelings built in his chest. The decision he'd been kicking around for a while suddenly seemed crystal clear. Funny how being close to Avery made a lot of the things he'd thought were important seem like they really weren't important at all.

By the time the concert was over, and he was outside opening her car door, he'd made a couple of life-changing decisions. But he wasn't going to rush into anything, and he definitely wasn't going to push Avery into anything.

"Would you like to go somewhere and get dessert?" he asked before he shut the door.

She fingered her earring, her face still flushed and beautiful from the emotions the music had evoked.

"I would love to," she answered.

He grinned and closed the door. Maybe she wasn't interested in any type of relationship with him. He wasn't even sure what he wanted, but he enjoyed being with her and didn't want the night to end. Not ever.

When she pulled into the all-night diner, he hopped out to get her door. She hadn't complained. Avery was quite capable of opening her own door, but he loved giving her that respect, showing that deference to her. He wasn't lying when he said he loved that she made him feel strong and capable. Protective. Manly traits that not all women appreciated anymore, but traits that were an integral part of who he was.

In Avery, he'd found a woman who wanted him to be a man. And who wanted to act like a woman. He wanted to lap it up. He opened her door instead.

"Thanks," she said as she emerged from the car. "It's gotten much colder since we left your house this evening."

"It's definitely below freezing now. I'm glad the weather held out for the celebration."

"Me too. I could have been sitting on the dunking booth facing a block of ice in that tank."

He laughed. "Oh, no. They'd put an ice melter in there. The town council has ways of making you suffer. Trust me." He held the restaurant door open for her.

"I'll keep that in mind for next year." She swept by him and he breathed in her scent.

"Just keep a hot chocolate handy for whatever new-to-town sucker they rope into doing that booth."

The hostess greeted them and led them through the mostly empty restaurant to their seats.

"I think you just called me a sucker," Avery said after the hostess left.

"If the shoe fits," Gator said from behind his menu.

"Oh, boy, does it ever fit. Better than it should. It won't fit next year. That's for sure."

The studied their menus until the waitress came over to get drinks and take their orders.

"Well, in the town's defense, they do make a lot of money from that booth," Gator said when she left.

"I believe it. There was never a time when there wasn't a line." She took a sip of her water and her bracelets jangled. A pretty silver chain with several charms hung around her neck. Her nails were painted and sparkling, and Gator loved how her classy femininity contrasted with his blunt masculinity. The contrasts between them drew him.

"Funny how humans enjoy making other humans suffer," he said.

"I don't think they really enjoyed my suffering."

"I think they enjoyed mine," he said with a grin.

"Thank you for that, by the way."

"You know, I had a good time then, and I am having a great time tonight. I enjoyed working with you in the barn. Whenever I'm with you, I have a good time."

"I do too. But Gator, you know anything between us will never work out."

"Really?" He tried to keep his tone light.

"Really. Also, I've steered clear of relationships since my fiancé left me for another woman. It just seems like it's a given that men leave."

"You really believe that?"

She shrugged and looked away.

He didn't think she really thought all men leave. Maybe she'd convinced herself she did.

The waitress brought their desserts. Avery smiled and thanked her. Gator's appetite was gone. There wasn't any way for him to convince Avery that he wasn't like "most men." It was something she would have to decide for herself.

"Jillian said you're the kind of man to put down roots."

"I like Jillian." Hope stirred in his chest.

"I think that's true. But I don't want to take that chance."

He'd hoped to change her mind and tried not to be disappointed that one night of fun together hadn't moved her on that issue. "Fair enough." He needed to change the subject before he got too depressed and became a bad date. "How are your party plans coming?"

Avery's face lit up. "I've been trying to find pictures of the barn from back in the eighties, but haven't had much luck at the newspaper. Ellie's former in-laws had a few, but most of theirs were older."

"My mom has tons of pictures. Did you already go through all of hers?"

"Some of them. I've hesitated because of her being so tired. I didn't want to make more work for her since she said they were in the attic and she'd have to hunt for them."

"I'll do it."

Avery smiled with surprise and pleasure. "Thanks. I really need to practice tomorrow evening, then I have the audition the next evening in D.C. but Saturday evening would work for me."

"Me too. I'll plan on it. I can have the boxes out and maybe some pictures sorted by then." He didn't like the idea of her going to D.C. alone in a snowstorm. Not because she was a woman and he thought she was weak. Not at all. He would question anyone driving that far in the kind of snow they were forecasted to get. The roads to Washington were not known for their safety, either. But he didn't say anything.

"Why did you decide not to team up with Kristen's project?" Avery asked after he'd paid the bill and they'd started for the car.

He really didn't want to talk about his ex.

"I'm not. It took me exactly a half a second to think about that and come to a decision."

She laughed, as he'd intended. But turned thoughtful after he'd settled himself in the car across from her. "Why not?"

"I guess the first reason that comes to mind is that the last time she made promises to me, she didn't exactly keep them. I can't see that she's changed. After all, she married that poor guy, got him to buy her what she wanted, and now they're divorcing too."

"Oh, I didn't know."

"My mom found out somehow." People might have thought he'd jump at the chance to work with her, knowing that she was single and available. It had only made him run faster. "Until then, I hadn't known either. Still don't care."

"You hate her?"

"Nah. Just now I can see where I made a lot of mistakes. Stupid decisions and choices. Not doing it again."

"Ah. You're wiser?"

"Yeah."

They rode in silence the rest of the way to his mother's house. Avery pulled in and he hopped out, as he had before, to open her door. She rolled the window down.

"I think I'll not go in. It's late."

Disappointment rolled through him. He hadn't realized, but a glance at the clock on the dash said it was after midnight.

"I'm sorry. I didn't mean to keep you out so long."

"I had fun."

"Me too. Let me check on my mom, then I'll follow you home in my truck." He barely kept from wincing as he said it, knowing that such a suggestion was something that would have garnered him a "women aren't helpless babies" lecture from most other women he knew.

"I don't want to put you out."

"It'd be worse to be here wondering and worrying."

She shrugged. "If you want."

"I want." He smiled and straightened. "Be right back."

He ran in, wiping his boots carefully, but not pulling them off. In the light coming in from the window from the decorations in the yard, he could see his mother slept soundly on the couch. Grabbing his keys, he ducked back out the door.

Avery waved as he jogged to his truck. She backed out and he followed her to the farm, where all the lights were off except the pole light by the farm office. Avery parked in front of the house, and he pulled in behind her, shutting his pickup off so it didn't wake anyone.

"Thanks," she said as he walked up. "I'm here safe."

He didn't give her a chance to back away, but strode up to her and put his arms around her. "Thank you. For the best evening I've ever had."

"That's big."

"I'm serious." She hadn't pulled away, so he drew her closer. "Don't be mad at my mom."

"What?"

"She really was tired."

Comprehension dawned in her eyes. "You bribed your mother to let you go!" Her arms, which had started to slide around his waist, stopped, and she gripped his shirt in her hands.

"No." He stroked the back of her neck, loving the feel of the soft skin meeting her hairline. "She was going to cancel at noon. I asked her to hold on and not make a decision until I got home. Which was later than I expected. I didn't cheat my mother out of a nice evening out. I just kept her from having you give her ticket to anyone but me." His other hand slid down to the small of her back with a little pressure, pushing her body into his.

"That's sneaky."

"I wanted to spend the evening with you."

Her narrowed eyes widened, and her hands loosened and slid the rest of the way around him. Her head started to bend down to rest against his chest, but he didn't want cuddling. Not tonight. Not now, at least. He was after more.

"I'm going to kiss you good night."

Her head jerked back up. Her eyes searched his out. "No, you're not."

His heart sank.

"You've held my hand, opened my car door, held my chair, followed me home. This move is mine." She blinked. "But you're going to have to bend down, because I can't reach you."

He laughed. "How about we fix that problem this way." He bent his knees and picked her up, pressing her whole body to his. But he didn't swoop down and take her lips, respecting her request to be the one to do the kissing. Gladly.

Her hands came up and cupped his cheeks, softly swishing against his stubble. "I love the way this feels."

"Makes two of us."

"I also like being able to look directly into your eyes." She leaned a little closer.

"They're nothing special. Yours, on the other hand, are amazingly expressive and beautiful." Her lips were so close his almost brushed them as he spoke. He resisted the urge to close that tiny distance. "You're soft and sweet and..."

"How do you know I'm sweet?" she murmured.

He smiled. "Prove me wrong."

Her lips brushed his, lightly. Almost intangibly.

He groaned.

She smiled that powerful smile that said she knew the effect she was having on him and was thoroughly enjoying it.

With her body pressed to his and her weight filling his arms, she could take all night long. Delectable torture.

More feathery touches that only served to heat his blood and weaken his knees. He turned, leaning against her car hood so that her weight was partially on him, keeping her face level with his.

Her hands gripped his hair, and he relished the slight pressure. Finally, finally, her lips settled on his. Firmly. And did not skip away. He pressed back with another low groan. Her tongue tiptoed out, and he opened to receive it, pulling her in, hot and welcoming. He caught her gasp, absorbed her sigh, and deepened their connection. The air around them crackled. He couldn't get deep enough, couldn't get close enough, couldn't get enough air.

He broke away, gasping.

She twisted, and he allowed her body to slide down his, eliciting another groan from both of them. Keeping her hands on his waist, she stood, panting as hard as he.

The wind ruffled the bare branches above them with a hollow, wooden sound. Her hair shifted around her flushed face and parted lips. He fisted his hands as she took another step back, but grabbed her waist again as she stumbled.

Their eyes met.

"I was right. You are sweet." She was a million other tastes that he couldn't explain, but already craved to taste again. And again.

She stepped back even farther. "Maybe we shouldn't do that again."

"Maybe your music was a little more powerful than I had given it credit for."

"It was the music?"

"I don't know what the heck else it was." He'd never felt anything like it.

She nodded rapidly.

He prepared to catch her again, hoping his shaking knees would hold them both if she did fall. "You're definitely right. Let's blame the music. No more classical music for you, mister. You obviously can't handle it."

"Me? That was your kiss. Last time I'm kissing a tuba player without protection," he continued, leaning against the car and crossed his arms over his chest. With any luck she wouldn't notice that his knees were still shaking too badly for him to attempt to stand.

"Protection?"

"A fire extinguisher, or something."

She let out a little, shaky laugh.

"Do me a favor, Avery."

"Yeah?"

"Go to the house. Now. You don't know how bad I want to do that again. And you're standing there all soft and warm. And sweet."

She blinked at him.

So help him, if she didn't move, he was going to find out exactly how steady his knees were.

"Have mercy, lady. Please."

Maybe she saw it in his eyes. She turned and ran up the steps, grabbing the door and slipping through, closing it softly behind her.

Gator leaned against her car a little longer.

Great. Now he knew exactly how she felt and exactly how she tasted. The only word that described both was perfect. Instinct told him there'd never be another woman who'd light his fire so easily and completely.

On one hand, he was thrilled. Avery wasn't just physically attractive to him. She had a beautiful, unselfish heart. She couldn't be any more perfect.

On the other hand, he'd been devastated tonight. That kiss had rocked him down to his toes. But the lady had already told him no. Firmly. He'd thought maybe he could convince her to change that no to a yes. But it seemed like he'd scared her off instead. Heck, that kiss had scared him.

He should have listened to his mother. Years ago, she's said, "If you can't have it, don't try it, because it only takes one to get addicted." She'd been talking about vices like drugs, alcohol, and cigarettes. He'd never tell her, but she should have added kissing Avery to the list.

No doubt about it. He was addicted.

Chapter Fifteen

Avery looked at the dripping roof in dismay. A drop of water hit her in her face, splashing down to Miss Prissypants who jerked and shook her head. Avery stepped back.

Why had the barn roof decided to pick this month to start leaking? After over a hundred years of standing in one spot, couldn't it have just waited thirty more days? Or even fifteen would have worked.

She moved the bucket that she'd brought over from the shed and the water starting pinging into it. Right in the middle of the barn floor too.

She could see it now at the party. Big orange cones and yellow caution tape right in the middle of the dance floor. Perfect. If she had time, she'd change the color of the decorations so they wouldn't clash. But that would be defeating the whole purpose of the party—to recreate Mrs. Franks' engagement party.

She kicked her foot on the floor, but didn't shake her fist at the ceiling like she wanted to. Apparently, some snow sliding off the roof had scraped the bit of rust off and had created the hole. At least there was only one.

The solution to her problem hadn't come to her yet, and she didn't have time now to think about it. The barn floor was completely cleaned and, thanks to Jillian, the lights were strung. All Avery had to do was decorate the large area. Hopefully, Gator would come up with a few more pictures for her.

Gator.

Every time she thought of him her heart started to quiver and her face flushed. Heat pooled in her stomach. How many times yesterday and today had she wanted to call him just to hear his voice? Each time the barn door opened, she couldn't stop herself from glancing up and checking to see if it were him striding through.

But it hadn't been. He'd not called. He'd not texted. And he'd not come.

She wasn't sure what to make of that.

Maybe he hadn't sent her inside because he just couldn't resist her any longer. Maybe it had been because she'd been such a huge disappointment to him. She couldn't trust her judgement, which said that he'd enjoyed that kiss every single bit as much as she did, because she'd barely been able to see straight, or walk, or form a cohesive thought for the next three hours. Three hours that she'd tossed and turned in her bed trying to figure out what in the world had happened out there in the dark with Gator's lips on hers. Nothing that had ever happened to her in her life before. That was for sure.

But it had been two days, and she hadn't heard anything from him.

The barn door opened and Avery, curse her silly heart, turned eagerly toward it.

Jillian walked in. "If you're going to make it to D.C. before the snow, you'd better get moving."

"It's not supposed to start until midnight."

"Oh. The storm must have missed that memo. It's snowing now."

"No way." Avery ran to the door. She couldn't miss that audition. She had to land that chair.

A hole in the roof threatened her party. Missing the tuba audition threatened her livelihood. Ellie and Fink wouldn't have any need for extra help after the holidays. She'd stayed at the farm long enough.

"I need to go."

Jillian placed both hands on her hips. "Avery. It's supposed to get really bad. They've been saying over and over all day that unless you have to be somewhere, it's best to stay home."

"I have to be somewhere."

"Fine. Give me Miss Prissypants, and I'll carry your tuba out to your car for you."

"Thanks!" Avery handed her cat over, then hurried out. She'd skip a shower. If the roads were bad and she got there early, she could grab a hotel room, although she'd really planned to save that money and come home tonight.

Less than five minutes later, she said good-bye to everyone and hurried out the door.

Just as she started her car, her phone pinged with a text. From Gator.

> You're not going to D.C.

Her eyes widened. An explosive kiss. Two days of silence and now a command? Not working. Not for her.

> I am.

There. That should put him in his place.

> I'm driving. I'll pick you up.

> No.

> Turn your car off. I'm here.

She looked in the rearview in time to see his pickup fill it. Irritation sizzled in her chest, but he was probably right. He had four-wheel drive and she didn't. Plus, she wasn't the greatest driver to begin with. If she didn't have to be at this audition, there's no way she'd go out in the snow.

She reached for her door handle, but Gator was already opening it.

His old jeans were torn and dusted with sawdust and darker dirt. His shirt sleeves were rolled up to his elbows. Light dust coated the fine hairs on his forearms and his hands were dirty. A streak of black went across one cheek and the other had dried blood on it from a cut just below his eye. It was scabbed over. He still wore his work boots and a red ball cap pulled low over his forehead. They were just as covered in dust and dirt as the rest of him.

"I'm sorry. Trying to get something done, but I didn't want you driving to D.C. alone in this weather."

She was staring. Goodness, she couldn't even open her mouth to tell him how good he looked, even if she thought that was something she should say. Which it wasn't. Most definitely not.

"You look good." The words came out anyway. Her mouth had disconnected itself from her brain.

"You're a liar. I'm filthy. And I stink."

"You're tired. And you don't want to drive to D.C."

"I'd drive to New York City. Heck, I'd try to figure out how to drive to Antarctica, if it meant spending time with you. Just wish I'd been able to stop about ten minutes sooner." He opened the door wider. "Come on. I don't want you to be late, and I'm not sure what the roads and traffic are going to be like."

After popping the trunk, she got out.

"I'll get your instrument. You go ahead and get in." He stopped. His hand reached up, but he dropped it immediately.

She stifled her disappointment.

"You smell good, by the way. Look even better."

Her face heated. She laughed and looked away.

"Hey," he said.

Her eyes met his.

"I know I probably sounded high-handed on my text. I was driving and didn't want to miss you and..."

"Shhh." A finger landed like a whisper on his lips.

He took it in his mouth, biting down gently.

She pulled it back, and cradled it in her hand. Not because it hurt, but because it tingled and burned. It took a few moments to remember what she was going to say.

"I was annoyed at first, but I really appreciate your offer because I'm not comfortable driving all that way in the snow. And now I can see," she deliberately looked at his dirty clothes, "you came in a hurry."

He studied her with a hard look. "Thanks." He turned. "Your tuba can go in the back seat of my truck?"

"Yes."

"Call my mom and check on her so we're not too far away if she needs something."

"Sure." She pulled up her contacts, clicked on his mom, then grabbed her bag and stuck it on the floor of his truck while waiting for the phone to ring.

Mrs. Franks sounded chipper when she answered the phone and assured Avery that she would be fine. Avery texted Jillian after she got off with Mrs. Franks and asked her to pop in or at least call before bed.

Jillian promised to check Mrs. Franks around suppertime and make sure she had something to eat.

"Your mom is taken care of." Avery connected her phone to his truck screen and typed in the address to the building her audition was in.

She leaned back in the passenger seat. "By the way, I'm glad I'm not driving." The windshield wipers rhythmically swept across the windshield, brushing snow into long, thick lines before pushing it from the glass. Black tracks between white areas marked the road.

"I'm glad you're not alone." Gator's jaw twitched but his gaze never wavered from the road.

Avery fiddled with the understated studs in her ears, wishing now that she would have had time to shower. Nerves cracked in her stomach. With nothing else to focus on, her mind went to the audition, trying to imagine any scenarios that might crop up and how she could best handle them. Ultimately, it would be the practicing she had done and the way she played that would get her the chair, but she was competing against the highest caliber of musicians anywhere, so getting the job could boil down to something simple.

Gator glance over at her. "Nervous?"

"A little, I guess."

"About the snow or the audition?"

"The audition. I trust your driving."

"I'd tell you you're going to do fine, but you know how much I know about music. It wouldn't be very convincing."

"It's okay."

"I just always figure that if it's meant to be, it will work out." He glanced at the dash clock. "What time is the audition?"

"Seven."

Gator blew his breath out slowly. "I'm not sure, at this rate, if we'll make it."

Avery studied her nails. She'd painted them a more professional-looking mauve for the audition. She supposed Gator's words were true of most things. If it was really meant to be, it would work out. The audition. Her relationship with Gator. The party. She couldn't even think about the hole in the roof right now. Maybe they could have the party anyway. After all, it wouldn't be leaking unless it rained or if the snow melted.

She shook her head to clear it and tried to focus on mentally preparing for her audition.

Gator checked the time on the dash for the hundredth time and shifted in the truck seat. He'd gone and gassed up the truck after dropping Avery off. Since then he'd just been waiting. How long did an audition take, anyway?

Snow fell heavily onto the windshield, obscuring the view before the wipers swiped it off, revealing Avery walking through the dark, snowy parking lot. Gator straightened, and turned the heater on high.

They had made it to her audition with less than five minutes to spare. Gator'd offered to go in with her, but she'd very politely declined without mentioning the condition of his clothes at all.

While he'd been waiting he figured he'd book them each a hotel room. Ha. That had been wishful thinking. The alerts on his phone had notified him that the turnpike was closed. There were other ways to go west out of D.C., but a state of emergency had been declared.

It all added up to some bad news he had to deliver to Avery.

The parking lot was mostly empty, so she had no trouble spotting him. He waited until she was far enough from the building so if anyone happened to look out at them, they wouldn't be able to see how dirty he was before he jumped out of the pickup. Not that he thought she was ashamed of him or anything. But he didn't want to be the reason anyone thought less of her.

He reached her and took her tuba. "I think that smile says you nailed it."

"No. This smile says I'm relieved it's over. I don't know anyone who enjoys auditions."

"They do seem nerve wracking."

"To say the least." They reached the truck, and he opened her door. "I'm starved," she said before grabbing ahold of the handle and pulling herself inside.

He put the tuba in the back and walked through the six inches of snow to the driver's side. "About that," he said after he climbed in and shut the door.

"About food?" she asked.

"Yeah." He started the pickup and looked over at her. "Everything's closed."

"Everything?"

"We can pick up something at a gas station. But every restaurant I passed was closed. All the stores. The turnpike."

"I kind of thought we'd have to stay here tonight."

"Yeah. Well," he rubbed a hand through his hair, hooking it around his neck before he looked at her. "There are a lot of other people who are stranded here tonight, too, it appears."

She blinked. "It does?"

"Yeah. I stopped at six hotels and called eight more. No rooms."

"No rooms," Avery said slowly.

"The ninth hotel I called had one room. I hope you don't mind, but I booked it."

"I don't mind," she said faintly.

"I don't even know where it is or if we can get to it. There are a lot of roads closed."

"I see."

Gator had his phone up, scanning his emails. "The man was supposed to send me an email confirmation. Honestly, I don't even know the name of the hotel. By the time I'd gotten to that one, I'd given up hope of getting a room. It was starting to look like we were sleeping here."

Avery gave a weak laugh. "That would have been...interesting."

Gator shook his head. "I wanted a shower. I *need* a shower."

"I need one too."

"There was just one room."

"I heard you."

"You can call around and see if you can find anything. I don't want you to think..."

"I don't think that."

"You must've if you knew what I was going to say."

She looked at him with that cute, direct gaze that made his heart flip every time. "You were going to say you didn't want me to think that you were taking advantage of me by only booking one room."

He hadn't been sure how she would take the news, so it pleased him that she was so matter of fact about it, and he couldn't help teasing her. "No. I was going to say I'm sorry if the hotel doesn't have a free breakfast. This beggar couldn't be choosy." He put the truck in gear.

She laughed.

"I was joking, of course, but I really don't know what it is. It might be a dump."

"I'm not worried."

"You can call and look for a hotel, if you want."

"Gator." She used a firm tone.

He stopped in the middle of the parking lot and looked at her. "What?"

"Whatever you did is fine. I promise."

He studied his hands on the steering wheel. "We can try to get home."

"No." Avery held out her hand. "Give me your phone and we'll figure this hotel thing out."

He took her outstretched hand in his.

"That's your hand."

He handed over his phone.

"Thanks." She reached with her outside hand, keeping her other hand locked with his.

After she typed the address in, they followed the directions, chugging through the snowy and mostly deserted streets, stopping only to grab a quick bite at the first gas station they passed. Even the fast food dives were closed.

It took thirty minutes, but the automated voice finally said they'd arrived at their destination.

"It's not the worst hotel I've ever seen," Gator said as they pulled into the parking lot.

"Me either. I'm ready for a shower."

"I'll check us in." He hopped out, leaving the truck running. A few minutes later, he opened his door, keycard in hand.

"We're clear down at the end. The receptionist said there was a door." There wasn't much parking, so Gator gave her the key and let her out before he drove down the parking lot and found a spot. He was soaked with the falling snow until he made it back.

Avery opened the door for him. "We're right here on the other side," she said.

The card opened the door easily, and they walked in to the stale smell of cigarette smoke. And two beds.

Avery paused, and Gator stopped behind her, still holding the door open. "You know. I just realized I have no clean clothes."

"Sometimes there's a washer and dryer." She stepped farther in and he followed and closed the door. "You shower first, and I'll see what I can find."

"Sounds great."

"I'll go look, and if you leave your clothes outside the bathroom door, I'll grab them if there's something."

"Thanks."

"No. Thank you. If it weren't for you driving, I would have missed my audition."

If she moved to D.C., he wasn't going to follow her. He might have just driven himself out of the chance of a relationship with the first woman he'd been interested in since his divorce. And, if that kiss was any indication, he had better chemistry with Avery than with any woman he'd ever known.

"I'd do it again."

She walked back out the door. In the bathroom he hesitated a moment—should he send out his underwear too? He decided he was being silly and added it to the pile. Who wanted to put dirty underwear on after taking a shower? And Avery had offered. Surely, she wouldn't be scandalized by his underwear. He grinned. Nope. Not Avery.

When he was done with his shower, he faced another dilemma. No clothes. The pile outside the door was gone, which he was thankful for, because he really wanted clean clothes. But...after making sure the towel was secure around his waist, he stepped out.

Avery sat in the middle of one of the beds, her shoes off, her fingers flying over her phone.

"I take it you found a washer and dryer?"

She glanced up. The smile on her face froze. Her eyes travelled over his chest, skimmed down, before shooting up to his face. "I—" She cleared her throat. "I did." Her smile returned, but she looked down at her phone. "I called your mom and let her know we were okay. Jillian was there with supper and home nursing just left. I told her you'd probably call, but I just wanted to check. I feel bad for taking you from her."

"You know, you could look at me while you're talking. All the important parts are covered. I checked before I stepped out."

Avery's lips turned up, but her head stayed down. The tips of her ears turned red. "I'm sure they are. You are a gentleman in every way. I just, I'm just not used to, um, you know. Being, like, well, being so, having..." She quit trying to talk and just laughed instead.

Uncrossing her legs, she slid off the bed. "I'll go shower. You, um, don't need to switch your clothes. I'll grab them when I'm done."

"So, you think I shouldn't walk around the hotel like this? Couldn't I pretend I just came from the pool?"

"I don't think there is a pool."

"Maybe I did the artic plunge?"

Her laugh sent shivers up his spine.

"Get in bed. I'll take care of your clothes. I promise." She walked by him without looking at him. "Oh, I hope you don't mind, but I did throw everything in together."

"You're apologizing for not separating the whites?"

"Yes."

He bit back a laugh. "Don't worry about it. Where's the washer at?"

"Down the hall. Just before the lobby you turn right." She grabbed her bag, which she'd set by the door and slipped into the bathroom.

She was tired, it was late, and he had more of himself covered than he would if he were swimming, so after she closed the door he grabbed the keycard and walked out to check the washer. He couldn't stand sitting in there listening to Avery rustle around in the bathroom.

Chapter Sixteen

When Avery stepped out of the bathroom, the overhead lights in the room were out. Gator lay in the bed she hadn't been sitting on, looking at his phone. Both of the lights between the beds were on.

Too bad she hadn't known she'd be sharing a room with Gator. She might have thrown something in her bag other than the ratty and oh-so-comfortable tee shirt and sweatpants.

"Hey." He looked up. One side of his lips kicked up. "I figured I'd get in here and get covered so I don't flummox you again."

"I wasn't flummoxed. I was just..." A liar. Oh, she was flummoxed all right. His shoulders looked broad under his shirt because they were broad. And muscular. And tanned. Like his arms. Like his back. Like his abs. She hadn't known that abs like that existed in real life.

"I'm just not used to seeing men undressed and sharing a room with me."

"I see." He still looked amused.

She felt very prim, but she wasn't going to discuss this any further with him. "I'll go switch your laundry."

"No need." He nodded to the open ironing board. "I just brought them back and ran the iron over them."

She gasped. "You went out like that?"

"No, I had my towel on."

She didn't feel any less scandalized. "Oh. I'd never thought of using the iron as a dryer," she said automatically. His towel lay over the back of the chair by the desk. That heat was back in her stomach. Burning.

"That's because it takes a man to think of using the iron for something other than ironing."

"Humph. Did you call your mom?"

"Yeah. Told me the same as she did you. That she was fine, fed, and ready for bed."

Avery laughed. "You've been waiting a whole twenty minutes to say that to me?"

"It was more like forty. I was about to send a search party in for you."

"It wasn't that long."

"It's okay, Avery. You had a long, hard day. Hot water is a good stress reliever."

"It did feel good." She set her bag down and climbed into bed. "Do you need the light?"

"Nope. I'm good."

She reached over and flipped her light out, plunging the room into darkness.

When she'd first realized that they'd need to share a room, she'd been more nervous about that than she had been about her audition. Although, when she'd walked in the room, she'd actually been a little disappointed that there were two beds.

"Gator?" she whispered in the dark. She hadn't heard a sound from him since she'd turned off the light. No rustling, no breathing, nothing.

"Hmm?"

"I've spent a lot of time wishing that you weren't going west, and I wasn't going D.C."

"Me too." His low answer vibrated along her spine.

"That's good to hear."

She waited a few minutes, trying to tell herself to just keep her lips closed.

"Gator?"

"Hmm?"

"I've spent a lot of time thinking about that kiss too."

He grunted. "I've spent more time trying not to think about it."

"Oh." She hoped she didn't sound as disappointed as she felt. "Really?"

"It was the best kiss I've ever had."

Her emotions did a complete about-face. "Yes. That's true for me too."

"I thought maybe it was a fluke. That it wasn't as explosive as I thought it was. That I exaggerated my response." The sheets rustled like he was shrugging or rolling over.

"I haven't had any of those thoughts. I'm sure about what I felt."

"Oh, yeah? What was that?"

"Like I wanted to do it again."

Gator groaned softly. "Isn't there some kind of music theory we could talk about? How about the history of the tuba dating back to the Middle Ages? Or maybe composers, including their birthdates, dates of death, and the number and types of pieces they composed?"

"You don't want to talk about the kiss? Why? Because there's no future for us?"

More movement, like he was turning again. "No. I don't want to talk about it because I'm never going to get to sleep if I'm thinking about kissing you. Especially with you...right there." He breathed out heavily. "I think I'd better go sleep in my pickup."

"I'm sorry. I'll be quiet."

"I don't want you to be quiet." He hesitated. "If you get this chair you auditioned for, you have to move to D.C.?"

She had never considered anything else. "It would be too hard to do it any other way."

"We'd better try to get some sleep."

"Good night, Gator."

"Good night."

THE ROADS WERE MUCH BETTER in the morning and they were able to get home by noon. Before he left for his construction job, Gator went

161

up to his mother's attic and brought a box of pictures down for them to go through.

Mrs. Franks felt well enough to sit at the table with Avery.

"Here's one of the inside of the barn." Mrs. Franks waved a picture in the air.

Avery glanced at it. "Hmm. I see." There was no party, but the colors of the photo were faded just right to indicate that it was from the same time period.

"Oh, my," Mrs. Franks said. "She tapped a picture that she'd just uncovered. "Here's one of Kristen and Gator."

Anticipation mixed with dread pushed through Avery's veins as she reached for the photo. She studied it. Gator, unsmiling, stood beside and a little behind Kristen, who wore heavy hiking boots, cargo pants, and a long-sleeved tee shirt. A gun stuck up from behind her shoulder and a knife was strapped to her waist. She knelt on one knee. A deer carcass spread out on the floor in front of her, its heavily horned head held up in her hands.

As she looked closer, Avery could see the dried blood on the knife and on Kristen's hands.

"She's tough."

"That's one word to describe her," Mrs. Franks said thoughtfully.

"You know, maybe I shouldn't admit that I like Gator."

"Honey, he likes you too."

"I think he does. But..." She tapped the picture. "After being with someone like her...it makes me feel like he couldn't possibly be interested in someone like me."

"Maybe after being with someone like her, he realizes how much more he wants to be with someone like you."

Avery snorted. "You look at everything in a positive light, don't you?"

Mrs. Franks laughed cheerfully. "I do."

"Well then, I need your positive thoughts. Snow fell off the barn roof, and now there's a hole in it. Fink was supposed to have someone out today to look at it, but I'm afraid I'm going to have to cancel the party."

"Because of one little hole?"

"It's right in the middle of everything, and it's not little. Plus, if we knew there was a problem with the roof and something happened, and someone got hurt, even if it had nothing to do with the roof, just the fact that we knew there was a problem and didn't fix it could land us in a lawsuit."

"That's true. People love to sue. Well, I'm sure something will work out." Mrs. Franks patted Avery's head.

They sorted through a few more pictures, finding several with good shots of the barn decorations, when Avery's phone buzzed with a text from Ellie.

> We dug up our homeowner's insurance. The roof replacement cost should be covered! Now we just need a contractor who will get it done before your party. :)

"Yay!" Avery read the text to Mrs. Franks.
"See. Think positive."

ONE WEEK after he spent the night lying in a separate bed with Avery only a few inches away, and didn't even get a good-night kiss, Gator was on the Finkenbinder's barn, working with Bret Shuff to put sheet metal roofing on.

He hadn't made as much money working with Bret as he would have made if he'd torn the Finkenbinder's barn down, but he'd not have the work of putting a roof on it if it had been torn down, either. Funny sometimes, how things worked out.

As he descended the ladder to grab another piece of roofing a crash came from above. Then swearing, then a "Look out!"

He looked up in time to see Bret's tool belt slide off the edge of the roof and bounce on the top rung of the ladder, headed directly for his head.

The two hammers and pockets full of metal could possibly knock him out. Jumping the last five feet to the ground off the side of the ladder would hurt less, he decided in a split-second decision that would haunt him.

He threw himself to the side, pushing with his legs, but his boot slipped and his leg fell inside the ladder while the rest of his body was on a trajectory to fall out and to the side of the ladder.

Cracking bones and shooting pain preceded the clash and clang of the ladder as it landed beside him, inches from his head. The entire world felt hazy red.

It wouldn't matter that he didn't know how to dance. He wasn't going to be dancing with Avery at her party for sure now.

Chapter Seventeen

Avery sat with Jillian and Mrs. Franks at Mrs. Franks' kitchen table. It had been hard to imitate the lacy table doilies, but they had found doilies online and were now gluing green and red glitter to the outside edges.

"I had no idea this was going to be such a huge undertaking. I really appreciate both of your help." She couldn't have done it without them, but Mrs. Franks was almost worn out and Avery needed to make sure she got a nap soon. She'd been dragging for the last few days.

"It's been fun." The words had barely left Mrs. Franks' mouth when she choked. Her face turned ash grey. The glue bottle that she held in her hand clattered to the table and onto the floor.

Avery and Jillian shared a horrified gaze for a millionth of a second before they both jumped up and reached for Mrs. Franks as she fell over, off of her chair.

They kept her from smacking her head on the floor.

"You call 911. I'll spread her out," Jillian commanded as she carefully lifted Mrs. Franks' legs from the chair, then felt her neck for a pulse.

"Make sure she's not actually choking," Avery said as she stood and dialed the emergency number.

"There's a pulse. Weak and slow."

The operator dispatched an ambulance immediately.

"As long as she's breathing and has a heartbeat, keep her comfortable until the ambulance arrives, which should be in less than five minutes."

Mrs. Franks moaned. "I need to clean up. I can't leave my kitchen in such a mess."

Avery almost laughed. Here she was, scared to death that Mrs. Franks was dying, and all the lady could think about was cleaning up her kitchen.

They assured her they would take care of it as the medics bustled in.

Jillian insisted she would ride in the ambulance so Avery could organize the decorations and clean up the kitchen. Avery had wanted to go in, but she couldn't leave everything scattered around Mrs. Franks' house and it wasn't fair to Jillian to try to have her sorting through things. Avery planned to head to the hospital immediately.

She was so deep in thought, worrying about Mrs. Franks, that the sound of her phone ringing made her drop the pile of craft supplies she had gathered up in her hands.

Fumbling for her phone, she drew in a calming breath before swiping the screen over a number she didn't recognize.

"Hello?" she said.

"Good afternoon. May I please speak to Miss Avery Conrad?"

"This is she." Avery bent down to pick at the mess on the floor.

"This is Dr. Evans, executive director of the Washington D.C. Eveningtide Orchestra."

The crafts slipped out of her hands. The knots in her stomach pulled tighter.

"Congratulations. You have been selected as the new tubists for our orchestra. Dr. Ramos and Dr. Alverzo both agreed they have never heard such beautiful tone and such exact rhythmic precision as you displayed at your audition."

"Thank you," she managed to stammer out. She had the chair!

"We will send you an official letter of acceptance, along with the Orchestra procedures, practice schedule, and tentative performance dates in the mail tomorrow, but I wanted to call and let you know immediately that you had been selected."

"Wow. This is thrilling and a huge honor. I can't wait to get started."

"Perfect. I'm sure I'll be seeing you soon. I hope your holidays are happy."

"Yours too."

Avery hung up the phone. Stunned.

Just like that, she had a position in a professional orchestra, playing her tuba. Her dream job.

Remembering about Mrs. Franks she dropped to her knees and began grabbing up the pieces.

Gator!

Gator would want to know that his mother had been taken to the hospital. This time, she set the craft supplies on the table before she grabbed her phone and pulled up his number.

Worry and anxiety warred with eagerness and excitement as she waited impatiently for him to pick up. His voice mail came on.

She didn't want to scare him with a message, so she hung up and called back. Still no answer. They hadn't talked a lot on the phone, but she'd never had trouble getting ahold of him before. But his voicemail answered again.

She finished cleaning up the last of the mess, and tried Gator's number as she walked out the door, closing and locking it behind her.

Four rings and then his now familiar automated message came on.

After the tone she said, "I guess you must be up on the barn roof and can't get the phone. We took your mother to the hospital. Call me when you get a chance." She swiped off. It was the best she could do, but she didn't know any more, and couldn't leave any reassurance other than she was still breathing and had a heartbeat. Hardly information that would ease anyone's mind.

Avery got into her car and drove to the hospital.

～

I'm at the hospital.

AVERY CHECKED her phone as the text came in, finally, from Gator.

> Great. They gave us a room on the seventh floor. 742. Can you find us?

She made sure that Mrs. Franks' feet were covered and tucked in. Not that Mrs. Franks had opened her eyes or moved since they'd taken her from the ER. Avery stuffed down the concern that choked her throat.

Jillian had gone home to feed her dog and help Fink and Ellie with the evening crowd, and since the doctor hadn't come in yet, Avery had really been hoping Gator would show up.

> I'm not going to be there right away.

Avery stared at her phone. How could he not rush to his mother's side? Disappointment trickled through her in a slow drip. Was he not the man she thought he was? He needed to be here.

Her thumbs typed out a response.

> The doctor should be in any minute. He's not going to tell me anything since I'm not family.

> Tell him you're married to me.

Again, Avery stared at her phone, surprised at how those words shifted her insides.

> I can't lie. He'll know right away that I'm not telling the truth.

> Call me when he comes in and put me on speaker phone.

> You're not coming here? I thought you were in the hospital.

> I am. I came in an ambulance, too.

Avery's knees buckled and she sat on the hard hospital chair with a thump. Questions and fear swirled in her head.

> What happened? Where are you? What room?

> Broken foot. Please stay with mom. How is she?

> Asleep. The nurses seemed to think it might be low iron or potassium. Hopefully nothing worse.

A young, clean-cut man in street clothes walked in just as she hit send.

"Hello." He walked toward her with his hand outstretched. "I'm Dr. Hess. Are you the daughter?"

Avery explained the situation, dialing Gator as she did so, while the doctor walked over to Mrs. Franks' bedside and gently shook her shoulder. Mrs. Franks blinked. Her eyes widened as they landed on the unfamiliar man standing in front of her. Her face relaxed as Avery put her hand on Mrs. Franks' other shoulder.

"I'm right here, Mrs. Franks. I have Gator on the phone too."

"Hi, Mom." Gator's voice came clearly through the phone.

Avery held the phone above the bed as the doctor explained that Mrs. Franks' tests had come back that she was low in both iron and potassium. Avery had trouble paying attention. How had Gator broken his foot? Wouldn't it be a pretty bad break if he were in the hospital? Or maybe he was still in the waiting room.

It wasn't that she wasn't concerned about Mrs. Franks, because she was, although it was a relief to hear that with a few additives to her IV, she should feel better in the morning. The iron would take a little longer to come up to normal range.

Ten minutes later, after answering a few questions from Gator, and telling Mrs. Franks that she'd probably be released in the morning, the doctor walked out.

Mrs. Franks gave a tired sigh. With her eyes closed she said, "Do either of you want to tell me why Gator is on the phone and not here?"

Gator didn't hesitate. "I fell off the ladder and broke my foot."

"This just happened?" Mrs. Franks asked skeptically.

"This morning."

"Gator." Mrs. Franks gave that motherly, threatening tone without even opening her eyes. Avery, too, wondered why he was still in the hospital if all he had was a broken foot.

"They're doing surgery on it tomorrow morning."

Avery's heart skipped. Surgery? No wonder he was still in the hospital.

"What time?" Mrs. Franks asked.

"They didn't say for sure, but they did say they start with the youngest cases first."

"Where are you?" Mrs. Franks asked.

Gator gave her the floor and room number.

"I'm sending Avery up to check on you. Is there anything else you want to tell me?" Mrs. Franks opened her eyes and gave Avery a tired wink.

"No, Mother. I've told you everything. And I want Avery to stay with you. If I need something, I know how to get it. But you're already weak, and I don't want you by yourself."

Mrs. Franks narrowed her eyes and looked at Avery.

Avery shrugged. He had a point. She couldn't exactly imagine Gator lying helplessly, waiting for someone to bring him a bed pan. Mrs. Franks, on the other hand, wouldn't want to bother anyone.

"I'll stay here," she said.

"Thank you," Gator said, his voice softer, almost intimate.

Mrs. Franks, who again had her eyes closed, smiled.

Avery tapped the red button. Relieved that both Mrs. Franks and Gator would be fine, she allowed the thought that had been plaguing the back of her mind all day to emerge to the forefront.

Tomorrow she was supposed to decorate the barn. The party was the day after. There was no way she was going to have everything ready. The food, the decorations, the lights, the tables and chairs set up. Gator had promised to help, but he couldn't now. Plus, the whole thing was moot if Mrs. Franks wasn't well enough to go.

Disappointment welled up within her, and she was forced to face the brutal truth. She wanted to plan the party for Mrs. Franks, that was true. But it was also for herself. She loved planning, she loved parties, and she had wanted to prove to Fink and Ellie that she could spearhead a successful celebration, possibly convincing them that keeping the barn could be a good business decision. That it would not only pay to have an event planner on staff, but that it would also pay to have insurance for such events and possibly even pay to renovate the barn. It had been her backup plan in case she didn't get the tuba chair.

The chair was hers. She smiled. She'd forgotten about that. Still, she could find a job around here teaching music and give lessons on the side and be perfectly happy. Happier. Because she'd be doing everything that she loved—music and events planning.

Plus, there had been a small window of opportunity with Gator. If things worked out, she might be able to pursue it.

Avery sat on the hard chair and looked out the window, over the lights of the city. Maybe, if she were being really honest, she'd admit that Gator might not have been the first reason she'd wanted to do the party, but he'd become the biggest reason.

Now all she had to do was figure out what she was going to do about it.

Chapter Eighteen

Gator's stomach rolled.

He'd never been under the knife before. The anesthesiologist had warned him that it might upset his stomach. The doctor had failed to mention that his insides were going to try to leave his body. Violently.

He kept his eyes closed and tried not to groan. He'd never felt sicker in his life. All because of his foot, of all things.

Suddenly, he needed a bed pan. Immediately. He struggled to open his eyes, to sit up, to call for help.

Gentle hands touched his bare shoulders. Avery's scent drifted over his senses. "It's right here," a soft voice said, taking one of his hands and helping him feel the container below his mouth.

His stomach heaved. Since he hadn't eaten since yesterday afternoon, not much came out, and he didn't feel any better after. But soft hands touched his forehead and tapped a napkin to his mouth.

He leaned back, resting. The voice and scent were Avery's, but he'd not told her where he was after his surgery, not heard from her since last night. He must be hallucinating. He opened one eye to check.

Blond hair. A concerned, familiar face. Sweet, rosy cheeks.

"How'd you find me?"

"I have friends in all the right places." Avery grinned, but she took pity on him and didn't make him ask again. "The trombone player from the Christmas parade is your anesthesiologist."

"I see."

"We exchanged numbers."

"I see." He cleared his throat and took a bit of the crushed ice she offered. "I was just thinking she didn't do a very good job of explaining just how bad I would feel." He moved the ice around in his mouth, breathing slowly and carefully. His stomach didn't seem to be in such a rush to claw its way up his throat when he moved carefully.

"You don't have to stay." But he wanted her to. He'd never thought of himself as someone who loved to be taken care of, but he didn't want to lose Avery's soft touch.

"Jillian is with your mom. They discharged her a few minutes ago and she's going to take her home."

"Did the doc say anything else?"

"Not really. They just made an appointment for her for Monday and told her to go to the ER if she felt anything out of the ordinary before that. He's pretty confident that the supplements will work."

"Good." Gator closed his eyes. Just for a moment...

When he opened them again, the nausea was gone and so was Avery. It felt like no time had passed, but the recovery room seemed to be busier with more monitors beeping around the hanging curtains and several nurses bustling in and out.

"Oh, Mr. Franks, are you awake?" A nurse carrying a clipboard and a plastic cup with shaved ice in it stopped when she saw his open eyes.

"What time is it?" He didn't have his phone and there weren't any windows.

"It's four."

Irritation at himself made him purse his lips. "I'd like to get out of here if possible." He wasn't going to be much help decorating the barn for Avery, but he was going to try. It wasn't going to happen until he at least had underwear on.

"Please lie still, Mr. Franks."

He tried to make his face not look as irritated as he felt. He must have succeeded somewhat since the nurse didn't run out. "Your incision was draining a little more than we expected. That, along with your severe reaction to the anesthetic, is causing the doctor to think that you might need to stay the night."

"No." He cringed at his tone, but didn't apologize.

"The doctor is just two patients down. He'll be here shortly. Your wife stepped out to use the restroom, and I bet by the time she's back, he'll be ready to talk to you."

The nurse must have meant Avery. It was the second time since he'd landed in the hospital he'd thought Avery and wife in the same sentence. The two words seemed to go together well. Regardless, he couldn't stay. He'd promised her he would help decorate, and he knew she was counting on him.

"I'll inform the doctor when he gets here that I'm not staying. Would you please bring my clothes in the meantime?" He lifted his head and neck off the bed as he spoke, phrasing it as a question, but the tone of his voice was commanding.

"The doctor will be here, soon, sir," the nurse said, obviously not intimidated by a weak, naked man with a broken foot. She strode out.

Gator gritted his teeth. He hated being treated like one cow in a herd of them. He also hated the fact that they had the upper hand since they had his clothes. His life had not consisted of waiting around for someone else to tell him what to do, and he wasn't so weak and wracked with pain that he was going to start now.

He sat up.

The room spun for a couple of moments, and he braced his hand on the edge of the gurney until it stopped. When he was sure he wasn't going to topple off of the edge, he reached around, adjusting the thin sheet that had been covering him so that it wrapped around his waist.

His foot throbbed and he grimaced. Probably the doctor would tell him he needed to keep it elevated. Hopefully, the pain meds didn't wear off too soon.

Bunching the blankets in one hand, he slid his butt to the edge of the bed, getting ready to slide off. He kept his broken foot up, not really wanting to damage it, but sure as heck not going to sit around waiting for someone else to decide when he was well enough to leave the hospital. He tightened his grip on the sheet and pushed with his other hand.

"Gator?"

His head jerked toward the incredulous voice.

"What are you doing?" Avery's brows were lost in her hairline. One hand rested on the curve of her hip. Her usually smiling mouth was set in a disapproving line.

She didn't wait for an answer, but marched over to the side of his bed and placed her little hand right on his chest.

"If you get out of that bed, I will chase you down and beat you to death."

"Kind of pointless, isn't it?" he mumbled, but he eased back. Not because he was afraid of her, of course. But because her hand on his bare chest did all kinds of things to his insides. He placed his hand over hers, curled his fingers around and threaded them with her fingers. The sparkly green nails with red tips made him smile. It was so Avery.

"Nice nails."

She had opened her mouth, most likely to give him another round of bossy commands or to possibly berate him more. Now, it hung open. Her lowered brows eased and lifted, pulling her face into a shocked expression.

The best defense was a good offence, or something like that, he remembered hearing. Not that his hunting and work had ever left much time to play sports. Anyway, he took advantage of her being off-kilter.

"I need to get out of here. I promised a certain very pretty and very sweet lady that I would help her decorate for the party that she is having..." He paused, trying to remember what day it was. "Tomorrow," he finally said.

Her shocked expression settled into a little smile. Just a ghost of her normal, light-up-the-room wattage. "I cancelled it."

"What?"

"I cancelled it."

"Why?" he asked, although it wasn't too hard to figure out the answer.

"Between your mother and you, I wasn't going to have time to do everything that still needed to be done."

"Me? You're blaming me?"

"No!" She pushed him back down on the bed, adjusting his sheets.

"I'm not. But I did have to choose. I couldn't be here, where I wanted to be, and also be at the farm, getting ready for the party."

He lifted a hip so she could pull the sheets out from under it, and tried to ignore the feel of her hands on his skin.

"You don't have to be here with me."

"Someone obviously needs to be here, if only to strap you down." She gave the sheets one final tuck, then crossed her arms over her chest.

He lifted a brow. They both knew that, even in his current condition, she wasn't strong enough to keep him anywhere he didn't want to be.

"I know." Avery dropped her arms and touched his cheek.

He resisted the almost overwhelming urge to close his eyes.

"Between you and me, it gives me a very powerful feeling when you do what I want you to, when you're so much bigger and stronger than I am."

He lowered his voice to barely a whisper and she leaned lower. "Between you and me, when you touch me like that, I'd do anything for you."

Her eyes opened wide, and her throat worked. "That's kind of why I had to cancel the Christmas party. I could have decorated without you, but I didn't want to be there, doing my thing, when you were here."

"We're a pair."

She nodded slowly.

His hand found hers again.

"Do me a favor, Gator."

"Anything." He'd do anything for her.

"Stay here tonight."

He snorted. "That sounded almost sexy, until I remembered that we're in a hospital."

"That wasn't a 'yes, Avery, I'll stay.'"

"It didn't have to be. I already said I'd do whatever you asked." He squeezed her fingers. "I feel really bad about the party, though."

"Sometimes things just aren't meant to be."

Maybe it was the way her eyes searched his. Or maybe it was the tone of her voice, or possibly just her words. Whatever it was, it made his heart plunge to his toes. The easy, teasing smile slipped off his face, and he stared into her eyes, barely breathing. Waiting.

She bit her lips.

"What?" he finally asked.

"The orchestra accepted me."

His throat tightened. His skin felt cold. But this was good news. For her.

He closed his eyes and drew in a deep breath. He had to be happy, and he had to be sincere. He swallowed and tried to make his lips smile, although he suspected he did not succeed.

"That's great news for you." His voice sounded strained. Her eyes showed what he already knew in his heart. It wasn't great news. Not for them. For her and her career, maybe. But it was the death knell for any type of relationship for them. Still, he held her hand tighter, as though that would ward off the inevitable.

"When do you have to be there?" he asked, having no idea how words were coming out of his mouth.

"Rehearsals start after Christmas, but I don't have a place to stay."

"I can go with you. Help you find one." What was he saying? The last thing in the world he wanted to do was actually help her leave him.

"I'd like that," she said.

"So, you're still here." The doctor walked around the side of the curtain. This one wore a white coat and carried an iPad. It wasn't the surgeon or any doctor he'd seen before. Not that it mattered. He barely paid attention to what the doc said, although he did notice that the doctor acted like Avery was his wife.

He glanced at Avery out of the corner of his eye. Her eyes were glued on the doctor and she hung on his every word, nodding and biting her lip. He half-expected her to grab the little notebook out of his lab coat pocket and start taking notes. Sure made it seem like she cared about him.

Maybe he could convince her that a long-distance relationship was possible.

Montana to Washington D.C. was almost an entire continent. But if he gave up his job and stayed in Pennsylvania, it was only a few hours. Four, maybe five.

A small part of him balked at giving up his job for a relationship. Especially a relationship that might not work out. One in which they'd not even discussed having a relationship, yet alone talked about any kind of permanence.

Two nurses came around the curtain. Gator noticed, but his focus was Avery.

"Is this thing between us worth doing anything about?"

The doctor stopped mid-sentence. The nurses halted at the foot of his bed. Avery's head swiveled to him, her mouth in a big *O*, her cheeks pink.

Awkward seconds ticked slowly by in church-like quiet.

"Sometimes the anesthetic takes a while to wear off," the doctor said slowly.

The nurses chattered in immediate agreement, but Gator didn't look away from Avery's eyes, which held awareness that it wasn't the drugs talking. It was the distance that yawned between them.

He thought he saw her nod slightly, but then she turned back to the doctor, who had finished his post-op instructions and was listing all the reasons he felt Gator should stay. The top among them was his severe reaction to the anesthetic, which his asinine comment of a few moments ago hadn't helped.

It had clarified in his mind, though, that Avery was worth it. Worth leaving a good-paying job that he loved and moving across the country. But only if she felt the same. He wasn't chasing another woman who was only in it for something other than him.

Chapter Nineteen

Avery pulled into the farm. Her headlights hit the house before she shut them off. Full darkness plunged down around. She sighed, both hands at the top of the wheel, before she grabbed for her second wind and shut the car off.

A room for Gator had not opened up until almost seven this evening. In the back of her head, she'd been thinking that she could maybe run home after getting him settled and maybe throw enough decorations together to possibly still have at least a shadow of the party she'd dreamed of.

Until he got taken to his room—grumbling and complaining, she might add—and settled, he'd completely missed supper, and the hospital cafeteria, both of them, plus the gift shop, were closed. He hadn't eaten since the morning before. So Avery ran to check on Mrs. Franks—Jillian had been caring for her in between helping at the Christmas tree cash register—grabbed a few things to make his room more cheerful and picked up fast food for Gator, who had very casually asked where his clothes and shoes were.

She, just as casually, had lied through her teeth and told him they were in the backseat of her car.

Thankfully, a nurse had come in before that whopper was out of her mouth. Avery had no poker face to speak of, and she had made a point, all of her life, to keep her lying skills rusty from disuse. Today, however, a lie had seemed fitting.

After all, she'd been lying to herself for a few weeks now. Because she'd realized today, while she was in the hospital holding the bedpan for that grumpy, surly, sleepy man, that the reason she'd told McKoy Rodning he could leave, that she was going to take care of Gator, was not because she'd felt like she had to, or even that she necessarily wanted to. After all, who wants to hold a bed pan?

But she couldn't get the guy out of her head, couldn't stop thinking about how much she loved being with him and how much fun they had together. She worried about him, wanted the best for him, admired him, and hey, she had to face it, she wanted the guy to kiss her again.

So, no. She didn't stay at the hospital all day today and give up the chance to have the party she'd always dreamed about, disappointing Mrs. Franks, and losing the possible opportunity to show Fink and Ellie that the barn could make a profit because of anything rational. She stayed with Gator today, watching him sleep, listening to the doctor's instructions, heeding the nurses' warnings and making sure they didn't give him the wrong drugs, because she loved him.

She loved him.

He was going to leave. It had scared her at one time, but after spending so much time with Gator, she had figured one thing out. He wasn't like her father or her ex-fiancé. He might leave, but not for the next flavor-of-the-month. And that, she could live with.

THE NURSES HAD TOLD them that the doctor usually made his rounds early, so Avery got up long before dawn, checked Mrs. Franks, fed Gator's dogs and rushed to the hospital.

No light shone from the door crack under Gator's door, so she knocked softly, and pushed the door open carefully.

"He was awake earlier," a friendly nurse said as she pushed a blood-pressure machine down the hall.

"Okay. Thanks," Avery said. She'd been blessed to have never spent the night in a hospital, so she had no idea whether she'd sleep well or not. Since Gator had spent most of the day yesterday sleeping off the effects of the anesthesia, and because he valued his independence and privacy, and because he had been in not-a-little pain from his foot the afternoon before, she was guessing he might not have slept well and might be just a little grumpy.

She pushed the door open a little farther and slipped through. Handel's *Messiah* played softly. Gator, who was not supposed to be out of bed, stood at the window, staring at the waking downtown. At least his foot wasn't on the ground. He had his leg bent with his knee propped on the lone chair in the room.

"Good morning?" she said softly as she walked closer. The table-top tree she'd brought in shone cheerfully from his bed stand, and the ornaments she'd hung from the window added a festive touch. To her, anyway.

Gator looked back. "Hey. Figured you'd be here early."

"Yeah. I'd have told you before I left, but it was in one of your dozing times when they finally kicked me out."

"It's what I thought."

She handed him the straight black coffee that she'd gotten for him, and pulled the tab on her hot chocolate.

Gator leaned over and sniffed her cup. "That smells good."

"Christmas cookie hot chocolate. One can never have too much sugar in the morning."

Gator grunted. "I was just thinking about that."

"Sugar in the morning?"

"No. About how different you are."

"Different from everyone. Or different from someone in particular?" she asked. Through everything that had happened yesterday, they had never talked about his comment mentioning "this thing between us." Because of the anesthesia maybe he didn't even remember it. She sure did. And she knew what her answer was.

"Different from what I'd always thought my ideal woman was."

"Oh?" He seemed to be in such a contemplative mood and she couldn't figure out whether he was thinking he'd been wrong, or if he was actually explaining why they didn't fit.

He waved his hand at the shiny bulbs hanging from the window, then over towards the tree and the bit of tinsel she'd arranged. "All this. I've always hated decorations. What a waste of time."

She drew back. If he'd have slapped her, she wouldn't have been more surprised.

"Knick-knacks. That's what my mother calls them. I trip over them. Knock them down. Break stuff. I'm not graceful, and a body this size takes some space."

"But you made all those decorations for your yard."

"Yeah. I think that's about the time I wondered what the point was. You know?" He shrugged. "I knew my mother liked the stuff and I spent a lot of time making it, but by the time I was done, I wondered why I'd bothered. You put the stuff out once a year. It clutters up the yard. You spend a lot of time trying to get the lights and stuff just so, only to take it down again."

He hadn't been overly enthused or impressed about the party, but he'd helped her some with the decorations and had promised to help her with the decorating. And now he was saying that he hated it all?

Avery squinted at him. The doctor said he'd reacted badly to the anesthesia. Maybe it had changed his personality. She made a mental note to ask the doctor if it was permanent.

"So," she hesitated, not sure she really wanted to know exactly what he was saying. "Do you want me to take the decorations down?"

Gator dropped his foot from the chair and moved his body around to look at her, his brows drawn down in confusion.

The lights fluttered on as a doctor walked in, a younger woman in a lab coat at his side. "You, sir, are not to be out of bed. If it's completely necessary for you to be up, you are to have your leg elevated."

Dr. Hess shook hands and introduced Dr. Bensten. Avery read "resident" on her badge.

"Were you on your way to or from the restroom?" Dr. Hess asked.

Avery stifled a smile. Nice way of telling Gator to get back in bed.

Gator gave her a last look, one she thought promised more conversation, before he lifted a lip at the doctor and leaned his weight on the wheeled tray before hopping to the bed. And, yes, Avery noticed that he barely glanced at the young, good-looking female "resident."

The older doctor pointed his clipboard at Avery. "If you want his foot to heal correctly, you are going to have to keep him in bed, or at the very least, off of his feet. When he's sitting, it needs to be propped, and he should not stand any more than it takes for him to walk from his bed to the chair to the restroom and back."

"Yes, sir," Avery said. Like she'd given Gator permission to get out of bed. Like he'd have gotten back in if she'd have told him to, and like she hadn't heard it all yesterday.

"It was all me," Gator said, as though he could read her mind.

The doctor turned serious eyes on Gator. "I know. Sometimes patients I work with aren't going to listen to anyone. Don't look so surprised. I've been in this a long time, and some people just don't listen. You're borderline." He narrowed his eyes at Gator. "My instinct tells me that if your wife wants it, you'll kill yourself to give it to her. That's why I was giving her the instructions."

Gator's eyes slanted to her. There was not a hint of a smile on his face. That slow burn in the pit of her stomach sparked and leaped.

He looked back at the doctor. "Pegged."

Avery's heart launched into a stunning rendition of Ave Maria.

As though he could hear it, one side of Gator's mouth quirked up. Avery turned toward the window to hide her own grin.

The doctor droned on about Gator staying off his feet and being careful not to bump the foot and things to look for with his anesthesia issues. Avery tried to pay attention around the thumping of her heart and the heat in her stomach and the nerves that still twanged because of Gator's decorations comments.

After telling Gator he should be discharged by noon, the doctor and the resident left.

Avery stood by the window, one finger trailing on the manger figurines she'd placed there.

Silence descended heavily in the room, broken only by the occasional clicking of the machines near the head of Gator's bed.

Avery looked around. At the sparkly wreath that hung on the back of the door. At the colored string of lights on the wall near Gator's bed. At the stained-glass throw in green, red and gold across the bottom of

Gator's bed. At the iPod docking station where she'd been streaming Christmas music.

"Maybe I went a little overboard on the decorations." It had taken five trips from her car to his room to carry everything. That was probably a little excessive.

"Come here," Gator said, softening his command with a quieter plea. "Please."

Avery smiled at Gator's barely polite command. She stepped toward the bed.

He reached out a hand and clasped hers. "I hate not being able to go where I want to."

"This will be good practice in self-control."

Gator gave a derisive snort. "It's going to take some soul-searching before I determine whether it will be worth the full use of my foot for the rest of my life, versus not being stuck in one place for the next six weeks."

"Stop. Six weeks versus the rest of your life." Six weeks would put them past the New Year. She'd be gone. Three weeks with Gator versus the rest of her life without him. The time was an easy choice when she was thinking about his foot. But what about her possible life partner?

Possible was the keyword.

"I was saying earlier about the decorations," Gator began.

"Yes, I know. You hate them." Avery tried to pull her hand away.

"No. That's what I was saying. It's not that I spent a lot of time thinking about the perfect woman for me, but I guess if I had, someone like Kristen would have come pretty close. And, I'd wager a guess that your idea of a perfect mate never looked like me."

Avery grunted. "No. You're right."

His thumb stroked her hand sending charges of excitement skimming up her arm.

"So, after spending so much time with you, I realized last night that I was starting to see the world from a different angle. I mean, it's nice to be with people who see everything the same way you do. No arguments." They laughed together. "But, no growth, either. Because I laid here and looked at the things you'd done—the homey blanket you laid across my legs, the

Christmas lights sparkling off of the bulbs you'd hung. Just everything you'd done to make my room look comfortable, festive and pretty. Before I spent time with you, I would never had appreciated it, or even noticed, really."

"Maybe that's why opposites attract?"

"Sure. Maybe that's why whoever designed us built us that way. Because we need to be more than our own opinion. Because being with people, a person, who is different than I am helps me be better."

"You're saying I help you be better?"

"Yeah. I'm better now than I was before I met you." He smirked. "But if you'd have told me that from the top of the light pole, I don't think I would have believed you at the time."

"So, are you going to be rubbing that light pole thing in for the rest of my life?" she asked with an eye roll.

Gator's look was serious. "Am I?"

"You're right about our differences. I fed your dogs last night and actually enjoyed it. I looked over the backyard at where your mom said the old hatchery used to be and I could see the potential. I would never be thinking like that if I hadn't met you." She smiled. "There's a lot more about you that I like because it's different from me."

"Yeah?"

She shrugged. "I like how you're bigger than me. I feel safe and protected with you. Actually, I like how you protect me—you drove me through the snowstorm. But I also like how we work together. Your strengths buffer my weakness. And mine yours, maybe. Just that idea makes me happy."

"So, you didn't really answer the question."

"What question?" She fingered the Christmas throw.

He squeezed her hand. "The one about whether I'm going to be teasing you about the light pole for the rest of my life."

"Knock, knock." McKoy stuck his head in the door. "Is everyone in here decent?"

"I am, and I'm working on her," Gator called. "Come on in."

"We both know the opposite is true between you two. Give her fifty years to work on you. Might be close to decent by then." McKoy grinned as he sauntered in. "Hey, Avery."

185

"Hello, McKoy." Avery greeted Gator's friend, then tried to pull away. Gator tugged on her hand.

McKoy's eyes went to their clasped fingers. "I actually *am* interrupting something, here. Aren't I?"

Avery shook her head. "No. Not at all. You come right in. Gator needs someone here who's big enough to make him stay off of that foot."

"That's not what the doctor said," Gator said in a low, almost husky, voice.

"Let's not argue about that now," Avery said. She gave McKoy another smile. "I appreciate you coming to visit."

"Can't let my friend languish in the hospital all alone. Not with all these cute nurses hanging around. And I'm pretty sure that one good-looking blond was a doctor."

"I wouldn't know," Gator said.

"I'm not going there," McKoy said with a wink. "What's this about the big party being cancelled? Lots of people in town are really looking forward to it."

Avery lifted her hand and shrugged. "My help broke his foot."

"And my mom was in the hospital too. Avery gave up her party to take care of us both."

"Jillian helped too," Avery said. She didn't deserve all the credit. And she really didn't deserve to be painted in such an unselfish light. Giving up the party hadn't been as easy as Gator made it sound. Maybe that was part of the reason she went so far overboard decorating Gator's room.

"The whole town is disappointed. That's all I heard about when I made my rounds yesterday." McKoy shoved his hands in his pockets.

"Maybe we can do something after Christmas," Avery said. Although if she was going to take the position in D.C., she would be too busy trying to find a place and...

Was she considering turning down the position?

Chapter Twenty

A very shut her car off in front of Fink and Ellie's house. Because of some kind of computer glitch which had caused a paperwork snag, Gator hadn't been released until early evening. Impatient wasn't a strong enough word to describe his attitude all afternoon. But now he was home, and she was back at the farm, thinking she'd relieve Jillian who'd been putting in way more hours at the tree farm than anyone had expected.

Only there were lights on in the barn. And a lot of cars parked outside of it. So Avery had driven by the farm office, curious.

Now, as she walked down through the dark yard toward the lights, she could hear voices and Christmas music playing. At least if Fink had hired someone to gut the interior, they probably wouldn't be playing Christmas music, would they?

Avery slid open the man-door and stepped inside, hardly believing her eyes.

Ellie, who was quite crafty herself, stood on a ladder hanging the pine swags Avery had just finished making last week. Other town ladies bustled around, setting up tables, hanging lights, arranging chairs along the knee-wall, and all the while, they checked the pictures that lay on the center table, making sure they had everything just as it was at Mrs. Franks' engagement party.

Mayor Higham did a double take, then threw up a hand in a wave, before leaning over and saying something to the man he was hanging the candle holders with. He set the holder down, then strode over.

"Avery! Does this mean Gator is finally home?"

"Yes, I just dropped him off."

"That's great. That's great."

Avery looked around. "So, what's all this?"

"Well, we're decorating for the party tomorrow, of course."

"But..." She'd cancelled it. On Facebook. It's not like anyone would have missed that.

"I know. You had to cancel it. But everyone in town has watched how hard you've worked, not just on the party, but on helping Fink and Ellie when Fink had his little mishap this summer, and how you've worked with Mrs. Franks, and how you've picked up the slack when Harper and Wyatt went to Chile. It takes all of that—successful small businesses, neighbors helping neighbors—and reasons to celebrate and get together to keep a small town like ours thriving." He gestured around the barn. "Right now, you see neighbors helping neighbors."

Avery just stared at him. This was the man who put her on the dunking board.

As though he could read her mind, or more likely her face, Mayor Higham said, "You were a great sport at the town Christmas celebration."

Good manners made Avery say, "Thank you."

The mayor clasped his hands together. "Jillian is really the one who organized this. But I, and the townspeople also, think it's a great idea. It's things like this that pull everyone together. We're all on board trying to recreate Patty Franks' engagement party. Patty's been a fixture in our town for years, and she's well liked by everyone. People admire you for helping her."

That people admired her was a shock to Avery. "I thought everyone thought I was odd."

"Well, we do."

Avery snorted.

"After you've lived here for fifty years, people might start treating you like you're almost normal."

"Fifty years?"

"Or so."

"It's not going to take that long." Ellie slipped her arm around Avery. "I think the good mayor forgets that you're family."

"Oh, yes. I did forget. There's not much resemblance."

Avery turned to hug Ellie. "Thank you so much, Ellie. This looks exactly the way I'd pictured it."

Ellie hugged her back. "I couldn't let all those beautiful decorations go to waste."

"I should have known."

"Plus, this could be really good business for the farm." Ellie looked around approvingly.

"That's what I thought."

"I hadn't realized how popular it's become to renovate old barns and turn them into bookable venues." She nodded. "This old place fixes up pretty nicely. I've already had two people ask about weddings here and one ask about having their reunion. Plus, I overheard a group of teens talking about having the prom here."

Avery's heart soared. "I knew it!"

"I don't think it will be hard to get Fink onboard. But we'll have to talk to him. Maybe after the party?"

Avery grinned. "It's still on, then? Tomorrow evening?"

"Yep. You don't think we're doing all this work for nothing, do you?"

GATOR SAT in a corner with his foot propped up on a chair, feeling more than a little bit surly. After all, he hadn't even been able to drive himself and his mother to this party, let along, pick up his girl. Girlfriend? He'd loved the pairing of Avery and "wife," but in truth he didn't even know if he could call her his girlfriend. If he'd been able to walk, he could steal her away for a few minutes and get their relationship straightened out. And kiss her. Mostly kiss her.

But with his confounded foot, he was stuck here, watching.

The words he'd said to Avery in the hospital came back to him. Words about learning to appreciate the things he hadn't appreciated before.

He tried to stop his negative thoughts. The barn was beautiful. Even his old self could have appreciated that. Candles flickered from the boxes Avery and he had built. And, because it was an old barn, they had discreetly placed at least ten or so fire extinguishers in easy to reach, but hard to see, places.

Friends of Avery's and local musicians had combined to provide live Christmas music. Some brave souls had even ventured out onto the dance floor, such as it was.

Still, the flickering glow from the open flames lent a romantic atmosphere to the whole party. There were more lights than just candles. And lots of shiny bulbs and garland to pull the reflections in and toss them out again in happy, shimmering waves of color and sparkle.

A Christmas tree in the corner had real gifts under it, and several fascinated children had already picked up the wrapped packages, shaking them and trying to peek through the slits in the paper. He'd laughed at that, because that would have been him twenty years ago.

But, best of all were the two women standing together. Avery glowed in a sparkling black dress with her arm around his mother, who wore an outfit very similar to the one she'd worn in the old picture he'd seen of her standing beside the man who'd sired him. His mother, the woman who'd loved him and raised him, shone with happiness and health. Hard to tell that she'd just been in the hospital only days before.

It was hard to take his eyes off Avery, too. She sparkled with life and laughter. He didn't know how he hadn't realized before that she had been doing all this work, not just because she loved decorating and organizing and planning parties, but because she knew how much it would mean to his mother.

To see his mother smiling and looking so radiantly healthy and happy made him love Avery even more.

He loved Avery.

He'd almost realized it that night in the hospital when he'd seen how much she cared for him by the way she'd fixed up his room. All that work just to make him feel comfortable and happy. How could he not love someone who put others ahead of themselves so consistently?

He was on unpaid leave, but he'd called his boss earlier in the day and given his two weeks notice. He didn't know how Avery felt, but in the end, it hadn't mattered. He was going to pursue her. If she didn't love him, he was hoping she'd eventually be able to. But he didn't have any hope of convincing her from Montana. Since there was no way she could move to Montana, and there was no way he'd expect her to, that left one choice—he had to give up his job.

Which he had done.

Now, somehow, he had to talk to her, but he couldn't walk, couldn't dance, couldn't even get her a drink.

So, he continued to sit in the corner, his leg duly propped up, frustration burning in his chest.

After what felt like hours, but was more like fifteen minutes, McKoy strolled over, carrying two cups.

"Hey, Gator. I'm kind of surprised you even came. Didn't the doc say to stay off that foot?" McKoy handed him one of the two cups he carried.

"Thanks." Gator took the drink. "Couldn't miss Avery's party. Even if I can't participate."

"What's up with you two, anyway?"

"Meaning?"

"It was pretty obvious yesterday that there's something there. Are you two a thing?"

Gator thought about hedging, but figured there was no point. "I'd like to be. But we need to talk and it's pretty much obviously not going to happen tonight." He took a sip of his drink while watching Avery. She led his mother to the dance floor. The mayor came up beside them and spoke. Avery smiled, while his mother laughed.

"I think your mother is blushing," McKoy said, his drink hovering half-way to his mouth.

"I guess the mayor is about her age."

"Younger, actually. But your mother has always acted much younger than she is. I remember that from high school." Shaking his head, McKoy downed his punch in a few swallows.

"Yeah. She's a good woman." McKoy didn't know about his mother and his history. There had never been any need to tell him. Still wasn't.

As the hours dragged by, Avery came over several times to check on him, but each time she was pulled away by someone who needed more food, or help with the music, or new candles to replace the ones that gutted out. She was everywhere. Laughing with guests, while keeping everything behind the scenes running smoothly, she balanced the role of party coordinator like a pro. If only he could help her, but at least he got to watch and admire.

As midnight rolled around, the mayor came to Gator's corner and asked if it was okay if he took Mrs. Franks home. Slightly flummoxed, Gator stammered out a yes. It worked out well, since fatigue darkened his mother's laugh lines, and she would have had to wait for Avery to take her, since Gator couldn't.

A small army of people gathered up the leftover food, but Avery shooed away anyone who tried to clean up, saying that she'd get it in the morning.

After standing at the door, talking to Fink and Ellie for a good twenty minutes, Avery floated to his side. The candles had been blown out, and the overhead lights were turned off, but the strings of Christmas lights still flickered. Silent Night played in the background.

He smiled up into her glowing face. "I think you can call your party a success."

Her eyes sparkled. "I wanted to recreate your mother's engagement party. I think it worked. Actually, the mayor was really paying close attention to her this evening."

"I noticed."

"Of course. I'm so sorry about your foot." She sat beside him.

"Yeah." He dropped his arm around her back and she laid her head on his shoulder. "You were amazing tonight. Everything you did was amazing." He indicated the still-beautiful decorations and the empty barn floor.

"Do you really think so?"

He squeezed her shoulder. "I do. And I think that everyone that was here tonight feels the same."

"Fink and Ellie asked me if I would accept a position of events coordinator on the farm. Part-time, as needed, of course."

"Wow. That's great," Gator said cautiously. She could probably do that from D.C.

"Fink wanted to talk to you because he'd already asked you to tear the barn down, but I told him if you had any problem with it at all, I'd hold off until it was resolved."

He'd managed to put his mother's financial problems out of his mind. The job he'd been working on would take care of some of it. Enough to keep it out of collections. Then he'd just keep chipping at the rest.

"Your mom was kind of the person of honor tonight. There was a jar for donations for her medical bills."

"Oh really?" That was news to him.

"Yeah. Several businessmen and the mayor made substantial donations. Jillian and Ellie are going to count it and let us know."

His chest was suddenly too small to hold the fullness of his heart. "That's great," he managed to say.

He turned in his chair and took Avery by the shoulders, making her face him. "You were beautiful tonight."

"Thank you." She blushed and looked down.

He took a finger and pushed her chin up.

"I love you."

Her eyes grew big.

"I love the way your heart is in serving others. How you enter a room and make it better just by your presence. How you're funny and sweet and sassy and I wish I could have participated in your party tonight. Holding you would have made it perfect for me."

"I love you too. That's what I was trying to tell you. Fink and Ellie offered me a job. It's only part time, but if I can book the barn and fill up the calendar, I can work myself into full time. In the meantime, there's a music opening at a private school not far away that Fink just told me about. He can give me a recommendation, and I might not get it, but..."

"I don't want you to give up your dream."

"I've realized that playing in a symphony isn't my dream anymore. I can't move to Montana, but I'll be here when you come to visit your mother."

"I'm not going back to Montana."

She tilted her head.

"I gave my notice today."

Her head swung back and forth slowly. "What are you going to do?"

"Nothing, right now." He indicated his leg. "But Bret offered me a job with his construction company, and I'd been tossing around the idea of opening up my Pap's old fish hatchery. He did construction and raised fish on the side. It's what made me go into conservation to begin with."

"But you liked your job. Didn't you?"

His hand cupped her cheek. "I like you more."

"But I don't want you to have to give up your job for me," she cried.

"You know. Maybe being married once helped me to see things a little more clearly. But I see it like this: I made the mistake of thinking that a woman who was just like me would make the best partner for me. In hindsight, it's obvious that I missed the red flags I should have seen. I didn't notice the defects in her personality because I was focused on our hobbies and interests. With that in mind, I don't think it's nearly as important that we share the same interests—we can learn to like each other's pastimes. Your character is what is so attractive to me." He grinned. "That, and you're a darn good kisser."

"No. I definitely need to practice kissing."

"No better time than the present." He lowered his head.

Epilogue

A small brass ensemble played wedding music which drifted into the small room that used to be a granary. Chairs had been set up, filling the newly renovated barn floor. Not only had the insurance paid for the new roof, but the money had included new beams and a new floor. In all, it was over half of the cost of the renovations.

Avery patted Gladys and Finch on their heads. Since she didn't have a dad, Fink had volunteered to walk her down the aisle. But after talking about it, Gator and she had decided there really wasn't anyone to give her away. So Gladys and Finch were going to escort her to her groom.

She peeked in the door. Gator stood at the front, his foot completely healed. The doctor had given him the go-ahead to take his boot off last week.

McKoy Rodning stood beside him as best man. They'd decided to keep the wedding party small and intimate.

Everyone was seated. Mrs. Franks sat beside Fink and Ellie and their children in the front row. A few guests checked the time on their phones. If Avery had hers, she'd be doing the same.

Where was Jillian?

She'd been there, helping Avery arrange her dress, not five minutes ago. She'd seemed a little flustered and Avery had asked her if everything was okay. She'd said it was.

Suddenly, the door to the old granary flew open and Jillian flew in. "I'm so sorry," she whispered.

"It's okay," Avery said. She hadn't minded the extra few moments to reflect on the huge step she was taking, too quickly, some said. "I knew there was something wrong. Tell me."

Jillian bit her lip. She glanced toward the barn floor despite the fact that the door was closed. "McKoy Rodning is the animal control officer."

"I know that. He's also the best man. And he's waiting on us."

Jillian pulled both her lips between her teeth and bit down. She drew in a shaky but determined breath. "There's an elephant in the barnyard."

Avery blinked. "I'm sorry. I thought you said there's an elephant in the barnyard."

"I did."

Avery put her hand on Jillian's forehead. The flu season had been mild until the beginning of March. Jillian obviously had a fever. A high one.

But her forehead was cold. "You are hallucinating, honey." She put a hand on her hip. "Are you doing drugs?"

"Please. You can't tell anyone." She swallowed, then spoke fast. "I'll walk up the aisle. This is your wedding day and I love you. I want it to be so beautiful. But I need to hide her. Her name's Heidi, by the way, and she's the sweetest thing."

"The elephant is Heidi?"

"Yes, we were in Mexico together. I worked with her for years." Jillian shook her head. "I don't have time to explain. I'll stand beside you. But I need to leave."

"Just go. This is relaxed anyway. No one will care."

"McKoy will notice. We didn't have a rehearsal, but he still knows I'm supposed to be there."

"I'll say you were hallucinating." Which could very well be true. "But I don't understand what the problem is."

"Avery, you can't keep an elephant in your backyard. It's illegal. They'll take her. McKoy will take her."

Avery fingered her pearl earrings. "What are you going to do?"

"I don't know." She smoothed her hands down her dress. "But come on. The next thing I'm going to do is watch my best friend get married to the most perfect man in the world for her." Jillian opened the door and started out. "Don't forget to smile," she whispered as she started down the aisle.

Like that would happen. Just looking at Gator made her grin. And when he caught sight of her standing in the open doorway, his teeth flashed in his tanned face.

Avery took a deep breath through her nose, smelling the scent of new wood and polish. The brass band began to play her song and she stepped out, toward the man whom she knew would never leave, toward the rest of her life.

Join Jessie's list and be the first to know about new releases and sales on her books!

Read Anything for You, the next book in the Sweet Haven Farm series where two people from completely different worlds are brought together by an...elephant. Keep reading for a sneak peek now.

Sneak Peek of Anything For You

The words elephant and wedding really didn't belong in the same sentence.

Even if the wedding in question was being held in a barn.

At least, that was Jillian Powell's experience. But what did she know? She spent most of her life in the Mexican circus where the word elephant and pretty much any other word in English or Spanish would have been perfectly normal. Possibly mundane, even.

At her current location, in central Pennsylvania at the wedding of her good friend and dubious relation, Avery Williams, though, elephant definitely did not fit.

"What did you say that noise was again?" Avery leaned over and whispered in Jillian's ear.

The brass ensemble that had been playing in the background while the guests had started eating had taken a break. The low murmurs of the guests had jerked into stunned silence when Heidi, the elephant, had trumpeted just a few seconds ago.

Jillian's palms started to sweat and her heart shivered like leaves that had been blown from a baobab tree by the lonely and sad trumpet of an African bush elephant.

"It's Heidi," Jillian whispered back, surprised her voice only shook a little. Heidi and her sister, Hazel, had been part of Jillian's act when she'd been in the Mexican circus. Not that she was going to go into her history with the elephant that currently stood below them in the long-unused barnyard.

That wasn't exactly the most pressing question on anyone's mind, anyway. 'How did the elephant get here, might be the top question in most peoples' minds.

Jillian, however, was more concerned about the best man.

No, she wasn't attracted to McKoy Rodning, although with his square jaw, strong nose, and broad shoulders, he probably was attractive. Maybe she did spend more than the average amount of time thinking about him. Only because of her recently opened dog kennel. Or maybe because of her general distrust of government employees.

But her current level of apprehension stemmed from the fact that McKoy Rodning was the animal control officer, and it was pretty much his job to question why an elephant would be trumpeting, independent of the brass band, at Avery and Gator's wedding.

And there she had it. Elephant and wedding in the same sentence, once more, sounding no more harmonious than they had the first time.

"And you know...Heidi?" Avery whispered, the pucker between her brows not matching the bright smile she flashed the curious guests who had slowly started conversing in low tones, throwing occasional concerned glances up at the wedding party table.

"Yes." Jillian rubbed her wet palms together, trying to remember she was wearing satin and not denim, and could not wipe her hands down her legs like she longed to do. Hopefully, the sweat that gathered in her armpits wasn't noticeable as long as she kept her arms pressed firmly against her sides.

The musicians began filing back to their seats. Avery pushed her half-eaten piece of cake away from the edge of the table and gave Jillian a nervous smile.

"If you leave before this dance, it will be noticeable, but I think once it ends, you could slip out and take care of whatever you need to. Maybe I can get Gator to distract McKoy."

"You two just enjoy each other. I can handle it." It's not like she hadn't learned plenty of survival skills growing up in the circus. Although how one would "take care" of an elephant problem in central Pennsylvania presented a quagmire she wasn't sure her skill set could handle.

Avery squeezed her hand, her shiny pink nails sparkling in the romantic barn light. "Thank you. Thank you for spending this day with me."

Jillian's smile was genuine as she squeezed back. Avery had been a great friend to her.

"Guess this is where I try not to step on your toes," Gator spoke, and Avery's head swiveled to him.

He had stood and held his hand out to her, his eyes full of love and admiration, even if his request to dance had been less than romantic. His jeans and plaid shirt looked new, though they weren't typical groom attire. They suited the barn wedding, and they suited Gator even more.

Just as the lacy white dress suited Avery.

Unfortunately, the coral satin dress Jillian wore might look fabulous next to her brown skin and black eyes and hair, but she would feel slightly more comfortable in a bikini standing at the South Pole than she currently did in the dress and the four-inch heels.

She wore outfits like this when she performed in the circus. Well, maybe not with the full skirt that fell below her knees. But definitely with heels this high. She could hold a hoop for the dog act, hang by her hair above the audience, twist herself into a pretzel, perch a monkey on her shoulder and ride the lead elephant's trunk around the show ring with no more nervousness than if she were sitting in bed, reading a book.

But somehow she felt she needed the security of comfortable jeans, worn sneakers, and a soft T-shirt to face Mr. McKoy Rodning, animal control officer and the only one currently in attendance at this wedding who had the power to remove Heidi before Jillian could figure out where she came from, who brought her, and what she was going to do with her. If he knew the secret that her hosts, the Finkenbinders, didn't know...Avery didn't even know...he could have her sent back to Mexico.

But she didn't have the security of comfortable clothes and he stood beside her, one hand behind his back, one hand held out to her, bowing slightly. The manners in his posture were impeccable, but the look in those powerful blue eyes was speculating.

Their relationship was not exactly harmonious.

They didn't belong in the same dance together any more than elephant and wedding belonged in the same sentence.

With a lift of her chin and a glint of her own eye, she met the challenge in his gaze, placing her hand in his.

Like sticking her fingers in a light socket.

Jillian fought to hold steady as shockwaves ricocheted up her arm, past her elbow, and slammed into her shoulder.

Her eyes flew to his, even as her automatic brain took over and her performing smile slid easily into place on her face. The net might have broken, but she would smile all the way to the ground.

Her fingers, long and slender like the rest of her body, rested lightly in his large, calloused hand.

The touch was light, but that crazy electricity that zapped between them felt stronger than the poles that held the big top up.

Her performance mask solidified on her face.

"Thank you," she said as she rose gracefully.

Something flickered in his eye as she straightened to her full height, her eyes square with his chin. Her stomach jumped in answer. Nervousness. It had to be. Had he recognized that noise for what it was?

He led her to the dance area, where Avery and Gator already danced to the dulcet tones of the brass ensemble.

She'd have to distract him so he wouldn't ask about the noise. But how? All she knew about McKoy she'd heard from the town gossips. He was the "dog catcher." Straight-laced. Followed the law to the T. Solid. Dependable. Still lived in the house he grew up in. Boring.

She could try to talk about stocks and bonds. That sounded boring enough to suit his personality. Except she couldn't hold even a remotely intelligent conversation about that. Maybe he was the kind of man who dominated conversations and tried to show by his verbosity how erudite he was.

It was too much to chance.

He stopped and she turned, her skirt billowing out, brushing his leg. Something about the soft satin of her skirt brushing the rough denim of his pant leg mesmerized her, and she watched as the material seemed to flow, smooth as cream over strawberries, across his strong leg.

She'd been required to do a lot of things in her time as a performer, but talking wasn't one of them. Her brain seemed to freeze as his large hand came up to settle with a whisper on her waist.

His lips didn't turn up, and he looked as serious as a pallbearer at a funeral. Apparently he wasn't any more eager to dance with her than she was with him. She'd just opened a dog kenneling business here on the farm, and so far he'd left her alone, but that didn't mean he wouldn't be visiting.

All of her paperwork was in order. Her business paperwork. Fink, who owned the farm with his wife Ellie, had filed it for her.

Her personal paperwork, on the other hand, was nonexistent. From what she'd heard of McKoy, he wouldn't hesitate to turn her in, but he shouldn't have any idea that she wasn't legal, unless she managed to stuff her high heel in her mouth in the next three minutes. Because of the different nationalities in the circus, she'd grown up speaking four different languages—Slovak, Romanian, Spanish, and English. Her Slovak and Romanian were rusty, but she was fluent in the other two languages. She'd been told her accent was faint.

Would he notice?

All of her upbringing had been focused on giving the audience a performance that made them feel their money was well-spent. It was time to put her talent to use.

He tilted his head, as though listening, then opened his mouth. He was going to ask about that noise, she was sure of it. She had to speak first. She had to distract him.

"Did you know that all monarch butterflies winter in one general area in Mexico?"

His mouth froze halfway open. His brows slowly formed a V, and if she read the look in his eyes correctly, he had just decided she was eccentric, if not slightly nuts. Perfect. He wasn't thinking about elephants anymore.

"It's beautiful to visit in the winter and see them almost covering every tree or bush within that certain square mile or two."

He blinked.

The circus had been playing a week-long show near the mountain on which the butterflies spent the winter, and she'd gone with her mother and several others to see it. "There's a lot of deforestation going on near that area, and scientists are afraid the monarchs will lose their home."

"Surely Mexico has laws in place to prevent that from happening," McKoy said with typical American naivete. Americans thought Mexico was like America.

"In Mexico, the person with the biggest bribe wins." She remembered just in time she wasn't supposed to sound bitter.

"Sounds like a nice vacation," he said. Ignoring the uncomfortable idea that monarchs might become extinct. Not surprising.

They swayed gently to the music. McKoy wasn't trying any fancy dance moves, which fitted exactly what she'd heard about his personality. He seemed uncomfortable in front of the guests, too.

She'd exhausted her monarch trivia, and he had that look in his eye, like he might be asking about the noise that had sounded suspiciously like an elephant trumpeting.

McKoy might not be her favorite person, but normally she wouldn't purposely do something that made someone uncomfortable. For Heidi, she felt she had no choice.

"Did I tell you I used to be a dancer?"

It was a rhetorical question, since they'd never spoken before five minutes ago.

He shook his head, his mouth still slightly open.

She gave him a little smile that might have had just a hint of deviltry in it. "I'm going to spin. Hang on."

A look very close to panic flashed across his face before she moved, grabbing his hand and stretching out their arms, then spinning herself up next to him. Their faces were only inches apart before she spun out, bending backward. She wasn't quite as flexible as she used to be, and her head was less than a foot off the ground, rather than the mere inches it would have been in her circus days.

The guests clapped.

She straightened slowly and twirled under his arm, turning completely around several times. Her skirt billowed out, but she refused to acknowledge it brushing his jeans. It wasn't herself she was trying to distract.

This time, as she twirled into him, he caught her, probably on accident, with his arm around her waist.

Her unconventional childhood had also taught her never to waste an opportunity.

She bent over his arm, careful not to lift her leg up too high. She hadn't been expecting this and her undergarments were not sufficient for *that* kind of show.

The song faded out on a low chord, she bent backward one last time, seeing Avery and Gator smiling before they kissed. The guests clapped.

She straightened.

McKoy offered his arm, which surprised her for some reason. His cheeks were red under his tan, and he didn't look her in the eye as she took it and he led her back to her seat.

She'd been trained since birth to be in complete control of her body at all times. So McKoy would never guess when she tripped and spilled the punch sitting on her table down the front of her dress that it wasn't an accident.

"Oh, no!" Jillian said with a glance at Avery and Gator, who were oblivious, wrapped up in each other's arms. "I'd better go blot this so the stain doesn't set."

She had plenty of experience in the circus of sewing costumes and getting stains out, and it didn't matter how much "blotting" she did, that stain was never coming out of her dress. But she was willing to sacrifice her pretty bridesmaid dress on the altar of saving Heidi.

McKoy jerked his head up and stepped back so she could go around him.

The restrooms in the renovated barn were around the corner at the far end in what used to be granaries. There were no windows in the small single user bathrooms, but there was a window at the end of the hall between them.

205

Jillian opened it, hitched her dress up, and climbed out.

~

Sign up for Jessie's newsletter! Get a free book, access to exclusive bonus content, get fun and funny updates on her life on the farm and more!

A Gift from Jessie

View this code through your smart phone camera to be taken to a page where you can download a FREE ebook when you sign up to get updates from Jessie Gussman! Find out why people say, "Jessie's is the only newsletter I open and read" and "You make my day brighter. Love, love, love reading your newsletters. I don't know where you find time to write books. You are so busy living life. A true blessing." and "I know from now on that I can't be drinking my morning coffee while reading your newsletter – I laughed so hard I sprayed it out all over the table!"

Claim your free book from Jessie!

Escape to more faith-filled romance series by Jessie Gussman!

The Complete Sweet Water, North Dakota Reading Order:

Series One: Sweet Water Ranch Western Cowboy Romance (11 book series)

Series Two: Coming Home to North Dakota (12 book series)

Series Three: Flyboys of Sweet Briar Ranch in North Dakota (13 book series)

Series Four: Sweet View Ranch Western Cowboy Romance (10 book series)

Spinoffs and More! Additional Series You'll Love:

Jessie's First Series: Sweet Haven Farm (4 book series)

Small-Town Romance: The Baxter Boys (5 book series)

Bad-Boy Sweet Romance: Richmond Rebels Sweet Romance (3 book series)

Sweet Water Spinoff: Cowboy Crossing (9 book series)

Small Town Romantic Comedy: Good Grief, Idaho (5 book series)

True Stories from Jessie's Farm: Stories from Jessie Gussman's Newsletter (3 book series)

Reader-Favorite! Sweet Beach Romance: Blueberry Beach (8 book series)

Blueberry Beach Spinoff: Strawberry Sands (10 book series)

From Strawberry Sands to: Raspberry Ridge (12 book series)

Swoonfully Jolly Holiday Stories:

Holiday Romance: Cowboy Mountain Christmas (6 book series)

Cowboy Mountain Christmas Spinoff: A Heartland Cowboy Christmas (9 book series)

New and Much Loved: Mistletoe Meadows (4 books and counting!)

Laughing Through the Snow: Christmas Tree, PA Sweet Romcoms (6 short reads)

Made in the USA
Columbia, SC
23 April 2025

**Sometimes a match that's all wrong,
turns out to be just right.**

While waiting to audition for a rare tubist seat opening, Avery Williams intends to cheer up her cancer ridden neighbor. She plans a throwback Christmas party in the barn where the sick woman got engaged forty years ago. It will be the highlight of the year, unless the building gets destroyed first.

In town for a short while to help his sick mother, Gator Franks expects to grab a side job and make some quick cash to help pay her hospital bills. Unfortunately, he has to get past the ugliest cat he has ever seen, which happens to be attached to a little blonde with sparkling pink fingernails, a city-girl attitude, and a fixation on saving the barn he just contracted to tear down.

Slowly, using simple words, Avery explains to the uncouth mountain man — the one with the ferocious, tuba-player-eating dogs — that she can't have a party in the barn if he bulldozes it first!

When circumstances force them to work together, it's a race to see who will win first, and if they'll give in to the growing feelings between them.

FIND MORE
SWEET HAVEN FARM
AVAILABLE NOW

13.99 US / 14.99 CAN

ISBN 9798808428379

90000

9 798808 428379